THE PREVAILING WIND

by

JOAN LINGARD

Paul Harris Publishing, Edinburgh

This edition first published 1978
by Paul Harris Publishing, 25 London Street, Edinburgh

First published 1964

© Copyright Joan Lingard 1978

ISBN 0 904505 56 1

Printed in Great Britain by offset lithography by
Billing & Sons Ltd, Guildford, London and Worcester

TO

THE MEMORY

OF MY MOTHER

ELIZABETH LINGARD

The city was busy that evening. Buses swung from stop to stop, loading and unloading; taxis slipped expertly in and out of the traffic; people milled on pavements, in theatre foyers and small dingy halls whose boards had been esteemed and sought-out for the last three weeks but would lie, dust-collecting, for the following forty-nine; tongues chattered in English, French, German, Russian, Japanese; cooks sweated over boiling pots and said thank-God-the-rush-will-soon-be-over; wine-waiters poised slim bottles, supine in wicker baskets, over wide-mouthed waiting glasses.

Khalil Siddigi walked alone through the streets. Despite the press and shelter of the crowd he felt the pinch of the wind through his thin clothes. It was time to put off the tropical jacket which he wore for three months of the year in a sublime effort of self-deception, for in all the years he had been in Edinburgh he had yet to experience the summer which was so much talked of but never came. 'It's here,' they would cry as the sun burst through the clouds above the battlements of the castle to dazzle the eyes of the west-bound Princes Street walkers; and at once, as if a wand had been waved, the street would be thronged with girls in cotton dresses and men carrying jackets and rolling shirt sleeves up over white forearms. They were a hardy race, the Scots. But though the sun sometimes shone, the air, to Khalil, remained cool and he gazed with awe at those who complained of the heat when the temperature rose a few degrees and even said it was *too hot*.

No one could say it was too hot now. He put up his shallow collar and fastened the top button of the off-white jacket. He had purchased it at a jumble sale where it had been placed by a former memsahib bent on unclutter-ing her husband's wardrobe after their return from the East. Khalil's friends and acquaintances would not have associated him with jumble sales, but he was a connoisseur of the subject and got most of his clothes from this source. The more prosperous the district the better the bargain, for how could the ladies of Ravelston Dykes be expected to buy the cast-off underpants of one another's husbands? Thus it was possible to acquire a pair of Y-fronts with sagging top or small darn in one leg, but otherwise whole, for the small sum of sixpence. The jacket had cost only one shilling – though that was a few years back and prices had risen since – for tropical clothing was not much in demand in this northern city.

Khalil enjoyed his visits to the church halls on winter afternoons. The ladies smiled on him as he humbly approached their stalls and fingered their wares: they thought him to be a Christian convert and said wasn't it nice for *them* to come about the church and support its functions? They knocked threepence off for him, complimenting themselves on being prejudice-free and also charitable. It was most satisfactory: pennies were put into the funds and the haunches of the ex-heathen were clothed. Often he was given a sweetmeat, usually a bar of sugary fudge known as 'tablet', as a reward and an encouragement to return. He seldom returned for he liked variety and there were many church halls in the length and breadth of the city, and in the course of a year many jumbles. He bought his underpants in Ravelston, his vests in Liberton, his socks in Corstorphine, his shirts in Goldenacre.

He halted on the edge of the kerb to let a vermilion and chrome beetle buzz past, then crossed the road and entered *Sandy Bell's Bar*. He infiltrated himself through to the front ranks at the counter, ordered half a pint of beer and put down his money. Holding his glass carefully in front of him so that none of the frothy golden liquid would spill, he retired to a corner and drank deeply. He had a great thirst but after the initial long drink he sipped slowly, knowing that he only had enough money for another half-pint tonight. Unless he met a friend. No sign of one here.

He tipped the last teetering drop down his throat, smacked his lips and went out. A few yards along the road he stopped off at *Greyfriars Bobby*. It was packed from wall to wall and bar counter to door with bodies that swayed, sweated, guffawed, drank. One or two nodding acquaintances nodded to him over the froth of their waving glasses but did not come forward with the offer of a drink. 'Philistines all!' he muttered. He bought a packet of potato crisps and ate them, scrunching noisily and licking the salt from his fingers after each one. As he scrunched he came to a momentous decision: he would leave Edinburgh. It was time for him to move; this he had known for a long time, yet he had lingered on, loath to leave the grey windy streets, the craggy spire-filled skyline, the green gardens, the colourful splashes of flowers in unexpected places. . . . He squashed the crisp bag flat and dropped it onto the floor. Yes, he would go. The end of summer was as good a time for departure as any other.

The crisps had renewed his thirst. He counted the coins in his pocket, put them back and resolutely left the den of temptation. He walked, hands in pockets, head bent, along George IV Bridge to the High Street. There he was brought to a stop by a vast army of men, women and children which surged up towards the castle, cheerfully carrying mackintoshes, umbrellas, mufflers, winter overcoats, old blankets, tartan rugs. They were headed for the early performance of the Military Tattoo. Khalil was in no hurry. He let them go, making no effort to break their ranks and pass between them. When the flood had eased to a trickle, he proceeded to the top of the Mound and looked down at Princes Street glistening with white and yellow lights like a stretched-out bracelet of jewels.

Down the long steep hill he went, drawing closer to the broad straight street until he stood at its middle point, waiting for a gap in the traffic to scuttle across. Then up Hanover Street and along narrow, shadow-pocked Rose Street where many pubs beckoned with beery breath and

9

noisy jingle. He went into *The Abbotsford*. A morose poet, red-eyed and unshaven, bought him a pint and they sat together in silence, each sunk deep in the recesses of their separate problems. The bar was warm and full, and ringing with noise that did not fit a mood of sadness. Khalil drank quickly and continued his journey.

He dropped down to the northern side of the town, to the mews where his friend Tim MacAuley lived. It was quiet in the lane after the main road. The windows of Tim's flat were open but the rooms beyond were dark. Khalil listened: no sound but the distant hum of traffic. Nevertheless, he banged on the downstairs door and called Tim's name several times. He should have known that Tim would not be at home on this Saturday evening: he would be sitting in one of the back street halls watching Ionesco or Pirandello, holding Isobel Robertson's small manicured hand in his.

He turned away.

He climbed back up to the centre of the city. The pubs were shutting, tumbling their beer-filled customers into the streets, dimming their lights, shutting and bolting their doors. On Princes Street the crowds were already gathering to await the fireworks that would soar up above the castle to mark the end of the Festival. A bus swerved into a stop in front of him. At one of the windows was a face that he knew, a face from the past. It belonged to a girl called Dolly. He waved. She gazed without expression into his eyes, and the bus slid away. He was disturbed. He licked his dry lips, straightened his tie, ran his fingers through his hair. Had he turned into a faceless man?

For a moment he did not know what he would do next; he stood in the middle of the pavement like an island around which a fast flowing current of people swirled; and then he remembered that he still had money in his pocket, enough for a cup of coffee. He chose a self-service café, large and impersonal, where he could sit unnoticed in a corner and nurse his warm cup. He searched the faces of the

10

young men and women who sat, two by two, smiling secret smiles, tapping their feet to the throbbing music that belched out of a leering juke box. Tim and Isobel were not amongst them. He sat back, resigned: tonight he would not meet anyone he wanted to meet.

He sat until the café emptied and the waitresses began to stack the dirty crockery high on their trays. The night was colder now and his feet were tired. The hole in the sole of his right shoe had been worn bigger by all the pavements he had passed over in the last few hours, and through it his toes felt the hard ground. He glanced up: the sky was astir with colour and movement. He watched, entranced.

Refreshed, he resumed his patrol. Down one side of Leith Walk and up the other, relentlessly, he plodded. People were disappearing, lights diminishing, noise abating. Back to Princes Street he came once more, his steps slow but determined. What was it he sought? He did not know but sensed there was something afoot he must not miss.

Suddenly he stopped and drew in his breath sharply. A few yards in front of him a woman was helping a small child into a taxi. He saw her face only for a moment and in profile, but he recognized her immediately. As he ran forward, she stepped in after the child and the door closed.

'Janet!' he called.

The taxi moved away, quickly gathering speed.

He sat down on a wooden seat and watched it go. He did not live a life in which one hailed another cab and shouted: 'Follow that car!' But he was untroubled. He knew how to find anyone he wanted to find, time being no object; and besides, Janet was Isobel Robertson's sister.

So Janet had returned. He had always known that she would and was relieved he had not gone before she came. During the five years she had been away he had thought of her often and wished to see her. He had questioned Isobel. 'She's fine,' Isobel had said vaguely, telling him nothing. He fished a cigarette-end out of his pocket and lit it. He would not go now, he would wait a little longer. . . .

11

He was surprised to find that the night had turned warmer and the wind had died.

CHAPTER TWO

Janet considered herself unfortunate to belong to a large, united family. As she stepped onto the platform at Waverley Station and smelled the smoke and soot, she thought of all the Robertsons lying in their close-carpeted lairs, ready to pounce on her. They did not yet know that she had returned but they would be ready nevertheless. They were as solid as the stone walls of Edinburgh itself and utterly convinced of their rightness. Herein lay their strength.

She turned and lifted her young daughter down from the high step. The child had slept for the last six hours; whilst she slept the tiredness had seeped out of her small, rather thin body to be replaced by new strength and energy. She skipped along the platform, exhilarated by the hurrying bodies lopsided and bent with the carrying of large cases, the navy-blue-clad porters trundling barrows, the wheeze of the engine, the vast canopy of the station roof, the strangeness of the hour. She surrendered the two single tickets to the collector with an air of importance and a coy smile. On the other side of the barrier she paused. Her eyes darted to left and right, taking in the gloomy, exciting station. Then she ran ahead of her mother into the Ladies Waiting Room.

Janet shut the door behind them. It was a pub-like door, ochre-yellow wood with patterned clear and opaque glass, and it had a large brass snib which her fingers itched to push home. Such a simple action could seclude them, give them shelter, keep at bay a dozen fears and doubts. Sally was circling the disinfected room, squinting hopefully up at the faded, obsolete pictures. She scratched her head, shook it and clambered onto one of the four chairs that guarded a small table in the centre of the floor. She swung her legs, drank an imaginary cup of tea and nodded at her unseen guest who sat opposite. Tiring of that, she ran to inspect the toilets. Janet put down their two suitcases, and decided to rest awhile on the red and grey plush that ringed the room.

It was time now to make a decision. She could have made it during the seven hours in the stuffy train but she had sat like a rag doll comfortably jolted by the regular movement, listening to the chuntering of the wheels on the line. They had spelled out no special message for her; she had merely heard their da-da-de-da, da-da-de-da, broken by a long thin whine as they entered a tunnel. Eventually she had fallen asleep and wakened only when the train achieved its final lurch and passengers trod on one another's feet in the frantic effort to be first to escape. She had wakened with a fugged-up mouth and the terrifying realization that the train was at a standstill.

She stared down at cigarette-ends, splayed matches, ash, sweet wrappers. Relics of passengers who had waited and moved on. They would have to move on too. Her life seemed to be spent in moving on—or back.

From the other room came the sound of running water and a child's voice shrieking above it. She found Sally washing her hands in the basin which was filled to the brim and flowing over. A woman was reddening her lips in front of the mirror. She pursed her lips and drew them back to bare a mouthful of stubbed brown teeth. She dropped her lipstick into a shiny black handbag, readjusted her right stocking and without a glance at Janet and Sally, turned to go. Her heels clicked sharply away.

Janet rescued her daughter's arms from the basin and dried them on the end of a dirty towel, only half listening to Sally's flow of admiration for the woman's hair which had been as yellow as a dandelion's head. The other half of her mind turned over the problem which nagged at her like a raw heel in a rubbing shoe.

They went back to the other room to collect their

13

luggage. Janet stopped in the doorway, bewildered: only one case stood on its end beside the ochre-yellow door. The other, the smaller one had gone. Her eyes scanned the room but there was nowhere for a suitcase to lurk. The woman must have taken it.

Quickly now, they left the room and hurried to find someone to help. Sally laughed, pleased with the further excitement, her voice echoing high in the gaunt station which seemed to Janet a desolate cavern designed to keep them prisoner. A few people stood around, waiting. Two porters lounged against a wall. They shook their heads: they hadn't seen a woman with hair as yellow as a dandelion's head. They twisted their heads to watch the woman and child cross the Booking Hall to the Lost Property Office.

The official was sympathetic but not very hopeful. He wrote down a description of the case: black leather, soft top, tag bearing name. Janet leaned wearily against the counter, knowing it to be hopeless. It was so typical of Janet, she could imagine her twin sister Fiona saying, to rush up to Edinburgh and lose a suitcase. And the woman? The man looked up with an enquiring smile. The woman had yellow hair, bad teeth and a black shiny bag. And the bag had a star on it that twinkled, Sally added. He noted it all down, then asked for their address.

Janet looked at him blankly. Of course everyone had an address. She hesitated and he frowned, showing disbelief in the existence of a black suitcase and a woman with yellow hair. She rattled off Fiona's address, and they left.

They walked up the steps from the Booking Hall and crossed the iron-sided bridge that straddled the empty track. The Waverley Steps stretched ahead, grey, steep, and uninviting. Janet paused at the bottom, reluctant now to abandon the warm fug of the station for the chill wind that would inevitably blow at the summit. Sally tugged at her hand and led her forward.

Sally reached the top step first. She gave a cry of delight

14

and Janet blinked, confused, as she, too, emerged at street level. The street was full of light and noise, more than one expected of an ordinary Saturday night. Something strange must have happened. And then she remembered what night it was: the last one of the Festival. As always, when she arrived too late for anything, she felt deprived. To have come three weeks earlier would have made a difference to this returning: there would have been extra life in the city and strangers for them to mingle with. Tomorrow would be a dead day: people converging on bus and rail stations, landladies sighing, dead posters ripped by wind.

'There will be fireworks later,' Janet said.

'Fireworks!' Sally skipped along the pavement.

They went to a café in Leith Street for they had not had a meal since morning. After they had eaten they sat on in the warmth, watching the passers-by through the window. Janet sat as if in a coma, knowing that she was wasting valuable time.

Midnight, and the firework display, drew near. They returned to Princes Street, to the top of the Waverley Steps once more, where the draught threatened to suck them back down to the station. They resisted its pull and reached the shelter of the wall. They crossed the wide cobbled mouth of Waverley Bridge; they passed the imposing monument where Sir Walter Scott sits in cold lonely splendour, the floodlit flowerbeds, the sentinel line of trees, the scrolled standards aglow with lights; they rounded the protruding steps of the Royal Scottish Academy and came to rest in the crowd that blocked the corner of the Mound.

'Will it be soon?' Sally asked.

Suddenly, splitting the darkness of the sky, rose a shower of brilliant coloured sparks. An 'oooh' went up from the watchers. The city quietened, darkened. Sally's hand tightened round her mother's. The fire soared and sizzled, twisted and dived, dazzling eyes, inducing gasps of wonder. 'As good as Blackpool,' said a woman with a tight anxious face. Her man nodded his flat cap and wished it were time to go for his feet were cooling and his belly rumbling. A baby cried, shoulder-high, and dribbled on the man's flat cap. The tight-faced woman said that people had no business bringing kids out at this time of night and they ought to be reported. The shoulder bearing the baby whirled round and a small hand knocked the flat cap askew. 'Wheest!' said an elderly man in a muffler, and eyes turned politely back to the Festival Finale.

A last glorious surge of colour, the crack of an explosion, and the sky was dark. 'That's it for another year,' someone said. The crowd sighed and began to disperse.

Cheered by the fireworks, Janet set about finding a room for the night. It was not easy: hotels were full or prices too high. She tried a few in the centre without success. By that time Sally was tired; she scuffed her feet along the pavement, arching her back and putting her weight on her mother's arm. Every few yards she asked if it was much further. They sat down on a bench to consider. Who would welcome them, unheralded, on their doorstep in the small hours of the morning?

Reflecting on her own inefficiency, led Janet to think of Fiona who was as efficient as she was not. Fiona's mind was like a well-managed alarm clock; it was always fully wound and the bell never failed to go off. They would go to Fiona's. Why not? They had to sleep somewhere.

Janet hailed a cruising taxi and they climbed in. As they headed out towards the suburbs Janet thought of Fiona and her husband Howard Bell. She had not seen them for five years but they would not have changed. They were not people who changed.

As a child Fiona had loved sport and little children. It had therefore been on the cards that she would marry. It had also been on the cards the type of man she would marry: clean-limbed and clean-shaven, he would have to have climbed every 'Monroe' at least once, played rugby for Scotland and swum across the Forth and back. Fiona had high standards. At nineteen she had met Howard who took

16

the air on the Braids golf course every Sunday afternoon and played rugby for the second fifteen Old Boys Association of one of Edinburgh's 'Better Boys' schools on Saturday afternoons; he had been to the top of Arthur's Seat twice and on one occasion had jumped from the top springboard into Portobello Pool. It was a compromise for Fiona but she had come as near to her ideal as anyone was liable to get and she was astute enough to realize it. After an engagement of three years she and Howard had married. Janet had not been present at the wedding but had received a 'family group': Fiona and Howard resplendent and beaming in the middle and flanked on either side by a sea of approving faces. The Robertsons had outnumbered the Bells who seemed not to mind.

In addition to his sporting abilities, Howard was very intelligent though he had the intellect of a fly. He earned his golf clubs and rugby boots by working out people's expectation of life and death for a large insurance company. Janet thought his knowledge of statistics helped him to be such an all-rounder at sport: he knew the extent of man's limitations but also his unexplored capabilities. He could tell you, for example, the number of men in Scotland capable of jumping from the top board in Portobello Pool, what age group they would be in, their build, the month in which they might make the jump and the likeliest day of the week. Thus, if one were to pursue it far enough, it would be possible to go to Portobello one Saturday afternoon in July and see a young man aged twenty years and two months, height five feet nine and a quarter inches, medium build, on the point of leaping into the chlorinated embrace of the green waters below. Statistics is a fascinating science and Janet could fully understand Howard's absorption, though she would not have wished to dabble in it herself since she would have hated to know how many years she would live and husbands she would have. She had a horror of fortune telling. This showed an inability to face up to life, Howard had once told her.

17

They were now in an area well known to Janet. She had cycled along the streets and dawdled on the pavements as a child. As they approached the road where her parents lived she slid back the glass screen and asked the driver to go slowly along it. He flicked out the right-hand indicator and they turned into the tree-lined road. It was quiet and asleep. Her parents lived in the third house, a solid stone detached villa, screened from its neighbours by leafy poplars which kept the downstairs rooms dim and sunless. Standing by the wall under the arch of an overhanging tree were two figures. The girl must be Isobel. Janet smiled and adjusted her mind to the idea that Isobel would no longer have plaits and wear a gym tunic. Through the bars of the gate she saw the pink glow of the hall light; then she glanced up at the dark window behind which her mother would be lying waiting for the sound of the key in the lock and Isobel's step on the stair. They were past now.

Half a mile further on they came to the warren of new houses where Fiona and Howard lived. The moon moved behind a cloud as the taxi deposited them outside a white wrought-iron gate. Magnificent sworls topped it. It was a gate that should have led to a Baroque palace or a Rococo mansion, not a semi-detached bungalow in pink brick. Janet put down the case. She had come on it too suddenly. She wheeled round but the taxi was turning the corner; the red lights disappeared and with them their last hope of escape. She said to Sally: 'Let's go for a walk.'

The child sighed and put her hand into her mother's. They circled the block slowly, passing all the other bungalows, and arrived back at the curly gate. The hinges creaked as Janet pushed it open. Remiss of Howard! They walked up the path, conscious of the ring of their feet in the quietness of the night. Janet pressed the bell. A little tune tinkled inside the house. Sally giggled. It was like the tune the ice cream men played. Silence. Maybe they weren't at home? At Sally's request, Janet put her finger back on the illuminated button. Dancing backwards in her excitement,

18

Sally kicked over a milk bottle; it clattered onto the crazy paving and fell apart.

As Janet was retrieving the pieces, Howard opened the door.

'Good Lord!' he said. 'It's Janet!'

She looked up quickly and a spike of glass jabbed the palm of her hand. It was not a good beginning: she entered the softly-lit vestibule with a suitcase in her left hand and blood flowing from her right one. Sally wrapped herself in the skirt of her mother's coat and stared at the bare-footed man in blue and white pyjamas. How many men wear blue pyjamas, piped with white, Janet wondered? This was one of the curious things about Howard: in his company one's mind began to work as his did. He ran a hand through his rumpled hair, surveyed them as though they had arrived from a distant planet, and called for Fiona. For once he had been caught unawares.

'You've come back to Edinburgh to live?' Fiona said three times. Then she gave Howard a knowing look which indicated that this could be discussed later and that practical issues must come first. They took charge: Howard bandaged Janet's hand and made cocoa whilst Fiona swept Sally off to be cleaned and laid in a comfortable bed. Her eyes were tender as she gathered up the child for she was soon to have one of her own.

Janet sat in a purple winged chair and drank the cocoa. Howard, now dressing-gowned and slippered, hovered around the curtains like a large uncertain moth, pulling them aside to look into the garden, then tweaking them straight. He cleared his throat and said that it was nice to see her again. To cover up the insincerity of his statement, he hastily began to talk of the Festival. He and Fiona had been to two late-night reviews and the Tattoo, at which they had been drenched to the skin and had narrowly escaped being struck down by lightning, and they had found time to pop into an exhibition for a few minutes but they hadn't thought much of it. Great splodges of paint, no shape or form to it, that sort of stuff. Fiona had said the children in her class at school could do better.

'There now,' Fiona said brightly as she came into the room. 'Sally's fast asleep, poor wee lamb. She was absolutely worn out.'

Further signalling by eye, and Howard decided to return to bed. The sisters were left alone with the two gleaming bars of the electric fire. Janet swallowed the muddy dregs of her drink and wished she could be allowed to sleep before the inquisition. That would not be possible. Fiona's eyes were smiling but blank: she was preparing her approach.

'Sally's very like you,' she said.

'So I'm told.'

Fiona put her hand on Janet's arm. 'You poor thing!'

Immediately Janet felt her hackles rise. In the taxi she had resolved not to let Fiona irritate her, but her resolution was wavering.

'You can talk to me, get it all off your chest.' Fiona smiled encouragingly. She was a good listener, Howard often said, and she thought that one day she might like to become a Marriage Guidance Counsellor. Janet did not exactly fit into the category of Marriage Guidance but this would be good practice nevertheless. She saw herself sitting behind a polished desk offering comfort to poor distressed women who had not enough character to manage their own affairs. She had helped quite a few of her friends over their little troubles. Janet remained silent. 'You can talk to me,' Fiona repeated. 'Get it off your chest.'

'For God's sake, Fiona! What do you want me to get off my chest?'

Fiona looked uncomfortable. Janet's voice had sounded so hard, but then one must make allowances. 'I thought maybe that if you were unhappy you'd like to talk. It helps to talk.'

'Sometimes it doesn't. It's so easy to exaggerate and give a false picture which you then come to accept yourself.'

'To define a problem clarifies it.'

'Very well. I am in Edinburgh, I have a child, I have no job and nowhere to live. Will that do?'

'There's no need to be facetious,' Fiona said, exasperated. She took a deep breath and calmed herself. The doctor had told her to watch her blood pressure.

'What do you want me to say? What do you expect of me?' Janet kicked off her shoes. 'I'm not unhappy, I'm merely tired. What do you want me to do to prove it?'

'But why have you come back to Edinburgh? I thought you had a good job. The last time you wrote you said it was a comfortable house and they were good to Sally.'

'It was a comfortable house and they were good to Sally, but I couldn't stand it any longer. I had a row with them this morning so I packed our bags and we walked out.'

'What was wrong with them?'

'They were elderly. She couldn't stand noise: it gave her migraine headaches. Sally tiptoed round the house, spoke in whispers and if she dropped anything she burst into tears. As for him! I couldn't stand the way he ate boiled eggs.' Fiona stared at her. Janet continued: 'He had one every morning. Sally and I ate with them – we were supposed to be part of the family. A nice little bit of make-believe that fooled nobody. I'd rather have been classed as a servant and done with it.' She decided to smoke her last cigarette. Fiona lit it for her with a heavy table lighter, still staring at her with troubled eyes.

'What do you mean? How did he eat boiled eggs?'

'He liked to imagine the egg was Khruschev's head. He would caress it gently, then lift his knife and go wheek! He cut the top clean off. He would lift his pink plastic spoon and scoop the yolk out of the head with great relish. "It's the only way to deal with the bastards," he would say.'

'Don't, please.' Fiona shuddered. 'You make me feel ill.'

'You see what I mean? It was an impossible way to begin the day. Sally used to play at "Khruschev's head" with her dolls.'

21

'Couldn't you have had your breakfast earlier and avoided the problem?'

'It's no good avoiding a problem. It pops up in another place. Anyway, that wasn't all. His conversation was peppered with damn swines, lower orders and all the rest of the claptrap. He thought we ought to teach the Russians a lesson, and everyone else he disagreed with. He had a long list. He was insane. He reminded me of father.'

'That's not fair! Father's a good man. He's a Christian.'

'So is the colonel. He's in his pew every Sunday showing the way to the peasants.'

Fiona spoke calmly: 'I can understand the noise problem being difficult but surely you didn't have to leave because of someone's political views?' To Fiona the idea was incredible, unless the people were Communists or something terrible like that. Politics bored Fiona though she would not have admitted it; she believed that women should take a healthy interest in the outside world so that they could be intelligent companions to their husbands. She belonged to a group on the estate called *The Seekers*; they were all graduates or college trained, and they met every Tuesday to discuss intellectual matters and current affairs. They took it in turns to prepare and deliver talks, it being too expensive to engage experts. The system worked very well. Last week she had given a talk on Jung; it had kept her frightfully busy for two afternoons. Howard teased her and said she was becoming quite the little intellectual but really he was pleased for he was very progressive.

Janet seemed not to have heard; her eyes were half closed. Fiona said: 'So many things are just a matter of opinion. Can't you live in the same house with someone whose opinions are different to yours?'

'Not those kind of opinions.'

'Sometimes one has to put up with a few unpleasant things for the sake of a child. A good home's worth a lot. It may not be easy for you to get another position.'

Janet laughed. 'Position' suggested lower orders. Perhaps

that was how her family saw her now. She said she was tired of keeping other people's houses in order and living at their pleasure. She intended to get a job and a place of her own where she and Sally could live and make a noise. Fiona was not encouraging. What kind of a job could Janet get? She had no training, no qualification, she had not completed her degree course. Janet had always been considered the most intelligent of the family but what did that count for now? She, Fiona, had known very early that she wanted to teach young children and had gone ahead and had herself trained to do just that.

'I'll find something,' Janet said. 'I'll buy the *News* and read the Situations Vacant.'

Fiona sighed, signifying that she would not get very far with such indefinite ideas. She wondered if Howard could get Janet a job in his office but decided not to mention it as he might find it an embarrassment to have her in the same building.

They stared at the two orange coils of heat, and behind them on the wall the golden hands of the clock ticked softly over its black face. Fiona's mind was busy turning over an idea for her next talk to *The Seekers*: 'The Position of the Unmarried Mother in Society'. There would be no need for the girls to know that she had a sister who came into this category. The Robertsons had kept the whole business as quiet as possible. After all, it was not a thing to boast about.

'Have you any money?' Fiona asked.

'A little. Not much.'

'Why can't you ask Sally's father for help? He ought to do something.'

'He gave me all he could.'

'I think he got off lightly. He can't be much of a man.'

Janet shrugged.

'Who was he anyway?'

Janet had been waiting for the question for the last hour. It had formed up at the back of Fiona's tongue a dozen times before spilling out.

23

'Why should I say now?'

An unpleasant suspicion lurked at the back of Fiona's mind: perhaps Janet didn't know who the father was. She claimed that she did by saying he had given her money but that might easily be a lie. Janet did not always tell the truth. As students, they had had different friends and she had not liked the bunch that Janet had associated with: an untidy, irresponsible lot of every shape and colour. In particular there had been a little Indian who wore funny clothes and a dreadful girl called Dolly, known to be little better than a prostitute. Fiona returned again to her talk. 'Such a tragic problem must be tackled at its very heart. We can do what we can to help these unfortunate women but we must not lose sight of the main issue: the declining moral standards of our times . . .'

Janet yawned. The golden hands showed that in another three minutes it would be four o'clock. Despite her pregnancy and a disturbed night, Fiona looked fresh and fit to sit till breakfast. Janet said she would like to sleep, and Fiona helped her make up a bed on the studio couch.

'It's a nuisance only having the two bedrooms and the second one is really very small, but we don't intend to stay here long. When Howard gets his rise next year we'll buy something better.'

'This is only a stepping-stone?'

'You might call it that.' Fiona smiled, refusing to be annoyed by the trace of mockery in the voice of her sister whose stepping-stones travelled backwards and not forwards in life. She looked at Janet's hand. 'You're wearing a wedding ring. It makes it easier for Sally, I suppose. Do you call yourself Mrs Robertson?'

'No. Crosbie.'

'I'll remember.' Fiona turned down the sheet. 'I'll phone mother in the morning. Goodnight, dear.'

Howard was still awake. 'I hope she hasn't been upsetting you,' he said.

24

'Of course not!' Fiona slipped off her dressing-gown and got into bed. 'Why should she? I feel sorry for her, and the child.'

'Is she short of money? Perhaps we could help. We could let her have twenty pounds, couldn't we?'

'Twenty pounds! Are you mad? We've got our own child to consider, Howard. Are you forgetting that?' she said softly. Then she pulled the cord that dangled over the bed and the light was extinguished.

CHAPTER THREE

Isobel Robertson awoke with a start and a sense of unfamiliarity. She moved her left leg and encountered another warm human limb that did not belong to her. She closed her mouth to stifle the rising scream in her throat and sank back into the man's arms. Now she remembered.

She slid her left leg across the crumpled sheet away from that other leg, and lay stiff and tense. It was cold in the room for the window was wide open onto the September night. She eased the sheet up over her shoulders, doing it gently lest she disturb him. The lights of a car passing along the mews glanced up and touched the surround of the window. When it was gone it was strangely dark and very quiet. She shivered.

'Cold?' Tim MacAuley said. He leaned on his elbow and looked down into her face. 'Can I put on the light now? I want to see your face. It's a pool of darkness on the pillow.'

'Don't do that.' She caught his hand in hers. 'I like lying in the dark like this.'

'Why are you so afraid of the light? Do you think I might see something you don't want me to see?'

'Of course not.' She ran her fingers over his hand: it was large and rough from the clay he handled, and the nails were probably not clean. She smothered a yawn and the effort called up another one. She wondered how long they would have to lie here like this. She wanted to go home and have a bath and go to bed and think about this new experience but she knew that she could not go away yet: it would be like leaving a party too soon. On the other hand she knew that it would be a mistake to stay too long. He must regret her going and feel deprived. The silence in the room was immense and suffocating. But there was not much to say, at least nothing for her to say. Shouldn't he be telling her how wonderful she was and how grateful he was? His continued silence made her resentful. She could not support it any longer. He must be made to declare himself.

'Have I made you happy?' she asked.

'Yes.' He squeezed her hand and then disengaged his. He stretched over to the bedside table and took two cigarettes from a packet and lit them. He gave one to Isobel who grasped it eagerly: whilst they were smoking he could not touch her. She did not want Tim MacAuley to touch her again that night. The idea of his rough hands moving over her body revolted her.

'Tim, have you slept with many women?'

He had known the question would be coming, a seemingly idle one which had happened to pass through her mind.

'Some.'

'How many?'

'I don't know. I've never counted them.'

He yawned. The conversation seemed to be an echo of hundreds of thousands of other such conversations whispered in darkened rooms, meadows in warm sun, woods scented with pine and filled with the noise of snapping twigs and twittering birds.

'How many?' Her voice was soft and lazy, suggesting indifference, but it was also insistent.

'Isobel dear.' He stubbed out his cigarette into the tin ashtray and put his arm round her. 'You're not being serious, are you?'

'Of course I'm being serious.'

26

'It doesn't matter, Isobel. None of it matters.'

'But I want to know,' she said, sounding now like a stubborn child. She sat up and leaned over him. He flapped the air to stop her cigarette smoke engulfing his face. 'Tell me, please. I won't hold it against you. I just want to know.'

Why? Why did she want to know? He knew: she wanted him to say that he had never slept with anyone else even though she knew it to be untrue. If he were to say it everything would be all right. He couldn't say it. He didn't want to say it.

'I'm not going to tell you,' he said lightly. 'A man and a woman can't reveal all their secrets to one another. We must keep some element of mystery.'

'I have no secrets from you.'

'That's not true.'

She was silent for a moment. Then she lay back and said in her softer voice: 'I'm sorry, Tim, I shouldn't have asked you that. I had no right to. Forgive me.'

'I don't have to forgive you anything.'

A clock began to strike somewhere beyond the open window. She counted out the notes under her breath. 'Midnight!' She sat up again quickly. 'I'll have to go.'

'You're not Cinderella,' he laughed. She will have to go soon, he thought, and felt happy.

'You know what my parents are like. They don't go to sleep till I come in.'

'Aren't you going to spend the night with me?' he asked. He did not want her to stay, yet felt compelled to ask her. He knew there was no chance that she would.

'Don't be silly. What would I say in the morning?'

'Tell them you stayed at Fiona's.' He almost wished that she would so that he could go with her in the morning and see the Robertson stronghold shaken to its foundations. He toyed with the idea but it would be too dangerous.

'They'd soon check up on me,' she said scornfully. 'Anyway, why should I stay at Fiona's?'

'I don't know. Surely there's some excuse you could give.

27

Don't you want to stay with me, Isobel? Do you want to go away? I believe you do. If you wanted to stay you would find some way of doing it. You want to go.'

'You know I don't.' She was near to tears. 'I want to stay but I can't.' She stiffened suddenly and listened. A key was being inserted in the lock of the downstairs door, feet sounded on the stair and another door opened. 'That's Murray. You said Murray wasn't coming back tonight. You said he had gone away for the week-end!'

'He must have changed his mind.'

'You lied to me! You knew he would be coming back but that I wouldn't stay if you told me.'

'Listen, Isobel, you offered to come here. Have you forgotten? Anyway, Murray isn't interested in who sleeps in my bed.'

'I suppose he's used to you bringing women in?'

'Certainly. I normally have three a night.'

She gripped his hand. 'You won't tell him?'

'Tell him what? He'll know you've been in my room.'

'But you needn't tell him what happened. Promise you won't. It's our secret.'

He promised. He hoped Murray had brought a couple of bottles of beer in with him for he had a fearsome thirst. Isobel's body was as tense as if it were her own mother moving around in the next room. He asked again if she would stay and agreed that he was being unreasonable. He pushed back the bed clothes and swung his feet onto the cool wooden floor. He went to the window and leaned out. 'Come and see the fireworks,' he said. 'They're beautiful.'

Isobel sat hunched up in the midst of the bedclothes, watching the dark figure at the window. She slipped out of bed and hastily began to dress.

'Come and see,' he said again. 'Quickly, before they finish.' She came and stood by his side. 'Why, you've got clothes on! You should have felt the night air on your body.'

She looked up to see the last flash of fire fade from the

28

sky. Tim closed the window and switched on the light. The unshaded electric light bulb was harsh; she put her hand across her eyes and turned back to look through the window, not wanting to look at Tim. She wished he would dress; it was disturbing and uncomfortable to know that he was standing there naked. When she looked round he was putting on his trousers. She smiled and relaxed. She enjoyed the feeling of intimacy this scene gave her whilst knowing that she was safe from having to be intimate with him.

'I really would like to stay, Tim,' she said, 'but you know how it is.'

'Yes, I know,' he said easily. He picked up his shirt from the floor and shook it out.

'Everything's all right then?'

'It's fine.'

'You don't feel I've failed you or anything?' she asked anxiously.

'Why should I feel that?' He pulled the shirt over his head and pushed it into the top of his trousers. She came over and tucked in a piece of the checked cotton which had escaped his notice.

'There,' she said and standing on the tips of her toes, kissed his mouth lightly. 'There'll be lots of other times for us to be together and one night I'll not have to go away and leave you. We're closer now, aren't we?'

'Yes,' he said, 'we're closer.'

'Tim!' It was Murray calling from behind the door.

Isobel put a hand to her throat.

'Is there any butter?'

'Under the sink.'

'I've looked there.'

'I'm just coming through.'

When they went into the living room and greeted Murray, Isobel thought that the look he gave them indicated that he knew very well what they had been doing behind that closed door. He was sitting at the table in front

29

of a loaf of bread and a pot of red jam. He sawed off a slice and spread it with the thick conserve. Tim disappeared into the kitchen leaving her alone with Murray. She did not like Murray, she thought him rather a boor. He had no manners and he rarely made any effort to speak to her. She sat down on an upright chair and watched him eat through the slab of bread. On the table was an open book which he was reading.

'Been to a show tonight?' she asked.

'Concert.' He flicked over a page without lifting his head.

She dismissed him as not worth bothering about, and turned her attention to her nails: she took out a nail-file and rubbed it gently against them, taking care not to chip the crimson varnish. She heard Murray wince and continued, with greater pleasure.

Presently, Tim returned with the butter. He tossed it at Murray and said: 'Come on then, Cinderella. We'll find you a coach.' He could scarcely afford a taxi but he wanted to be rid of her as soon as possible.

In the taxi she said: 'I don't know why you share a flat with Murray. He's barely civil.'

'He suits me. He goes his way, I go mine and we don't interfere with one another.'

'He doesn't like me.'

'Nonsense!'

'Do you like me?'

'Of course.'

She pressed his hand and leaned back against him. Of course he liked her. Hadn't he made love to her a couple of hours ago? She closed her eyes. She was very tired.

When they reached her house Tim paid off the driver and got out with her. They stood by the wall under a tree with their fingers locked together. At the end of the path the hall light gleamed out its warning message to Isobel.

'I'd better go,' she whispered.

A taxi turned into the road and passed along slowly. Tim bent his head and kissed her. 'See you tomorrow,' he said.

She caught his hand. 'Tim, do you love me?'

'Yes, I love you, Isobel.'

Although she was so tired she found that when she lay down she could not sleep. Her body was aching. In her mind she went over the whole evening, remembering what they had said to one another. She was glad to be in her own bed: it was narrow and she had it to herself, she could stretch her legs and not touch any other flesh, she could pull the bedclothes tightly round her and keep out all the draughts, she could think and no one wondered what she thought. She would rather be with Tim, but since she could not she was pleased to be alone. Everything would be all right. He loved her and the next time would be better. Everyone said so. And taken all in all, the first time had not been too bad. She had expected it to be much worse.

Tim MacAuley closed the gate behind Isobel and walked briskly away. It was a fine night and he felt disinclined to return to the empty crumpled bed which would smell of cigarette smoke and Isobel. Now that he was free of her high restricting heels and small hand in the crook of his arm, he could walk with long easy strides. This was the way he liked to walk: unhampered and evenly balanced. There were times when he liked to walk with a woman and feel the brush of her body against his but this was not one of them.

Further on he came to the estate where Isobel's sister and her husband lived. He turned into the midst of the houses. A certain curiosity drew him along to Howard and Fiona's house, a desire to see it with its curtains drawn and its occupants asleep. Perhaps he wanted to see the kind of house that Isobel would like to have, though she said flatly that she loathed new bungalows. He stopped on the corner. Howard was framed in the open, lighted doorway and on the path knelt the figure of a woman and a small child. Tim smiled for he had not imagined that anything would be happening at the Bells' house in the small hours of Sunday morning. The woman straightened herself, picked up the suitcase and went into the hall followed by the child. The door closed and a moment later a light went on in the sitting room.

Intrigued, Tim moved along to the wrought-iron gate. What was happening in there? Something strange, something unexpected.

He had twice been inside that house, for supper with Isobel. The first time, as they had stood on the step waiting to be admitted, Isobel had whispered: 'I loathe Fiona.'

'Why are we here then?'

Isobel had been saved from a reply by the opening of the door. He knew very well why they had been there: he was being edged into the family and Isobel preferred that he should be disapproved of by her relations rather than not recognized at all. To know what was revolving in her head had amused him and made him willing to be a party to it. Standing in the narrow, inconvenient hall giving up his coat to Howard, he had felt like a conspirator. He had been acting a part: Isobel's boy friend come to meet the family. When he had seated himself in the purple chair and accepted a glass of sweet sherry from Fiona's square capable hand, he had known with certainty that he would never become that part in fact. The second time a visit was proposed he had protested but in the end given way. Isobel had sat on the studio couch with her feet tucked under her, smiling happily as he and Howard argued and Fiona eyed him with distaste. Tim was not sure why he had bothered to argue – it had been about abstract art which Howard regarded as the biggest swindle ever invented – and he had been very bored. Fiona had been unable to keep her eyes off his hands. 'My hands are never clean,' he had said. 'Chalk from school and clay from my pottery.'

After they had left he had said to Isobel: 'Never again! Not for anything.'

'Very well,' she had said submissively. 'They're ghastly, aren't they?'

Tim MacAuley patted the gate and left the Bells to their

32

mysterious visitors. He went back by the same route, repassing Isobel's house which was now dark. Was she asleep or thinking of him? What was going on in that small, well-shaped head? Often he could guess but tonight he could not and was a little troubled. He wondered why she had suddenly decided to sleep with him. Her announcement, for such it had sounded, had come to him as a not altogether welcome surprise. She had said it in the way that she might tell him of a decision to buy a new frock. During the past few weeks he had lost all desire for her and had been awaiting an opportunity to create a row and end the friendship, but when she had nestled up against him and said: 'I've decided to let you sleep with me,' he had felt the reawakening of it. But after he had taken her he had known that he would never want her again.

He returned to the mews and slept soundly.

A few hours later he was wakened by Isobel sliding into bed beside him. She giggled at his astonishment.

'Surprise,' she said, and kissed him.

He found that it was quite pleasant to be wakened in this way, and more civilized than by a shrilling alarm clock. Gropingly he put out his hands and touched her smooth body.

'You slept soundly,' she cooed in his ear. 'Were you exhausted after last night?'

'Not too exhausted,' he murmured, still a little dazed. 'What time is it?'

'Midday.'

'How did you get in?'

'The door was open and there was no sign of Murray.'

She kissed him again, then lifted her head, laughing down at him with the tip of her tongue showing between parted lips. He was conscious only of the pink soft lips, limpid grey eyes, curling hair the colour of a copper beech in summer, the feel of warm flesh under his hands. The mouth came back again and his head swam.

33

He made love to her. As he said afterwards to Murray, what else could he do? It would have been churlish to push her out. Murray was of the opinion that if you found a naked woman in your bed you were entitled to her. 'There's probably a law about it somewhere that was never repealed,' said Murray, whose mind was frequently preoccupied with obscure laws. 'But you realize you're more deeply committed?'

'I wouldn't say that,' Tim said. He was not one to worry unnecessarily. He had made love to a girl, he might make love to her another two or three times, and then he would withdraw from the scene. He had done it before and emerged unscathed.

CHAPTER FOUR

Earlier on that Sunday morning, Agnes Robertson had gone into the hall and called her daughter Isobel for the third time. The smell of breakfast was filling the whole house. She wrinkled her nose with distaste, knowing that when they returned from church they would be greeted by the odour of stale bacon fat. During the week they had eggs boiled, scrambled or poached: they left no mark on the house. But on Sundays Fergus liked his bacon. She undid the cap of the bottle of air-freshener that she kept on the hall table and pulled up the long green wet tongue. She took a deep sniff and called Isobel for the fourth time.

The girl appeared at the top of the stairs. Her hair was uncombed and her face unwashed. She descended slowly, trailing a hand behind her on the banister rail. She avoided looking down at her mother's face.

'You were late last night.'

Isobel shrugged.

Agnes Robertson sighed, straightened *The Monarch of the Glen*, which had an annoying habit of becoming squint, and returned to the kitchen. It was useless to say any more: Isobel became sullen when questioned. She hoped that Fergus would not bring up the matter for she felt unequal to a family row this morning. She had lain awake for a long time after Isobel had come in, listening to Fergus snoring and wondering what Isobel could have been doing out so late. The trouble was that she had too clear an idea of what Isobel might have been doing. A stab of fear made her pause with the cooking tongs suspended over the frying pan. If Isobel should turn out like Janet! She closed her eyes. Oh God, that mustn't happen! One disappointment in a family was enough. When she opened her eyes she noticed that some grease had dropped from the tongs onto the cooker. She took a damp cloth and carefully wiped the stain from the white enamel.

From the dining room came the sound of raised voices. Soon Isobel's was blotted out by the voice of her father. It rumbled on without pause. Fergus had excellent breath control and had no need to rest. When all was quiet, Agnes Robertson swallowed two aspirins with a little water and carried in the breakfast.

They seated themselves at the gate-legged table which was too large now that the other four children had gone away. Robert, the youngest, had not gone completely since this was still nominally his home and he came for his school holidays when he had nowhere better to go. Fergus Robertson said grace, giving weight to each word and pausing between the phrases; after a pause of extra length came the solemn amen. He opened his eyes and stared in front of him for a moment before piercing one of his two eggs with his fork. His wife kept her eyes closed for five seconds longer, during which time her lips moved slightly but inaudibly. Isobel, who had been gazing through the French windows at the rose petals lying on the wet lawn, moved her head to complete the third face in the family circle. As she looked down at the congealing, half-cold food on her plate she felt sick. Her father's plate was covered with thick

35

egg yolk and a fringe of yellow clung to the edges of his grey moustache. Her nausea increased. She wondered if it could be morning sickness. If she had conceived last night could she be affected by it so soon? She had stopped Tim taking precautions by telling him that it was the safe time of the month for her. A thrill ran through her body and as she lifted the cup to her mouth she noticed that her hand was trembling. It was possible that somewhere inside her a tiny seed had started to grow and that in nine months' time it would emerge from her as a perfectly formed baby. Isobel was not daunted by the idea nor by the fact that she would be thrown out of the family to join the ranks of the unmentionables. No, she welcomed the idea. It was not that she wanted a baby particularly; she could not imagine herself as a mother; but it would solve a lot of her problems.

'Eat your breakfast, dear,' her mother said. 'It's getting cold.'

'I'm not hungry,' Isobel said. She pushed away her plate, thereby earning a ready frown from her father.

Isobel had three problems. First: she wanted to leave home and this, she felt, was a perfectly reasonable desire. Second: she was about to begin the third year of her mathematics course at the university and at the end of the first year she had discovered that she hated mathematics. Third: she was in love with Tim MacAuley and wanted to marry him.

'Are you coming to church, Isobel?' her father said.

'No,' she said, and this time deflected her eye to avoid the frown.

Isobel had known Tim MacAuley for a year. They had met at a meeting of a left-wing group, which she had attended because her parents were True-Blue Tory. She knew that her reason was an obvious one but she had never cared much about subtlety. Once she had had the idea of going to a Communist Party meeting but that would have been going a bit far and could even have been dangerous. She did not want her name on the police files: she only

36

wanted to dig a few thorns into her father's thick hide and prove that she had a mind of her own. It was necessary to assert one's individuality, or one might lose it.

Half way through the meeting Tim MacAuley, whose name she did not then know, had said to her: 'I could do with a drink. What about you?' Rather amazed at being spoken to like this by a complete stranger (although she had suspected that this sort of thing would happen at this sort of place) she had got up and followed him over the line of sprawled protesting legs out of the dingy brown hall. She had stood on the pavement wondering what would happen next. It had been a moment of excitement and anticipation. Her sixth sense, which she valued highly, had told her it was a moment of importance in her life.

'Thank goodness for fresh air,' he had said. 'Drumming feet and raised voices oppress me. You looked as fed up as I felt. Let's get some beer.'

Later he had asked her to come to his flat and had even said why he wanted her to come. Although she had been shocked by such a direct approach she had been careful not to let him see it. She had laughed in the manner of a woman of experience but discretion. She had said that she didn't know him well enough.

'I know you well enough.'

'It's different for a man.'

He had not persevered and of that she had been glad. She had half expected him to make the suggestion and indeed would have been a little hurt if he had not, so when he accepted her refusal without pique she had warmed to him. Her pride was satisfied and her virginity kept intact. He had asked to see her again and she had assented happily, pleased to find a man who wanted her for herself and not for the sole purpose of going to bed. She was tired of the students who took her home from dances in the Men's Union and breathed on her face with hot beery breaths and tried to slip their hands under her clothes.

After that first evening Isobel and Tim MacAuley met

37

regularly and sometimes he would say in a lazy detached way: 'When are you going to sleep with me, Isobel?' She would reply equally detached: 'This year, next year, sometime . . .' She enjoyed these little interchanges: to discuss the possibility of sleeping with someone and know that it would not happen unless she had fully made up her mind made her feel sophisticated and in charge of the relationship. Isobel was not inhibited about sex: she liked to talk about it. With Tim she was safe for he would not try to coerce her. He kissed her goodnight and that was all. He said that he had long since passed the stage when he wanted to writhe round on the back seats of cars and have everything but consummation of the act itself for this half-intercourse was sex at its meanest and most cowardly. Isobel had been in complete agreement.

'Why won't you sleep with me?' he would ask as they stood under the overhanging tree. She had never given him a direct answer nor had she given herself one. But underneath all her pseudo-reasons was a real one: she prized her virginity highly and thought it was not something to be given away cheaply on an impulse. It had to be put to good account. She knew it would have to go sometime but she would keep it until it was absolutely necessary for her to surrender it. The time had come last night.

She had had yet another row with her father in the afternoon and when she had gone upstairs to weep into her pink eiderdown she had realized with a shock that next month she was due to return to the nightmare of those horrible symbols and formulae. Two more years of it! She had sat up and punched the pillow hard. She couldn't do it. In addition, she had been aware of a restlessness in Tim and she had begun to wonder if he was tired of waiting. At his age – he was twenty-six – a man could not be expected to lead a celibate life indefinitely. It was trying for a man, Isobel fully understood and was sympathetic. She had made her decision: she would give herself to him that evening. She had sunk back into the soft eiderdown and smiled at

38

the pale blue ceiling, caressing the idea in her mind. Down in the garden her father had been running up and down with a mower, working off his bad temper on the lawn, and in the kitchen her mother had been dropping tears into a Madeira cake mixture, and neither of them had known what was happening to their youngest daughter in her pink-and-blue bedroom. Isobel had not looked forward much to the actual love-making itself but it would not last long. The main thing was that Tim would know that she loved him and he would love her and want to marry her. To marry Tim and never have to do mathematics again! She had not imagined that she could be so happy.

The burr of the telephone disturbed her thoughts. Her father, who always answered the telephone when he was at home, rose and went into his study. He closed the door behind him so that they would not hear what he said. Isobel lit a cigarette.

'You'll make yourself ill eating nothing and smoking so much,' her mother said.

Isobel smiled. The cigarette was increasing her nausea. Poor mother, she thought, she's had five children but she's as barren as Rannoch Moor. What did she know of life with her church committees and her Madeira cakes and her husband who was more Calvinistic than Calvin himself?

Fergus Robertson returned to the breakfast table frowning. He sat down and said abruptly: 'Janet's back.' His wife's hands began to flutter, which increased his annoyance. Her mouth was full of unspoken questions and her eyes were ready to fill with moisture. 'She's at Fiona's,' he said. 'She arrived in the small hours of the morning – as irresponsible as ever! I said we'd call in on our way home from church.'

'The child?' Agnes Robertson faltered.

'She's there too. Look like a couple of refugees, Fiona said. And of course they have no money but Janet needn't think I'm going to support them. She made her bed years ago and she can get on with it. Anyway I can't afford to keep another two people. Robert's school fees are nearly breaking me and it costs a fortune keeping Isobel at university. She goes through money like water just as Janet did. How is it that Fiona managed on so little when she was a student?'

He received no answer though Isobel would have liked to make one. She thought over this new development. She was excited that Janet had come back: it seemed a good omen for her. She might need some support in the next few months and Janet was the person to give it to her. One thing was certain: she would not end up as her sister had, with a child and no husband. She got up to help her mother carry the dishes into the kitchen.

Fergus Robertson remained at the table. It was so like Janet to return to Edinburgh with a child and no money and throw herself onto her family. She was the most intelligent of his children and he had not allowed himself to get over the disappointment she had been to him, and never would. It was strange in his family that the three girls outshone the two boys when it came to brains. He had hoped one of the boys would have been able to follow in his footsteps as an accountant and come into the firm. Ian, who had been described as average at school and not university material, had solved the problem of a career himself. After doing his national service he had taken himself off to Canada where he had found employment in advertising. It sounded vague and unsuitable to Fergus Robertson but Ian's letters assured them that he was doing well. As for Robert! He was another matter. At his day school in Edinburgh he had been described as below average and lazy, and the headmaster had said that since he did not seem to be benefiting from the type of education the school had to offer, he thought it expedient that the boy should be removed to a more suitable establishment. He had gone then to a boarding school in the Central Highlands where his lack of intelligence and industry did not matter so much. He had friends who invited him to shooting lodges

40

and country houses at vacations so that he seldom came home. This suited Fergus Robertson reasonably well. He felt a little uneasy about Robert. The uneasiness was something he had not tried to analyse nor wished to. It was easily offset by the enormous amount of hard cash that Robert cost him. About Janet he had no such doubts. She had had brains and the ability to succeed and she had thrown her advantages away by a deliberate act of wrong-doing. Fergus Robertson tilted his chair backwards and took his liver pills from the sideboard. He would take an extra one this morning.

In her blue-and-white kitchen Agnes Robertson was bending over the sink. The steam was bringing the heat into her face; she wiped her forehead with her upper arm and glanced quickly at Isobel over her shoulder. Isobel was examining her face in the mirror above the dresser: it was a small elfin-like face and Isobel seemed very pleased with it. Her mother looked back at the foaming suds in the stainless steel sink and once more was afraid. Janet had come back and Isobel regarded Janet as a guiding star that could point out the exciting paths of life. One day in a fit of depression Isobel had confided to her mother that she was disinclined to pursue her mathematics course to its bitter end, and since then Agnes Robertson had found it difficult to sleep. Fergus would be furious if he had wasted his money on Isobel for nothing as he had on Janet. It was not that they expected any return from their children but it was a bit hard when they spent all your money and then walked off and left you.

Agnes Robertson knew that Isobel went out often with Tim MacAuley. She disliked Tim on several accounts. To begin with, he was a Glaswegian and she found Glaswegians tended to be vulgar and over-familiar. She had once had a cleaning woman who belonged to Glasgow and she had been both; in the end she had had to sack the woman for reading the letters behind the clock. The woman had denied the charge, saying that she had only been dusting.

41

The obviousness of the lie and the cheerfulness with which the woman had accepted her dismissal had left a nasty taste in Agnes Robertson's mouth. Then, Tim MacAuley was a primary-school art teacher and this was a poor occupation for a man. But Agnes Robertson's main dislike of Tim was personal: he spoke with a marked Glasgow accent and it was not Kelvinside, he dressed shabbily and he was ill-mannered. Isobel had brought him home to tea one Sunday afternoon and the visit had been disastrous: he had contradicted Fergus five times.

'Will I dry the dishes for you, mother?' Isobel asked.

'No, don't bother.'

'Give my love to Janet,' Isobel said as she glided out of the door. She stopped in the hall to tilt *The Monarch of the Glen* sideways before running up the stairs. She took three steps at a time, rejoicing in the agility of her slim legs. On the top landing she turned a somersault; then sat down on the Wilton carpet, alarmed, for she had forgotten the baby. She must be careful from now on, she must take no chances. Solemnly she went into the bathroom and filled the bath. She lay down in the warm scented water. She regarded her body dispassionately: it was an *objet d'art* which she was fortunate enough to own. It was slender but well proportioned and she regretted that soon it would swell and she would lose the nice flat stomach and neat waist. It was inevitable. Isobel, although she had renounced presbyterianism, still believed in predestination. 'It is inevitable,' she said aloud to the ten pink toes that lay against the far end of the bath. And it was wonderful, for at last she knew what it was to sacrifice herself for love.

When she had dressed she would go down to the mews and see Tim. She wanted to see him again as soon as possible, to know that last night had not merely been a dream.

Janet sat in the purple chair listening to the boom of her father's voice. During the years away she had forgotten how deep and loud it was. It thudded against the thin walls of

42

the room, bouncing on her eardrums, making her long to press her fingers into her ears as she had often done as a child. The action used to infuriate him. He stood in front of the fireplace, his favourite position. The grate was empty but he held his hands behind him as though warming them at a fire. He was roaring like a hippopotamus on the edge of a dried-up pool, his face was red and splotchy, and the words spluttered wetly from under his moustache; yet she fancied that he had lost some of his fire, that there was a forced quality about the tirade which, five years ago, would have been completely spontaneous and impassioned. She realized, too, that she was listening to him with indifference.

She wiped the spray from her cheek and pushed her chair backwards until she was out of his line of fire. Fiona frowned at the dents left on her pale grey carpet and, thinking that a child ought not to be present at such a conversation, took Sally by the hand and led her into the kitchen where Howard was tending the lunch. Agnes Robertson lifted her face from a lace-bordered handkerchief to watch them go.

Fergus Robertson paused, trumpeted into his handkerchief, wiped the excess mucus from his moustache, and continued. Janet had never known on which side her bread was buttered and she probably never would, but she needn't think she could come running to him for money when she was short. Why hadn't she stayed in her job? What did she want to come running back to Edinburgh for, upsetting everybody? Did she mean to sponge off Howard and Fiona? The questions were rhetorical and demanded no answer.

The meeting was terminated by the offer of ten pounds on his part and its refusal by Janet. He clapped his black Homburg onto his bushy grey hair and stomped off down the crazy paving, calling to his wife to hurry or the joint would be burnt to a cinder.

Agnes Robertson hesitated in the doorway. 'I wish you

43

could come and stay with us,' she said to Janet. 'But it wouldn't work. Your father – '

'I know.'

'Agnes!'

'Coming, Fergus. Come and see me one afternoon, Janet, and bring Sally.'

Agnes Robertson hastened down the path into the waiting car. The engine started up, and Janet closed the front door.

Fiona and Howard stopped talking as she came into the kitchen. Howard pulled open a drawer and brought out a carving knife. He began to sharpen it, drawing the long blade over the steel with slow careful movements. Sally stood by his side, mesmerized by the flash of the metal. He lifted a tin-foiled roast of beef from the oven and laid it on the draining board. He unwrapped the foil; steam rose, clouding the spectacles he wore for close work. The smell was delicious, and Janet's mouth watered.

Fiona continued to shuttle about the kitchen pouring water off brussel sprouts, stirring gravy, wiping plates, filling salt cellars with an air of efficiency that made Janet's head swim. In reply to Janet's offer to help, Fiona said that everything was under control and why didn't Janet go into the sitting room and have a look at the papers?

Janet did not move. She stood with her back against the refrigerator and kept her feet out of Fiona's way whenever she passed. Her stomach was noisy with hunger; she wished they would hurry up with their carving and stirring. Howard cut the dark brown top off the meat and laid it neatly at the side of the plate. He shook his head gently at Sally whose fingers fumbled round it. He said that the knife was sharp and she must stand back.

'Did father give you any money?' Fiona asked.

'I refused it.'

'You are a fool. The trouble is you have no sense of values.'

They sat down to lunch in silence. Howard cleared his

throat and said grace; in the middle of it Sally knocked a glass of orange juice over the hand-painted damask cloth. Janet thought that the child was showing every sign of having inherited her clumsiness. She started to apologize but was cut short by Fiona. The table was cleared, wiped dry and a clean cloth spread. The food was now tepid and did not taste to Janet as delicious as it had smelt.

'Janet,' Howard said, unrolling his serviette, 'it's not that you're not welcome here – you know you are – but how long do you intend to stay?'

CHAPTER FIVE

The following morning Janet left Sally with Fiona and went into town.

It was a sparkling clear morning so she decided to walk. As she set off she knew that Edinburgh would look its best. A tang of woodsmoke scented the air though there was no sign of burning wood in any of the gardens she passed, and the leaves were speckled red, cinnamon and bronze. Autumn was a good time in Scotland. Spring came late and was usually a disappointment; summer often did not come at all. She had been right to return to the city. Last night on the studio couch she had tossed, unable to sleep, wondering why she had come. The drizzling Sunday in the L-shaped sitting room had crucified her with depression, but now it was erased from her mind. She marvelled how quickly her mood had changed, quelling the thought that tomorrow all might seem grey and useless again. She was full of hope: somewhere there would be a job for her and a place for them to live.

First she went to Marchmont, the Mecca of bed-sitters. A notice in the window of a ground floor flat said: ACCOMMO-DATION. She pulled the brass bell and listened to its clumsy ring. It was a long time since she had pulled such a bell.

45

Coming home from school, the rows of shiny bells had been a temptation.

The heavy door was tugged open as though it was stuck with damp, and an elderly woman wrapped in two grey cardigans and a dirty university scarf pinned across her chest appeared. A smell of cabbage and boiled mutton wafted round her spare form. She eyed Janet with suspicion. Yes, she had a vacant room with two beds. And it had a kitchenette.

'Wonderful! Could I see it, please?' Janet smiled generously but the beady eyes remained cold.

The room was gloomy. Thick net curtains clung to the windows and at their sides hung thick brown drapes, unpleasant to the touch. The woman put on the light. The walls were dun coloured, the ceiling had no colour at all; the furniture was sparse but heavy and the divan beds sagged under scratchy grey blankets. The kitchenette was a cupboard; it contained two gas rings and a shelf with a hole which held a polythene basin. The walls were spattered with grease.

Janet was undaunted. 'How much?' she asked.

'Thirty-five shillings and cheap at the price. Pay your own gas. Ye're lucky it's free. It'll be snapped up as soon as the students get back.'

Janet took it. It was a day for decisions and action. It was a horrible room but it was somewhere to come at once. Soon they would move to a better place. She gave the woman a week's rent in advance and said they would move in that afternoon.

From there she went to the nearest day nursery and arranged for Sally to start the next day. Pleased with her progress, she retired to a café to examine Saturday evening's paper. She ran her fingers down the long list. No shortage of jobs. None very exciting. Cinema usherette, mother's help, photographer's assistant . . . That sounded better. She folded the paper and left the cup of coffee, unable to wait till it cooled.

46

She walked with a long rhythmic stride, letting her body absorb the smells and sounds and sights. The warm smell of food as she passed the grilled windows of the Caledonian Hotel kitchens, the aroma of ground coffee from a grocer's shop, the sweet, pungent scent of a tobacconist's. Sound of traffic, and for a moment a curious stillness at the West End with a lull in the flow, the thud and boom of the one o'clock gun fired from the castle, startling her, for she had not realized that the day had progressed so far. And her eyes taking in all aspects of the city: charcoal-grey tenements, gracious squares, the green of the gardens, dark red and white buses bearing familiar names. Things well known and part of her but seen as though for the first time. And Princes Street with its split personality: on the northern side plate-glass windows offering gowns and green-grocery, settees and shortbread, books and bales of cloth; and a historic, jagged skyline flanking its southern side with smoke puffing up from the trough of the gardens against the black silhouette of the castle and rock.

She turned off Princes Street into the New Town. The photographer inhabited a shop in a side street.

His name was P. Smiles. She stared at the sign and laughed. She opened the door and stepped inside. A little bell tinkled behind a faded black velvet curtain. She looked round. Passport photographs curling at the edges, a few studies of constipated women with bared throats and strings of pearls, three awkward wedding parties, a bride with buck teeth and an enormous bouquet, two round-eyed children. Hardly a top flight photographer, but better than nothing.

The black velvet swayed and P. Smiles emerged, straightening his bow tie. He was a tall thin man with a tiny head. He wore a maroon smoking jacket and tapered black trousers.

'Ah, good morning, madam.' He rubbed his long white hands together, producing a sound like rasping sandpaper. 'What can I do for you? Passport photographs? Three for

47

five and sixpence. Or would you like a study?' He cocked his pimple of a head to indicate the constipated women. 'You have a very fine bone structure. You'd make an excellent subject.'

'I've come about the job.'

'Ah!' He took a cheroot from his inside pocket. As he lit it he watched Janet with narrowed eyes.

'It hasn't been filled?'

'No, no.'

'Good. I expect you want to know about my qualifications.'

'Yes indeed,' he said, though he had already been studying them.

'I'm a keen amateur photographer,' she lied. She owned a Box Brownie and had not taken a photograph for five years. 'I don't mind hard work and I'm quick to learn. Would I do?'

'I expect so.'

She thought this a most unsatisfactory interview and irritating in her present desire for action.

'Actually you wouldn't need to know much about photography.' He went round to the back of the counter and leaned across it. 'Let me explain. Most of my business is outside work, going to the clients' homes. I specialize in child photography,' he said, glancing at the two round-eyed children for confirmation. 'I want someone to go round making a survey, finding out in which houses there are children. Preparing the ground, one might say.'

'You mean you want a canvasser? Door to door. A bit of persuasive talk and leave a leaflet.'

'You've got the idea.' P. Smiles smiled enthusiastically. 'I'm sure you'd be just the right person for me. You're obviously quick on the uptake and an attractive girl like you would make the right impression.'

'What'll you pay?'

'Well now, this isn't a very lucrative profession. I can hardly keep myself in cheroots. Talk about the welfare state! It doesn't do a thing for me, dear girl, not a thing.

I even have to pay for the whole of my insurance stamp. I mean to say it's not worth it, is it, unless one's ill all the time or something? And they won't let me draw the dole when business is slack. Four pounds a week?'

'Hours?'

'Nine to four. No Saturdays,' he added hastily.

Thirty-five hours a week for four pounds. Slave labour! But he wouldn't be able to keep tabs on her and she needn't work seven hours a day. It would do till something better turned up.

'Can I start tomorrow?'

'Delighted!' He shot round the counter and seized her hand. 'Delighted! I'm sure we'll have a very happy association.'

Janet doubted that but at least it was a job. Back now to Fiona's to tell her she had a job, a place to live, a nursery for Sally to go to.

'How much is he paying?' Fiona asked at once.

'Six pounds a week.'

'Hm.' Sniff. 'How far do you think that'll take you?'

'Far enough. It's only a temporary situation anyway.'

'And what are you paying for the flat?'

'It's not exactly a flat. It's a big bed-sitting room with a kitchenette. A pound a week.' Janet sat on the lid of her remaining case. She had not told Fiona about the one she had lost. She had called at the police station on the way back but they had not found the dandelion-haired woman. 'Cheap at the price.'

'That leaves five for everything else. You'll never manage.'

Fiona was full of gloom: Janet was impractical, Sally would starve and develop something horrible like rickets, they would be back at her door before the month was out. Her voice rolled on like the steady beating of a drum foretelling doom and disaster. Janet remained outwardly cheerful but inwardly she was a little uneasy. Her exhilaration of the morning had vanished. You'll never manage to keep that

49

child. It's not fair to push her into a nursery all day while you go out to work. A housekeeping job was the best thing for you: then you were sure of your bed and board. A bed-sitting room's no place for a child. It's not a normal life.

Janet and Sally departed to Marchmont, leaving Fiona's sorrowful face behind them. The landlady's chest wheezed and she hoped the child wasn't noisy. Sally liked the kitchen cupboard and jumped on the divan beds. When they had unpacked they went out to buy food. Janet counted the money that remained in her purse: they would have to be careful.

After their meal Sally went to bed and fell asleep, exhausted after all the excitement of the day. Janet sat by the spluttering gas fire trying to read but too restless to concentrate. She wanted someone to talk to, she wanted to go out. She smoked half a cigarette and saved the rest for later. Economy was her watchword, no money to waste on luxuries. She stood by the window, peering through the net screen. A bus passed, its windows lit up. She wished she were on it. She lay on the bed, staring up at the cobwebbed cornice that belonged to an elegance of a century ago. She smoked the other half of her cigarette and told herself she must give it up. She lifted her book again and laid it down after a moment. She opened the door and looked into the long narrow hall. She counted eleven brown doors. Were there people behind all those doors? What could they be doing? It was so very quiet. Somewhere in the nether regions a woman coughed. Was it the landlady clutching her cardigans over her thin chest? Janet shut the door.

It was a hellish room, dismal and depressing. They could not stay here for long. She couldn't sit, evening after evening, watching the buses pass and listening to a woman cough. She must get out of it even for five minutes. She turned off the fire, took a last look at Sally and slipped out.

It was a relief to be in the street and see the sky above the roofs. She walked up Marchmont Road towards the lighted windows of a café ahead.

50

As soon as she opened the door she saw Isobel. She was sitting in a corner gazing at a man. As she turned her head she caught sight of Janet.

'Why, it's Janet!' she cried, leaping to her feet and rushing to meet her. 'I knew you at once.'

They hugged one another, laughing and chattering breathlessly in short unfinished sentences, feeling that there should have been something more to say than they were saying. Five years is a long time . . . How you've grown . . . Janet had not yet adjusted herself to the idea that her young sister had grown up and Isobel was too pre-occupied with the fair-haired young man in the corner. He had the build and jaw of an Australian tennis player, but he was not as clean. Isobel took Janet by the arm and led her across to him.

'Janet,' she said solemnly, 'this is Tim.' She made the introduction as though Janet had known all about Tim and had been eagerly awaiting this moment.

Janet and Tim shook hands and then he went to the counter to buy another cup of coffee. He stood there with his back to them, the sides of his jacket bunched over his hands in his trouser pockets. The set of his head was jaunty. Everything about him suggested that he was pleased with life – or himself. Janet's first instinct was to shrink from such a person: she suspected him of forced jokes, hearty laughter, back-slapping, crassness. She reminded herself that her snap judgments were often wrong and she could not imagine Isobel with such a man. Turning round, she saw that Isobel was gazing at him with a small, rather absurd smile playing round her lips. So Isobel was in love! It was impossible then to guess what kind of man he was.

He returned to them, bearing a cup and saucer swimming in coffee.

'It's lovely to see you,' Isobel said again.

The sisters talked idly of family affairs, smiling self-consciously when they looked directly at one another. Tim

51

leaned back in his chair and studied their faces with interest. There was a family likeness but Isobel's pretty little face looked like that of an animated doll beside her sister's stronger, broader one. The greenness of Janet's eyes was startling and exciting; he had to look back at them again to check that they could be so green. A flicker of her eyelids told him that she was aware she was under observation. He whistled softly under his breath. Life had taken on a different taste in the last five minutes.

The conversation trickled out as all the members of the family were disposed of, and finally died. Janet searched her memory for names of Isobel's schoolfriends she might enquire about. Nothing came. She looked at Tim.

'Is maths. your subject too?'

'Tim's an artist,' Isobel said.

Tim sat up straight and said: 'Nothing of the sort. Don't listen to anything Isobel tells you about me. She's got some grandiose ideas about my role in life. I'm a travelling salesman in art. I tour around ten primary schools calling at each once a month. I once estimated I tear up paper and give out chalks to four thousand children every four weeks. Everywhere I go in Edinburgh kids call after me and I don't even recognize them.'

'He's really a potter,' Isobel said to Janet, ignoring him.

'Stop labelling me!' he said, half-laughing to hide his annoyance. 'I mess around with bits of clay whenever it comes up my back. I'm not what you'd call a commercial success. I haven't got enough energy to become one. I'm too lazy.'

'Aren't we all?' Janet murmured.

'No,' Isobel said.

'I'd better be going.'

'Where are you staying?' Isobel asked.

'I've got a room down the road.' Janet hesitated. The thought of the dun-coloured walls and the silence in the lobby choked her. 'Would you and Tim like to come in for a cup of coffee? Or have you something better to do?'

Tim opened his mouth but Isobel was quicker. 'We'd love to but we're going to the pictures. Perhaps another time?'

'Doesn't matter,' Janet said. 'I'll have to go. There's Sally —' She had forgotten Sally.

'You haven't left Sally alone in the house all this time?' Isobel was horrified. 'Oh Janet, how could you?'

'I don't know. I only meant to go out for a few minutes.'

'But she might have wakened and called out for you.' Isobel glanced at Tim but his face was non-committal. A slight shrug had settled round his shoulders.

Janet muttered something inaudible and dashed out of the café.

'Poor Janet,' Isobel sighed. 'I don't know how she could leave her child alone even for a few minutes.'

Your trouble is you don't know very much at all, Tim thought. He yawned and did not bother to cover it with his hand.

Isobel was even more cheerful than usual; her eyes shone and her lips parted in frequent smiles to reveal her perfect white teeth. It was her vivacity that had largely attracted him to her in the first place. He had attributed it to *joie de vivre* but on further acquaintance had decided that it was simply a biological attribute and that whatever joy Isobel had was directed not towards life, but herself. She gloried in her own existence which was fine for her but boring for those who were cast as admirers. Tim was bored now and he could not revive his interest in her. But he would have to drink coffee with her a few more times for if he were to give up now she would think that he had only wanted to get her into bed and having achieved that, lost interest. He balanced his spoon on his index finger. Did it matter what she thought of him? He admitted grudgingly that it did: his pride wanted her not to think too badly of him. And now there was a further consideration: her sister Janet. Stupid ass! he thought, and replaced the spoon in the saucer with a clatter.

'What'll we do tonight?' she asked.

'I thought we were going to the pictures?'

'I don't feel like going to the pictures. I just said it on the spur of the moment.' She laid her fingers on his wrist. 'I didn't think you'd want to spend the evening in Janet's bed-sitter. You wouldn't have wanted to, would you?'

'I don't know. I rather liked Janet. Yes, I think I would have liked to spend the evening in her bed-sitter.'

She lifted her fingers. He had hurt her and he was glad. Her eyes grew wet; he looked away uncomfortably.

'You don't really love me,' she sniffed.

'For God's sake!'

'You don't, do you?'

'Of course I do.'

Why had he said it? God, he might have been married to her the way the lie popped out so easily! Her smiles returned and the tears were whisked away on the edge of a pale blue handkerchief. They were back where they were half an hour ago.

'Let's go,' he said.

They stood outside on the pavement wondering what to do next. It was only half-past eight, too early for him to take her home. He said that Murray was having some friends in for the evening so they couldn't go to the mews. She squeezed his hand and said: 'Never mind, darling. We can't go to bed every day. There'll be lots of other times.' He suggested that they go for a drink but she didn't want to do that for if they went to a pub they might run into some of his friends, none of whom she liked. She suggested that they go for a walk in the park.

'It's a lovely warm evening,' she said and her voice was full of meaning. He said he didn't feel like walking. 'We don't have to walk,' she said softly.

'The grass is wet.'

She giggled and said that he was full of wicked ideas.

'The trouble is my ideas are not wicked enough,' he said. He had a sudden notion to go down Leith Street and pick up a woman, any woman, so long as she had no name and no family. He could take her to a pub and drink beer, then they could go somewhere quiet and afterwards he could give her money and not have to worry how he was going to tell her he didn't want to see her again.

'What would *you* like to do?' Isobel asked.

'Go to the pictures.'

She pouted, but what else was there to do?

Sitting in the cinema holding Isobel's hand and trying not to listen to Isobel predicting the next move in the film, Tim thought of Janet. He hoped that Isobel might take him to visit her one evening. As they sucked iced orange juice during the interval, he suggested it casually. Isobel was evasive: she had noticed how Tim had looked at Janet and remembered Fiona telling her that whenever she had taken a boy friend home Janet had tried to get her claws into him. Fiona claimed that Janet had even tried to take Howard away from her but this Isobel doubted, for who would want Howard but Fiona?

'I'll see,' Isobel said.

She went to see Janet the following afternoon, and in the evening said regretfully to Tim: 'Janet didn't like you much. Fiona's been poisoning her mind against you. All my family seems to be against you. Except me,' she added. She stirred her coffee. Her conversation with Janet had disturbed her. Tim had not been mentioned.

'I think father's fed up with himself,' Janet had said.

'What on earth do you mean?'

'He's tired of sustaining his role as head of the family, trying to keep his children on the narrow path, his path. He'll be glad when we've all gone our own ways and he can retire. Dictators must get weary as they grow old and begin to wonder if it was all worth it.'

'You sound almost sorry for him. What do you know about him now? You've been away five years.'

'Maybe I don't know. It was something I sensed during the few minutes I saw him at Fiona's. I'd never thought

55

before that he could doubt himself. I did then. I felt he wanted to act differently but didn't know how to.'

Isobel had left Janet feeling that something in her life had been challenged. Her father *was* impossible, she told herself. To her friends she had given a picture of him as a figure of fun, a hangover from the Edwardian era, a religious maniac who dwelt on the wages of sin and insisted on thanking God before eating a crumb, a despot and tyrant who denied his daughters their natural heritage of freedom. She had exaggerated a bit of course but then everyone did when telling a story. He gave her an extra dimension to her personality. 'Your poor dear Papa,' as her friends called him.

Janet had become a bit odd, Isobel decided, and forgot it. She had no time to waste pitying her father; she was sure he didn't deserve it anyway. Her mother she did pity and had resolved quite young not to follow in her footsteps. Money and a stone house weren't everything. Love mattered more.

Tim yawned, loudly.

Isobel took a sip of coffee: it was cold.

'What'll we do tonight?' she said.

CHAPTER SIX

Janet reported at the studio each morning for instructions. She rapped on the frosted glass door, then waited for a few minutes whilst Smiles dragged himself off his couch in the back room. The blind would go up with a rattle and the door open a few inches so that she could squeeze round it. Fresh air disagreed with P. Smiles; it was an enemy he kept at bay with remarkable success. He would stand in the middle of the floor, clad in a Paisley dressing-gown and leather slippers, yawning. The hot flow of his breath and the sight of the grey furred tongue arched in the pink cavity of his mouth nauseated her so early in the morning.

56

'Just nip across the road, my dear, and fetch some morning rolls. And half a pint of milk. I'll put the kettle on.'

When he had discovered himself to be without change for three mornings running, she refused to go before receiving the money. He assumed an expression of hurt but fumbled in the till and produced one and sixpence. 'I'll give you the rest when I pay you on Friday.'

When he had fortified himself with food and drink and a few puffs of cheroot, he told her which part of the town she was to cover that day. He spread the counter with maps and tackled the project with the air of a military commander planning an invasion. He confided that he had held the rank of major during the war but his natural modesty prevented him using the title in civilian life. 'Such a piece of affectation I always think, don't you, dear girl?' He lectured her on strategy and after each session told her to tell his prospective customers that he was a family man and an expert at handling children. She recoiled at the idea of him handling Sally.

She liked being out in the fresh September mornings, talking to people, stopping to watch the children playing. When her feet tired she sat on a low garden wall or shared a park bench with a couple of old men; she smoked a cigarette and read a morning paper. If it rained she retreated to the nearest café. Four pounds a week did not cover wet feet. It wasn't a bad job, she decided: no one was watching or hounding her, and roaming the streets brought its own feel of freedom. Often the women asked her in and over cups of tea told their troubles: most were short of money, some were bored and glad of a bit of company, some had children who wet their beds, others had husbands who came home only to eat and sleep. Often Janet forgot the purpose of her visit and went away without leaving a leaflet. She doubted if she was much good as a saleswoman but was unperturbed: she doubted if Smiles was much good as a photographer.

At one o'clock she knocked off for the day for by then

her feet were hot and she considered that Smiles had had enough for his money. At four she returned to the studio with a list of addresses. Nothing in the studio indicated that a photograph had been taken or that Smiles had done anything other than lie on his couch and smoke cheroots, though he always declared that business had been brisk.

'Good girl!' He would massage her shoulder with his bony hand as he perused her notebook. 'So nice to have someone trustworthy working with one.'

On Friday afternoon his compliments were more effusive than usual. Janet watched his face carefully but he avoided her eye. 'See you on Monday,' he said with a smile that was intended to charm. Then he retired smartly behind the black velvet.

She followed him. He was holding up a negative which he was studying intently.

'My money, Mr Smiles.'

He held the negative aloft between two fingers and gazed at her, astonished.

'But, my dear Mrs Crosbie, I thought we agreed that I'd pay you monthly?'

'We agreed nothing of the sort. You quoted a weekly wage.'

'But I always pay monthly.' He squinted again at the negative which was blank. 'Assistants, bills, rent, everything.'

'Come off it! I want my four pounds – I need them. I have rent to pay and a child to feed.'

'Couldn't we come to a little arrangement? I'll pay you double next Friday. You see, my dear, I am temporarily a trifle embarrassed. It's a terrible business this,' he sighed. He put down the negative and lit a cheroot. 'People never pay their bills. But I expect money next week.'

'I want it now.'

He waved the cheroot in the air. 'No can do. But perhaps to oblige you I might be able to let you have a little something.' He turned his back to her and fished in a wallet. He brought out a pound. It was dirty and almost torn in half. 'You can fix it with some sellotape. So useful, sellotape. One wonders how one used to manage before.'

'Now you'll write me an IOU.' She thrust her notebook and a pen in front of him.

'Don't you trust me, my dear?'

'No.'

'Very well.' He shrugged. He wrote out 'IOU three pounds sterling' and signed his name: P. Smiles. He wrote it with a flourish. His signature was worthless anyway.

And much good will it do me, she thought, as she tucked it away in her pocket.

She would not have returned for a further week if she could have found another job. And she still had hopes of getting some money out of Smiles. The second week she finished each day at twelve. Calling at doors was beginning to bore her and the same stories were repeated from new council house to tenement to bungalow. The snippets of humdrum life were no longer comforting; they left her with a sense of greyness and depression and she longed for the extravagant or extraordinary. Even Smiles was a welcome sight at the end of a day of housewives in floral aprons and curlers with their harassed faces and shrieks of censure at erring children. Whenever she saw a garden hung with washing or a buckled bicycle straddling a garden path she pushed a leaflet through the letter box without bothering to knock. Other houses were obviously childless: neat rows of flowers, an ordered quiet, glimpses of tidy rooms through clean windows; these she passed by.

On Tuesday afternoon *The Seekers* visited the National Gallery. The previous week one of their number had instructed them on Allan Ramsay, the painter, and now they were coming to see examples of his work. The bus disgorged them in the middle of Princes Street, a bundle of women, three pregnant and nine not-at-the-moment. They streamed across the road, chattering gaily, giggling a little as

59

a bus threatened their advance and then halted, patiently, to allow them to pass. These outings were so pleasant and took one out of oneself for a little while.

They swarmed up the steps of the gallery into the entrance foyer, exchanging pleasantries about culture being free and how seldom people took advantage of the city's amenities. They had the place to themselves. Almost.

Sitting on a bench in one of the rooms was Janet. Fiona frowned when she saw her. Her sister wore an old duffle coat and tartan slacks she had had as a student.

Fiona greeted her and the girls clustered round to be introduced.

'Twins, do you say, Fiona? You're not a bit alike.'

'We're not identical twins.'

'We didn't know you had another sister, Fiona.'

'Janet's been away for some years.'

'It must be wonderful to have a twin. Do you always know what the other's thinking?'

'Not always,' Fiona said. She shifted her heavy weight from one foot to the other, then sank down onto the seat beside Janet.

The Seekers streamed away across the polished parquet in pursuit of Allan Ramsay, filling the high gallery with their noise as they went.

'What on earth are you doing in here with that bunch of women? Is it a convocation or something?'

'We've come to see the paintings of Allan Ramsay,' Fiona said stiffly, mistrusting the look in Janet's eye.

'Are you afraid to come alone? Or are you playing at schools?'

'We're not playing at anything. We're a serious-minded group with wide interests.' Fiona knew she had sounded pompous but blamed Janet for making her so. She said irritably: 'Anyway, that's not what I want to speak to you about. What are you doing in here at this time of the afternoon? Have you lost your job already?'

Janet explained. Fiona was horrified: that was dishonest.

60

Janet told her about P. Smiles but Fiona was not convinced for two wrongs did not make a right.

'Stop ramming your schoolgirl phrases down my throat!' Janet said.

The sisters parted a trifle coldly. Fiona was rattled at having met Janet and her visit to the gallery was spoiled. Later she could remember nothing of Allan Ramsay's paintings.

Afterwards *The Seekers* went to a tea-shop. Over the cups interest was expressed in Janet. Fiona was not surprised at their reactions.

'What an unusual face! Interesting.'

'Those green eyes are rather startling.'

'She has the look of having suffered deeply.'

Janet had always had that look, Fiona thought, her irritation increasing. It had earned her a great deal of attention in the past.

'Is she married, Fiona?'

'No.'

'I thought she was wearing a wedding ring?'

'Well — ' Fiona paused. Eleven pairs of eyes were turned towards her, eleven pairs of ears were waiting. Honesty was the best policy. She took a deep breath and told them.

They were not in the least shocked. She should have known that they would not be and was a little ashamed at having doubted their breadth of mind and understanding. To compensate for her lack of trust, she began to talk about Janet, telling them the circumstances of her unmarried motherhood, everything she knew, in fact. The heads closed over the cups, cigarette smoke rose in thick blue spirals, soft sympathetic murmurs fluttered round Fiona's clear voice.

'So you can see,' Fiona said, straightening her back, 'it's not been easy for her.'

The heads nodded and lifted, backs were straightened.

It was suggested that Janet be invited to join the group even though she didn't live in the estate. An exception could be made in the circumstances. One more timid

61

member pointed out that that would bring the numbers to thirteen, but the rest were too intelligent to be superstitious.

'Janet must certainly join us. She'll bring a different point of view into the group.'

'We want new ideas. We must guard against insularity.'

'Hear, hear!'

'I wouldn't say we were insular,' said Fiona, who disliked the idea that Janet was being brought in to broaden their outlook. 'After all, we have a wide range of interests. No, I think *we* might help Janet.'

'It should be one of the purposes of the group to help those in need.'

'Hear, hear!'

Fiona was commissioned to invite Janet to come to the meeting on the following Tuesday: a talk on Zoroaster. Howard drove her over to Marchmont in the evening to present the invitation.

'You know I dislike institutions, mothers' meetings, women's guilds, etc.,' Janet said.

'This is not a women's guild,' Fiona said. 'We're discussing Zoroaster next Tuesday.'

'I don't care about Zoroaster.'

'Well, it's time you did! You're letting your mind run to seed.'

'In that case I wouldn't be able to keep up with *The Seekers*. I'd be a drag on the company.'

Fiona tried to press the invitation for half an hour, without success. Going home in the car she said to Howard: 'It's no good trying to help Janet. There I was offering to share my friends with her but she just tossed the offer back as though it were a rotten plum without a thankyou or a hint of gratitude.'

'Don't distress yourself, dear. You ought to know Janet by now.'

As they sipped their coffee on Friday morning, Janet reminded Smiles that it was pay day.

'I haven't forgotten,' he said with a coy smile. 'I'm going out today on business and I expect to collect some money. By the way, my dear, I suppose you wouldn't be interested in making a little extra?'

'What would I have to do?'

'Why do you always look at me with suspicion? It's nothing very much really. Just a few poses. You have a lovely figure, dear girl. What do you say?' He held up his hand. 'All right, all right. I didn't think you'd be interested. You have a hard puritanical stare. John Knox's influence is rampant in this city. Some day I shall have to set myself to counteract it.'

At four she stood again on the doorstep of the studio. The door was locked, the blind drawn and her hammering brought no response from within. She sat down to wait.

Twenty minutes later she crossed the street to the dairy. She asked the woman if she had seen Smiles.

'He went out early this morning, hen. Early for him, that is. About ten.'

Janet bought a sugar bun and sat on an empty milk crate to eat it.

'Owes you money, does he?'

'Seven pounds.'

'You'll be lucky. He owes money all round here. Wouldn't trust him with a tanner. Sleekit as they come. I'm surprised at a nice young lady like you working for one of his sort.' The woman moved the tray of sugar buns and leant across the counter. 'They tell me there's some queer goings on behind that velvet curtain?'

Janet said that as far as she knew nothing went on behind the curtain; that was the trouble. She finished her bun and returned to the studio. She listened: nothing moving inside. She slipped down the vennel at the side and found herself in a back yard cluttered with old boxes and two rusty dustbins bulging with rubbish. Above her head was a small window with a broken catch. She looked round quickly, then hoisted herself up onto one of the bins. The

63

window swung inwards. She crawled through and landed on her stomach on Smiles' unmade couch. The bedclothes stank of feet, stale sweat and cheroot smoke.

The studio was almost in darkness. As she fumbled round the velvet curtain it brushed against her face making her shudder. She pulled open the drawer of the till and counted out the few coins that lay on the mildewed baize. She swore. He owed her more than that for bus fares and milk. As she put the money in her pocket she heard a noise.

Someone was trying the door handle. She listened to the faint squeak as it gyrated in its socket. She moved round very slowly until she faced the door. A dark shape stood at the other side of the blind. The handle turned again, then the figure moved away. She let out her breath.

She went back to the other room. Beside the couch stood an old bureau; the drawer was locked but gave way with a tug. She rummaged through it: bills months old and crumpled, a few receipts, an empty cheroot packet, a leaflet advertising rubber trusses. At the bottom lay a pile of pornographic photographs. She shut the drawer and left as she had come.

Climbing back up to Princes Street she wondered if she could keep the landlady at bay for a week. She had not had to worry about rent before and had not thought that such a small sum could ever have worried her. For the last two weeks she had thought about little else but money, her mind was beginning to work like a calculating machine and her last conscious thoughts before going to sleep were about shillings for the gas and a resolve to stop smoking. The suitcase had not turned up and she had been forced to replace some of its contents. As she crossed George Street and narrowly missed being knocked down by a large cement lorry, she concluded that she was not making much of a success of her rehabilitation.

'You're looking very grim.'

She looked up to see Tim MacAuley blocking the pavement in front of her. He was swinging a brief-case in his right hand and he was grinning.

'I was reflecting on my inadequacies.'

'That's a terrible thing to be reflecting on. I wouldn't dream of it myself. Do you think a drink might help to lighten your load?'

They walked up to a pub near Tollcross. The bar was long and mirrored and smelled of beer rubbed into the wood. Janet chose an octagonal table which had a map of Edinburgh under its glass top and Tim joined the crush of small men in fawn trenchcoats at the bar. She relaxed against the dark red leather, pleased with the smooth barrels, the round gilt-edged tables, the stuccoed ceiling.

Tim came back with the beer and joined her on the leather couch. She took a long drink and said: 'I've had a hectic afternoon. Been doing a spot of breaking and entering. It's surprisingly easy.'

He looked at her hands cradling the glass. 'You look a bit dusty.'

'I had to climb on a dustbin. I dislodged the lid on the way down and grabbed a handful of ashes.'

'I trust the loot was lucrative?'

She shook her head. 'I could have had a bundle of pornographic photographs but I wouldn't have known how to start selling those.'

'I expect there's a ready market somewhere or other. Perhaps we could set up in business together. You do the breaking and entering and I'll handle the disposal.'

'I might be forced into it in the end.' She drank again. 'Tim, I need a job. Badly!'

'I see.'

'I've got hardly any money left. An old poof of a photographer owes me seven pounds but I haven't a hope in hell of getting that and even if I did it wouldn't last long. Know of anyone who'd like to employ me – and pay me?'

He thought for a moment. 'I do know of someone who wants an assistant. He runs a bookshop, mostly second-hand

65

stuff. I don't know if he could pay you much but he's reliable. Shall we go and see him now? He's open till six. We'll make it if we hurry.'

They hailed a taxi and picked up Sally on the way. The lights were still on in the bookshop when the taxi stopped outside.

'Why it's Mr Boland's Bookshop!' Janet said. 'I used to come here often.'

As they went in through the doorway they saw a postcard sellotaped to the window: 'Assistant Wanted. Apply within.'

They applied within. Mr Boland remembered Janet at once though he said she looked thinner. And older, she added. No, no, he protested. He shook hands with her several times, polished his glasses vigorously on the corner of a yellow duster, and fished a peppermint out of his ticket pocket for Sally. He would be delighted to have Janet as his assistant but . . . His smile faded. He couldn't pay much: six pounds a week.

'Could I have a word with you, Mr Boland?' Tim said.

They retreated to the back of the shop, where they spoke together in whispers.

Mr Boland returned to Janet and said: 'I could throw in a flat. It's not much,' he added quickly. 'An old basement. I don't know that you'd like it. It's round the corner in The Crescent.'

'A flat,' Janet echoed.

He locked the shop and they went to see it. It was dark and smelled damp. There were two rooms each with a closed stove, a bed recess and some elderly pieces of furniture, a long narrow kitchen, a w.c. without a window. The kitchen had a door which led onto the back green. The term was a euphemism for what they stood in was a great stretch of yellow-green wasteland broken by upright poles and a tangle of sagging clothes lines. A few pieces of washing flapped listlessly in the soot-specked breeze. The Crescent might have looked dingy from the front but from the back it looked so ancient and grimy that it might have stood there since the Middle Ages. The windows had a curious impersonal air which made one doubt if anyone really lived behind them. Tim waited anxiously for Janet to speak. Tenements, back greens, dimly-lighted stone passages, communal smells, kids scrabbling over tin cans, had all been part of his Glasgow childhood but Janet had been brought up in a detatched stone villa with apple trees in the garden. To her this might seem like the end of the line. Standing here, watching the darkening sky and the tracing of pink round the roof tops, he might have been in his own back green at home; he almost expected a window to go up with a rattle and his mother to bawl out that tea was ready.

'No bath, I'm afraid,' Mr Boland said apologetically as he wiped the dust from his hands onto the seat of his trousers. 'And you'd have to get a cat. You might be troubled with mice.'

'I'll take it,' Janet said.

Tim was delighted. It was a good omen for him: he had helped Janet find a job and a place to live, and now they had the basis of a relationship that had nothing to do with Isobel. He returned to the room in Marchmont with them and played boisterously with Sally whilst Janet fried sausages and made tea. She hummed tunelessly over the frying pan and laughed at their antics.

After their meal Tim rose reluctantly. 'I have to meet Isobel. Can I come and visit you in The Crescent?'

A slight frown creased Janet's forehead. 'Yes, do,' she said with formal politeness. 'Come with Isobel.'

Isobel had been waiting for ten minutes when he arrived at the café. She glared at him over an empty cup and asked what he had been doing.

'Nothing,' he said. He wanted to keep his few hours with Janet to himself and not have them pawed over by Isobel.

He would have to break with Isobel, and it would have to be soon. It was ludicrous to spend one's evenings in such a manner. Lots of people did it, thinking it was better to have the company of a member of the opposite sex than walk the streets alone, but it was not for him.

Even before she opened her mouth he knew what her next words would be.

'What'll we do this evening?'

CHAPTER SEVEN

Janet and Sally moved to The Crescent the following morning. When the rooms had been scrubbed and fires lit, they went out. They acquired a fluffy grey cat, whom they named Muffin, and some coloured travel posters to brighten the walls of their new home.

Coming back along The Crescent, they met one of their neighbours. She was the fattest woman Sally had ever seen. She was polishing the bell of the ground floor flat which sat on top of their basement. She moved round slowly when she saw them and watched Janet undoing the catch of the gate.

'You the new tenant in 31B?' she said.

She eased herself down the three steps onto the pavement, leaned back against the railings and put her hand on top of the gate. She introduced herself as Mrs MacNab and repeated Janet's name three times as though she might have read it in a sensational Sunday newspaper. She had eyes like a dead fish but they were misleading for they saw clearly. She had a smell of old wash-coppers, soap suds and steamed cloth, but though she smelled like a laundry she was certainly not clean: when she turned her head to note a movement along the street Janet saw the dirt standing out in the folds of her neck. Standing there, feet astride in fawn felt slippers, she resembled a vast suet pudding oozing out of its cloth. Sally, staring up at her, looked like a Lilliputian gazing on Gulliver.

Mrs MacNab blew her nose on her polish rag and said:

'Yer man working near here?'

'No.'

68

The small eyes grew larger in their surrounding mass of flesh. Mrs MacNab shook the Brasso tin in her right hand and cocked her head to one side. 'Stranger, eh?'

'I belong to Edinburgh.'

'Not this part?'

'No.'

The next few questions were addressed to Sally who was too astonished at the proximity of such a large body to answer. The cat was mewing and scratching the wicker; a stream of liquid flowed out of the side and spotted the pavement. Janet moved the basket to her other hand and looked longingly down at the green blistered door bearing the black numbers 31B, but the fat beige hand had a firm grip of the gate.

'Mondays and Thursdays is bucket days. Cart comes at seven. Nae puttin' yer bucket oot the night before, mind. I'm nae wantin' a' the muck blawin' intae my front windaes. The last yins that lived doon there was a lot of mucky pups.'

She treated them to a saga of the previous tenants' dirty habits; at the end of it Janet firmly edged her out of the way and got her hand on her own gate. Her own gate! She had never felt such a pride of possession before as she pushed it open. Mrs McNab remounted the steps to continue the polishing of her clean bell. The doorbells and name plates of The Crescent shone like pure gold: the women were to be seen rubbing them up at all hours of the day and night. When anything special was happening in the street, a wedding, a funeral, a burst gas main, there was a great flurry of bell cleaning. What a flapping of dusters and shaking of Brasso tins! Janet was sorry that her bell was hidden in the shadow of the area. Perhaps that was why she did not clean it all the time she lived there.

They spent the afternoon rearranging the few pieces of furniture and decorating the walls with the posters. Sally was delighted with it all; she went around talking to her imaginary playmate as though they were playing at houses.

69

To Janet it had the same rather unreal quality. She would be glad when the rest of their possessions arrived from the south for then the flat would look more like their own.

After she had put Sally to bed in the smaller of the two rooms, she sat by the window watching the light fail over the grey worn steps. Dry leaves were rustling in the wind. One hovered between the railings before drifting down to land on the dead geranium in the window box. The wind was rising and soon the leaves came swirling fast. To-morrow she would sweep them up along with the squashed cigarette packets and limp chocolate wrappers that lay on the cracked cement outside. The wind bore the refuse of the street down to the basement dwellers of The Crescent.

The Crescent was not shaped like one: it was straight and lined on either side with solid blocks of tenements. Whoever designed them had set the windows of the basements too low and the pavement too close to the windows. Had The Crescent been designed? Janet thought rather that it had been made by men in overalls who had piled grey stone upon grey stone; all day they had worked without looking up until at the end of it they had realized that they had made it straight instead of curved, and by then it was too late. But its name was no more ridiculous than many another.

There was little light left in the street now, though in the sky there would be more. A flicker, and the street lamp cast a yellow pool in front of the railing. Feet were hurrying past, eager to reach their Saturday night destinations. She watched the thin heels of the girls and women going clickety-clack on the hard pavement and the longer, firmer strides of the men. She could see nothing above the knees. The world from her window was one of ankles and shoes and flapping trouser-legs. All these feet had somewhere to go whilst she sat watching them go. So many evenings now she had had this sense of isolation. The removal had solved very little.

She continued to sit by the window in a state of apathy

tinged with fatigue, mesmerized by the line of railings, the lift of the feet on the pavement and the quiet regular breathing of Muffin behind her in the room. She sat on the edge of the room but she was not in it, nor was she out there in the street where her eyes rested. She became dulled, emptied of all feeling. Nothing could ever touch her: she was wrapped in a cocoon of disinterest which muffled the sharp edges of the world. Even the noise of passing traffic and the clack of shoes came to her as though through a wad of cotton wool.

Get up, she said to herself. Go out. Walk the streets. Feel the air on your face and the wind in your hair. Don't sit gazing with blank eyes, listening with half-closed ears.

She jerked herself out of her trance. There was a sleepy reluctance about her limbs: they felt soft and woolly. Pins and needles shot through her left foot; she rubbed it gently, wincing at the pain as the circulation gradually returned. She looked into the other room to make sure Sally slept, and went out.

The street was curiously empty and very quiet. Had she imagined all those feet? Where had they gone? She was surprised to see that it was still so light. Opposite her scattered yellow squares broke the dark bulk of the buildings into strange patterns. She turned up the collar on her coat against the cut of the wind and walked briskly towards the Meadows. Once there she slackened her pace and wandered idly along the paths, stopping to look at the lights of the traffic blinking along Melville Drive, the line of roof tops and spires that stood black against the sky, the spread of the branches above her head. This part of Edinburgh she loved. Her depression slipped away.

She went up Middle Meadow Walk and round the streets near the university, glancing in the café windows as she passed. There were several that she did not know, brightly-coloured and nickel-plated, but even the old ones looked unfamiliar. None of the faces behind the glass were known to her. What had happened to all those she had known?

71

They would have turned into hard-working doctors, black-coated lawyers, young matrons pushing prams and deploring the menial jobs to which they must put their superior intelligence. . . . Most she had known had been predictable. And then she thought of Dolly for it was impossible to imagine what had happened to Dolly.

Dolly had been unlike most students who tended to be the same from day to day: she could transform herself from hour to hour if it were necessary and it often was. A chance meeting in the street, and her whole personality changed. She was full of enterprise and liked variety. She claimed to have been made love to in ten different languages. Amongst her lovers Janet recalled a Norwegian who lived in a flat off Leith Walk with five other Norwegians and two hundred and twenty-three dirty milk bottles, an Egyptian doctor who wore long woollen combinations to protect himself from the chill of the Scottish winter and whose breath stank of garlic unsuccessfully masked by the extra-strong peppermints which he chewed, a kilted Scottish Nationalist whose mother was a good plain cook and from whose lips fell succulent details of stew and dumplings whilst he forked amongst Dolly's concoctions of rubbery spaghetti or curried eggs. There were many others and for each one Dolly became a different person. She worked on the theory that men liked women to be the opposite of the women in their own country so for the Norwegian she was dark-headed and sultry, for the Egyptian pink-cheeked and brimming with good clean fun, and for the Scottish Nationalist volatile and provocative. And she always fell in love with them. Her versatility was breathtaking. For her there were no half measures: she changed the whole mode of her dress, her walk, her voice and she dyed her hair. Her hair was in turn ash blonde, strawberry blonde, chestnut brown, soot black and even pink, green and pale blue. (Once it was Belisha beacon orange but that was a mistake.) Janet did not know what colour Dolly's hair really was, and thought it likely that Dolly did not either.

72

She said often that Dolly should become an actress but Dolly would bat her long false eyelashes and pretend not to understand. When she had no assignations – dates was too paltry a word for her meetings – they would sit in a horse-boxed café and she would tell Janet of her latest *amour*. In comparison Janet's life was dull, a point Dolly made daily. She urged her to dye her hair, change her name, leave home, do something! 'You don't want to be Janet Robertson all your life. It's such a solid, uncompromising name. You want something more fluid.' To Janet, coming each morning from the stone villa, Dolly was refreshing and exciting.

But where would Dolly be now? Anywhere between Edinburgh and Katmandu. And what would Dolly be now? That one Janet could not begin to answer.

She looked at her watch and saw that it was time to go back.

At the top of Middle Meadow Walk she collided with a small dark figure. They both stepped backwards, apologizing, and then Janet realized that his voice was familiar.

'Khalil!' she gasped.

If she had given it any thought she would have known that Khalil was the one person from that old life she was liable to come face to face with in the city. How had she forgotten him?

'I am so pleased to see you again, Janet. We must have a drink to celebrate.'

'I can't,' she said. 'I have to go home – now. Come with me if you like, but you'll have to run.'

He asked no questions, did not protest; he trotted by her side along the shadowy paths to The Crescent.

All was peaceful in 31B. Muffin and Sally were both fast asleep. Khalil pushed the stuffing back into the drop-end settee and laid himself out on it; Janet pulled the faded blue curtains and turned to look at him. He hadn't changed. She laughed and was reassured: it was as if her own identity had been finally confirmed and her right

73

to be in this city acclaimed. Khalil, without any emotion, accepted that she was here and that she had been away for five years was of no importance.

'It is all right for you to laugh,' he said, 'but I am not used to such exercise.' His little black eyes darted round the room, not judging or approving, but looking. 'Have you a cigarette, Janet? I seem to have mislaid mine.'

She laughed again and gave him a cigarette. His thin wrists and ankles protruded like twigs from a blue Harris tweed suit, patched on the elbows and frayed at the cuffs. One of the buttons on the jacket had been lost and replaced by an overlarge bottle green one. Under the jacket he wore a red and black tartan shirt and a yellow tie. He grinned at Janet and flicked his tongue down over his bottom lip like a frog catching flies.

'You haven't changed a bit,' she said.

'But you are wrong! I change every day: the cells in my body grow older, my hair shows pepperings of grey and I have to ink out the offending strands, my cynicism grows with the hours. But not my wisdom, alas! And now you are smiling at me as though I am a figure of fun. And you are pleased because my fortunes have not improved, that I am wearing the same suit or one very like it, that I have cadged a cigarette from you because I have none in my pocket. If you had met me wearing striped trousers and black coat, stepping from a limousine with bowler hat in one hand and gold cigarette case in the other, you would have been sad.'

'Yes, I would.'

'And your fortunes – have they improved?'

'Obviously not.' She laughed. 'I've got a job at Mr Boland's Bookshop. This place belongs to him.'

'It is much better than no place at all.'

'Yes indeed. Khalil, what are you living on?'

He waved his cigarette in the air. 'This and that.'

He looked as though he were living on very little. She cooked a meal which he ate greedily. 'So you have learned

74

to cook,' he said with admiration. 'I did not imagine that. You always had such a loathing for domesticity.'

'I haven't had much option. A loathing for domesticity is something only the young and the rich can afford. At seventeen I thought it smart to declare an antipathy to all things domestic and I was too wrapped up in my own affairs to devote any time to washing dishes or tidying my room. My mother despaired of me. She would have laughed then if she had known I was destined to become a housekeeper. And so would I for I thought I was too intelligent for such things!'

'And now from housekeeper to book-keeper. A step up or a step down?'

'Up or down, it doesn't matter. I don't intend to sell books for the rest of my life. That is the thing about every move I make – it's temporary. If I look ahead into the future I see myself leading a richer fuller life, I don't imagine that things are always going to be like this. But how to get this something better?'

'I am the wrong person to ask,' he said.

She smiled. 'I often worry about Sally but she seems adaptable. She goes where I go and accepts it all. I don't know that a child wants security and a settled way of life above all else.'

'You didn't?'

'Oh, no! I was always longing for something new to happen that would alter our whole life. I wished father would lose his job and we'd have to go and seek our fortunes in the outback of Australia or Peru or somewhere miles from Edinburgh. I didn't realize how improbable it was, how impossible. It irked me that we lived in the same house year after year, and every summer we took a house at St Andrews for a month. When we went on a journey I willed the car to break down and isolate us in a lonely spot. If visitors came and the house was crowded I was delighted to give up my bed and sleep on the dining room floor; waking in the morning was like being born into a new life and the

75

day was full of possibilities. But nothing much new ever did happen in our house: we went on in the same old way, father didn't lose his job because of course he owned the job, the car was never permitted to break down or run out of petrol in an inconvenient place and we didn't often have people to stay. Mother liked the house to herself. "Thank goodness they've gone!" she would say. "Now we can get back to normal." Normal! I loathed that word.'

'It is not an inspiring word, I agree.'

'I'm glad I met you tonight, Khalil. It's good to have someone to talk to again. I've had no one for such a long time.'

They sat in front of the fire and exchanged their news. Later Janet realized that this was not true: she told him some things about herself but he told her nothing. At the end of the evening she knew no more about the facts of his life than she had done five years ago. He liked to keep an air of mystery about himself and his activities. She had known him for three years at the time when he was supposed to be reading for a degree in political economy though to her knowledge he had never attended a class; he had existed with the aid of a grant which appeared at irregular intervals from the Indian Government and he had dwelt somewhere in the shadows off Leith Walk. Questioning, whether bantering or serious and purposeful, could not penetrate the wall of secrecy which shielded him. He was there, reclining on the settee, talking, listening, smoking one's cigarettes, and what did it matter how, where or with whom he lived? One evening she and Dolly had tried to follow him but the task had proved impossible for within minutes he had eluded them and Janet had been relieved for she had feared tracking him to a squalid room which would contain a bed, rotting linoleum and no secrets. When she had confessed this to Dolly, Dolly had said with a pout: 'You're an incurable romantic!'

'So you've come back to Edinburgh,' Khalil mused. 'I wonder why.'

76

'I like it. I like its harsh edge, even its chill wind and the greyness. I belong here.'

'You're a true Northerner.'

'And you?'

'I belong anywhere. And nowhere.'

His answer brought Dolly to her mind. She asked him if he had seen her.

'I saw her the last night of the Festival. She was sitting on a bus wearing a black hat. Not a fashionable hat, you understand, just a hat. I waved but she didn't know me. She had a man with her.'

'Of course,' Janet said.

It was late when Khalil left. She went up to the top of the steps with him. He looked both ways along the street before opening the gate and stepping out onto the pavement. Then he walked away quickly, keeping close to the railings. She stood listening to the sound of his feet dying away and went back down into her room feeling happier than she had done since returning to Edinburgh.

CHAPTER EIGHT

Emptied trunks and a broken tea-chest stood in a pile against the wall, dwarfing the low room; clothes, books and toys lay strewn across the floor. Janet pushed a hank of hair out of her eyes and looked up to see her mother's feet come along behind the railings and stop at the gate.

Agnes Robertson descended the steps slowly, not trusting the smooth worn edges, trying each one tentatively with the sole of her soft suede shoe. A heather tweed skirt with two swinging pleats came into view, then a jacket with three purple buttons and a pale lilac jumper showing at the neck straddled by two rows of neat, unostentatious pearls. The face appeared at the window, and Janet realized with a shock that her mother was getting old.

Agnes Robertson picked her way through the various

objects and seated herself on the edge of a springless chair. She accepted a cup of tea which she held on her lap with both hands. There was a dirty thumb mark on the side of the cup; after a few minutes she laid it aside without touching the tea. The place smelt. Her nostrils twitched, trying to discover what it was that was so offensive. She came to the conclusion that it was a collection of smells: fried food, stale tobacco smoke, dampness, cat. She made a mental note to bring a bottle of air-freshener the next time she came. She wiped her hands on her handkerchief and watched Sally with an air of wistfulness that made Janet want to scream. She had brought a plastic doll in a pink frilly dress but after a cursory glance the child had tossed it onto the bed in the recess, preferring the things on the floor.

'I thought you might have come to see me?'

'I meant to.' Janet poured herself another cup of half-cold tea. 'I've been working. I've not had time.' It was a lie: she could have gone when she was out on her canvassing rounds. Once she had walked along the road, hesitated with her hand on the gate, and turned away.

'This is a terrible place.' Agnes Robertson stared at the stove with its spewed porridge enamel and cracked mica windows. 'Surely you don't mean to live here?'

Janet swallowed the remains of her tea. Of course she meant to live here. What else was she doing here? She meant to distemper the walls, put up new curtains, hang some pictures. . . . A bird was chirping on the railings and she thought she could smell burning leaves. Sally began to transfer the coal, lump by lump, from the bucket to the window sill. Agnes Robertson looked at the child and then at Janet.

'It doesn't matter,' Janet said. 'She's playing at shops.'

Agnes Robertson sighed. No, perhaps it didn't matter. The room was filthy anyway. This daughter of hers had never had much idea of cleanliness though she had been brought up in the same way as the others. Even as a child she had differed from the rest: she had fought with her father, roamed the streets after dark, came home with dirty hands, cut knees and an unsuitable vocabulary. In her teens she had been wayward and uncontrollable, she had refused to go to church, to tell them where she spent her time and most of the time she was at home she had locked herself in her room. What had gone wrong? What had made Janet so different? She had spent many sleepless nights pondering the question. Fergus blamed an eccentric old aunt on her side. Aunt Emily had been housekeeper to a retired civil servant from Rangoon but it was said she had done more than keep his house. Fergus said that Aunt Emily's wickedness had come out in Janet.

'It can't be healthy down here. I smelt the damp as I came into the hall. Why can't you live in a decent place?' She knew a woman, a member of her church, who had recently been left a widow and wanted to let part of her bungalow. She had declared herself willing to discuss terms with Janet. 'She remembers you, dear, when you were in the Guides. You cut her grass during Bob-a-Job week.'

'I'm no longer a Girl Guide.'

'Consider it, please, Janet. It's a nice house and there's a big garden for Sally to play in.'

Janet considered the idea and rejected it at once. Her mother tried to reason with her but, as she said to Fiona afterwards, it was impossible to make Janet see reason once she had made up her mind about something. At the end of it all she said that Janet was stubborn and did not deserve sympathy, then she wept. Janet, although she had anticipated the tears from the moment she saw her mother's legs come down the steps, was surprised and uncomfortable.

Agnes Robertson soon had herself under control again. She dabbed her eyes and smiled bravely at her daughter. In the silence that followed Janet raked desperately round in her mind for something to talk about. The subject scarcely mattered: it was only to mask the blankness. She started to talk about a book she had read, talking quickly and animatedly. Her mother stared past her with glassy eyes.

'You should read it, mother. It's very evocative. You went to Bruges for your honeymoon, didn't you? I could write down the title for you.'

'Do you remember Betty Parker?'

Janet started. 'Betty Parker?'

'She married Bob Morrison. I met her the other day. She has two lovely children and a house on the Braids. Bob's got a good job, straight in line to be managing director.'

'I'll write down the name of this book . . .'

'I've had to sack my daily woman. She would bring her two-year-old child with her. He had dirty habits. It was disgusting – stains on the carpet and pools on the linoleum. I warned her several times but it was no good. She had to go.'

Janet began to tear an empty cigarette packet into strips.

'It's so difficult to get help these days, and they ask three and sixpence an hour plus bus fares. I can remember when you and Fiona were babies . . .'

Janet tore the strips into small pieces like confetti.

'Of course they can get big money in the factories now. People like me can't hope to compete. It's perfectly true that it's our class that's been hit the hardest. Before the war . . .'

There was a clatter of feet on the steps outside. Janet swivelled round to see Khalil's brown face pressed against the window.

He came in and shook hands politely with Agnes Robertson before settling himself on the settee.

'I see you have a typewriter,' he said, prodding it with his foot. 'I have a friend who wishes to borrow one. I will bring him to meet you.'

All of Khalil's friends wished to borrow something. Janet protested that she needed it herself. Khalil said that nevertheless he would bring his friend and they could discuss the matter. Agnes Robertson preserved a prim-lipped silence interspersed with quick vacant smiles; Sally sang over her black knobbly patterns; Khalil told them of a typewriter he had once owned – this Janet did not believe – which would

80

only work in a downhill position. On fine summer days he would take it into the Queen's Park, lay it on a soft green slope high above the smoky tenement roofs and gently tap out love poems. 'Love poems to your city, madam,' he added with a little bow towards the skewered felt hat under which flickered another of those lost anxious smiles. 'Ah yes, on the few days of summer it is beautiful: sun on grey stones, the smell of grass, flowers . . . But in winter' – he shivered – 'the blood runs cold in my veins, the wind cuts me like a thin wire, I waken in the morning with icicles on my lashes and my breath freezes against the sheet. Soon it will be winter again. I feel it in my hands.' He stretched out his thin fingers, then linked them together behind his head. 'And yet I stay. Do you love your city, madam?'

A faint blush stained Agnes Robertson's powdered cheeks and she looked away from the dark inquiring eyes as though she had been asked something vaguely obscene. The word 'love' was a difficult one for her. Janet had never heard her say she loved anyone or anything. She had often said: 'You know I'm very fond of you, dear,' when she had meant something more.

'There are worse places to live,' she said, rearranging the pleats of her skirt.

'Yes indeed. I have lived in them all. Places where nothing ever freezes, where the sun beats hot all day on dry earth, where flowers push through the stones only to die, where are no sheets for the breath to freeze against. And places the sun never finds, where all is cold and green and grey.'

Agnes Robertson coughed and stole a glance at the wrist watch under her tweed cuff. 'Yes, we are fortunate here. We have no extremes. I must go, Janet, or I'll be late for your father's tea. It's been nice meeting you, Mr – er – '

'Khalil. Just Khalil.'

Janet walked up the steps with her mother.

'Who on earth is that? What rubbish he was talking! I know you've got to lead your own life and all that but I don't think it's good to have someone like him hanging round you. People start talking. I mean you've got to think of Sally too, haven't you? Poor wee mite. I'm sure he hasn't had a bath for a month: his neck looked filthy to me though of course it's hard to tell when his skin's that colour anyway. I don't know what your father would say. I wouldn't trust him if I were you. There's something shifty about those dark eyes.'

They embraced, skiffing one another's cheeks with their lips, caught for one moment into a feeling of pure tenderness where all judgments were suspended. Then they drew apart and the wind swirled between them. Agnes Robertson looked back from the corner to wave. Janet moved forward a step. She wanted to run after her and tell her that she would be all right, that Sally would be all right, that she need not carry her worry home with her in the bus; but she went back down the steps into the room where Sally and Khalil were playing with a red and yellow beach ball, where Muffin purred in the folds of a faded rug, where all the objects of her life lay on the floor like exhibits for all to see and pick over.

'You think I made a hit with your mother?' Khalil asked. 'No?' He flicked out his tongue. 'At the top of the steps she said to you: "Beware, this man is dangerous"! They laughed and Sally joined in. 'She is a nice lady even though she thinks I am not nice. A nice Edinburgh lady who is never late for her husband's tea.'

An Edinburgh lady who is loyal to her husband, who loves her children and worries over them during long sleepless nights, who goes faithfully to church, delivers its magazines along suburban roads, stands behind cake stalls with hands sticky from soft sweet icing and shiny red cherries, who works diligently sweeping the dirt from the corners of her house, whose tear-washed eyes betray a self-induced martyrdom of sadness; a wife and mother who has known what it is to be peacefully content with a fire at her feet and children sleeping in upstairs rooms but who has never known what it is to be wildly, deliriously happy and want to shout it out of every window up to the stars in the sky. An Edinburgh lady, standing now at a bus stop, feeling the chill of a September afternoon round her legs, waiting for the dark red bus to come and carry her back to her close-carpeted villa where she can take the long pin out of her hat and sit down beside a tidy hearth to drink tea from a thin cup that bears no mark of a dirty thumb. Standing on the pavement thinking. Thinking of her children. Ian: he is all right, he is in Canada, he has a good job, a nice home, a big car, he has two children whose eyes laugh out of their photographs making her sad. Fiona: she is all right, she has a good husband, a nice little house, fitted carpets, a wrought-iron gate, a car, she will soon have a child. Isobel: so far she is all right, she stays out late sometimes but not too late, she is not as openly defiant as Janet was, she is not as sensible as Fiona but not as irresponsible as Janet. There is hope yet for Isobel. Robert: he is not clever but he seems to be all right, he has some nice friends who will help him. But Janet: she has a child who has no father and whose face is black with coal dust, she has a dark dank basement where paper clings to the walls like burst blisters and chairs erupt their entrails onto stained coconut matting that hides the rottenness of the floor, where strange men lie on the sofa and say strange things. No, Janet is not all right, she has made a mess of her life . . .

'You look sad, Janet,' Khalil said. 'Are you?'

'Sad! Why should I be sad? Come on, help me clear up this mess. It looks like one of mother's jumble sales.'

Khalil departed in the early evening and returned an hour later with a carrier bag full of beer and the friend who wished to borrow the typewriter. The friend was Tim MacAuley.

'We've met,' Janet said. She had been wondering when he would come.

Khalil nodded. He set the bag on the table and began to

83

unpack it. Tim had of course bought the beer but had been generous enough to allow him to carry it in. Khalil lined the bottles up and lovingly wiped the dust from their shoulders with the corner of the table cloth.

'I didn't know you two knew one another?' Janet said.

'You sound suspicious,' Khalil said, regarding her with an air of innocence. 'I know everyone it is necessary to know in this city.'

'It's very good of you to lend your typewriter,' Tim said.

Janet started to speak but was forestalled. Khalil's tongue moved with the speed of a rattlesnake on the strike. 'Janet is very kind. She likes to lend things. If one lends one may borrow.' He removed the top from a bottle with a neat flick of the wrist. 'Perhaps you will have something she would like to borrow?'

'I hope so.'

Janet opened the doors of the stove and they sat round it. As she drank her beer she was aware that Tim MacAuley was watching her, and he was watching her with an interest that was not altogether due to her being Isobel's sister or the possessor of a typewriter. His candid gaze said: you attract me. She was irritated by his lack of subtlety and his easy disloyalty to Isobel. Isobel was her sister. She must remember to tell him how fond they were of one another and how close. Nevertheless she could not help feeling flattered, and admitted to herself that she was allowing herself to respond a little. The admission made her contemptuous of herself and of him, and she hoped he would not come back, except of course to return the typewriter.

'It is interesting to watch two people who want to know one another better,' Khalil said. 'I have been making observations: you are like two boxers circling in a ring, jabbing at the air to show that you intend to land a blow when you find a suitable opening.' He smiled blandly at them. 'I hope you two will not fight one another?'

'There's no reason why we should,' Janet said tartly and Tim laughed.

84

He leaned back in his chair and relaxed. 'You have a lot of books. Could I borrow one or two?'

'As long as you return them.'

'I'd certainly return them.'

'You see,' Khalil said, 'he will go away with a typewriter and six books, then he can come back seven times. After that there will be no need of excuses. Borrowing and lending has its uses, as I said.'

'You're talking rubbish tonight,' Janet said. 'You've drunk too much beer.'

'Not too much. When I left you I went to *Greyfriars Bobby* and there I find Tim. Have a beer, he says, so I do not refuse. I do not like to insult people. I have found a beautiful young woman with a typewriter, I tell him. His eyes light up. He says: Have another beer, so again I do not refuse. I will take you to her, I say, it is a beautiful typewriter with a leather case and a zip fastener and it can be carried round in one hand, so he says: Have another – '

'All right, Khalil.' Janet stopped laughing and said to Tim: 'Why do you want to borrow a typewriter?'

'But it is not for me,' Tim said, surprised. 'Didn't Khalil tell you? It's for a friend. He shares my flat. He's writing a social history of Scotland.'

The friend had reached the reign of Duncan the Meek. Janet groaned and said that she didn't want to lend her typewriter for a year.

'What do you want with a typewriter?' Khalil demanded.

'I may want to address envelopes or take it to a pawn shop.'

'Nonsense! You know, I may borrow this machine myself one of these days. I could write the story of my life.'

'I would lend it to you if you would do that.'

'No one would ever read it! It would be written and then burnt. Ceremoniously. Perhaps in this stove. I would sit in contemplation whilst my life burst into flames and then dwindled away to grey ash.' He decapped another bottle. 'Do you think it would be a valuable experience for me to poke the pus out of the boils of my life? It's a long time since they have been visible to the naked eye: I keep them well sealed down with sticking plaster. No one is interested in a beggar's sores.'

Khalil talked most of the evening. Beer frothed down his supple throat and words bubbled back up. When all the bottles were empty, he went down on his knees on the coconut matting and prayed, Muslim fashion. 'You see,' he said, looking up at them, 'I have no reverence for anything.'

'You don't expect us to believe that, do you?' Janet said.

Tim and Khalil went away as the church clock on the corner was striking two, Khalil with a pound note tucked into his trouser pocket – he was expecting money by the next post – and Tim with the zippered typewriter and half a dozen books.

'What's the matter?' Janet said.

'Nothing,' Isobel said, staring moodily at the green beer bottles which Sally was arranging in a circle on the floor. 'I'm just fed up, that's all. I didn't see Tim last night. I usually see him on a Friday night. He phoned to say he had to go and see someone on business.'

Janet thrust the poker into the fire and raised a shower of sparks.

'He was phoning from a pub. I could hear glasses clinking in the background and people laughing. He could have been out with another woman.'

Sally completed her ring and sat down in the middle of it like a tailor. She closed her eyes, crossed her fingers and made a wish.

'You've been drinking a lot of beer,' Isobel said.

'Khalil brought it.'

'Khalil! I don't like him. I wish Tim didn't see so much of him: he's forever borrowing money and whenever they go out together Tim drinks too much. Khalil took us to a party one night down at Leith Docks. I'd never seen such an odd collection. Some of the women were prostitutes –

I'm sure of it for they looked horrible. There was a Sikh with a turban – you know the type that comes round the doors with battered suitcases full of pink satin blouses – and a couple of drunk Dutch sailors and two men who looked like tramps.'

'You can't expect everyone to look the same.'

'I don't. But they gave me the creeps. Tim laughed. He seemed to think it was a great joke. We came away early and Khalil has never asked us again. I'm sure he tries to put Tim against me.'

Janet protested, but Isobel insisted that Khalil was a sly character and not to be trusted. 'You may well laugh but there's something evil about him, and he looks so dirty.' She wrinkled her small nose.

'You sound like mother.'

That roused Isobel from her lethargy. The colour in her cheeks flamed to a deep rose, making her look very pretty.

'You ought to get angry more often,' Janet said complacently. 'It suits you.'

The compliment softened Isobel, who hurried away a little comforted. She decided to have a row with Tim tonight, and when he saw her with her cheeks flushed and eyes sparkling, a new admiration would be awakened in him.

She went down to Princes Street and bought herself a lemon-yellow sweater one size too small. With a finger hooked through the string of her parcel, she strolled along the street in the midst of the Saturday morning parade, stopping to talk to a couple of friends for almost an hour. When it was time for the pubs to open their doors, she walked along Rose Street, but saw no sign of Tim.

She returned home to see how she looked in the mirror when she was angry. Janet was right: it did suit her.

CHAPTER NINE

Janet settled in quickly at the bookshop. Something akin to a fever gripped her whenever she found herself in a room entirely walled with books: her eyes flitted from title to title scarcely able to believe that all these things existed, her fingers fluttered over bindings and flicked over pages, her brain reeled at the thought of all the millions of words waiting to be read. She smiled as she moved about. 'You can read when you've nothing else to do,' said Mr Boland, who seemed to do little else, except when he donned his black coat and once-black hat and set off with a fibre suitcase in search of more books.

The shop was divided into two parts. On one side the new books gleamed and shone, and when opened, gave off a fresh invigorating smell. On the other side was the second-hand department which smelled like a dusty museum that had been locked up fifty years ago; it was a place of mystery and surprise where one encountered things forgotten or never known. The little shop was so rich after the mean dark one of P. Smiles. Janet took the bus down to the studio one lunch-time to try and recover her money but the blind was drawn and the woman in the dairy said that she hadn't seen Smiles for days.

The hours passed pleasantly in Mr Boland's bookshop. Khalil often came in and sat on the floor in a corner. He kept his legs tucked well underneath him and did not get in the way. Mr Boland did not mind him reading through the stock without ever buying anything; he minded no one who could keep quiet. The customers were for the most part uncommunicative; they lounged against the bookcases reading furtively, and when they wished to leave they would wait until they were unobserved and slink out with a guilty air which they would shake off in the porch before marching boldly away along the street. Several times a day a sale was made. The ring of the till was pleasant and lifted everyone's head, even Mr Boland's. Janet enjoyed wrapping the purchases in shiny brown paper and securing them with golden sellotape that adhered to the fingernails at the slightest provocation. The second-hand books were not wrapped: they were carried out under the arm and exposed immediately to the perils of the weather. And the paperbacks were slipped into flimsy white bags.

At lunch-time Mr Boland and Janet sat in the back shop, their sandwiches spread out on the table and their books propped against the milk bottle and tea pot. They rarely spoke of their personal affairs. She knew that he was married and had one son who wanted to be a boxer: that was all. He asked no questions about her life outside the shop, and he paid her every Saturday morning.

The only thing that caused alarm in the shop was rain. The mornings opened on a speculation about the weather, staring up at the sky, sniffing the air. But they nearly always took a chance on it. As Mr Boland said, the shop looked half-dressed without its trolleys on the pavement. When the first drops of rain appeared they dropped books, extricated themselves from the sellotape and rushed outside to bring in the two trolleys, one of sixpenny books, the other of shilling ones. The trolleys had lost their wheels a long time ago and had to be carried; loaded with books they weighed several hundredweights so that the customers had to be called upon to lend a hand. If the rain was not apprehended early enough the shilling books were reduced to sixpence and the sixpenny ones were given away. Janet marvelled that Mr Boland was able to support a wife, a son who wanted to be a boxer, and was also able to pay her six pounds a week.

On Friday mornings she cleaned the two big plate-glass windows. First, she smothered them with soap suds so that the shop looked as if it had been hit by a freak snow storm which had ignored its neighbours on either side; then she drenched them with buckets of warm water and watched the suds scurrying down to meet the ground. After that

89

came the polishing up: she stood on a pair of rickety steps which swayed dangerously, alarming the passers-by who executed a wide nervous arc that took them at its widest point to the brink of the kerb. She breathed on the glass, rubbed vigorously and shook out her duster, feeling as pleased with herself as the housewives in The Crescent did when surveying their bells. Fiona said that there were more labour-saving methods of cleaning windows but Janet was not interested. She liked her little flood on the pavement on Friday mornings. Afterwards she took a stiff yard brush and swept the water into the gutter where it gurgled into a nearby drain and dropped down to the dark underworld. Fiona said that it wasn't nice for Janet to have to clean windows in a public street, but Janet told her that it was very nice.

During the operation she had short rests which gave her time to observe the life of the street. The top of the steps was an excellent vantage point. Directly opposite was a greengrocer's which was a riot of colour: yellow grapefruit, lemons, bananas; red tomatoes, peppers, apples; green curly lettuce, cabbage, parsley, cress; white heads of cauliflower, sticks of celery; amber onions; purple beetroot; soil-brown potatoes; fawn and mauve turnips. And then there were the flowers. The profusion of colour made her feel dizzy so she would turn her eyes to the fishmonger next door where all was blanched and clean and cold and water ran incessantly down the inside of the window. Beyond it was a butcher's shop, a study in red and white broken by the blue and white aprons of the men who wielded their choppers on the stained counter. Then came the chemist, old-fashioned and sombre, its windows filled with gleaming jars of mysterious liquid, its pestle and mortar a dull yellow. The shops comprised the ground floor of a block of tenements. All day women passed up and down examining the produce, going in and out of doorways, stopping to talk with their shopping bags propped against their legs. They carried the largest shopping bags Janet had ever seen, and

90

with their spare hands they pushed prams in front or tugged unwilling children behind. Mrs MacNab was a professional shopper: she ambled up and down a dozen times a day, her small efficient eyes noting and weighing the proffered bargains.

Janet's view was rarely uninterrupted for long: a bus would pass, a car, a message boy on a bicycle, a van intent on business. The street was full of noises: the skid of tyres, bleat of horns, rumble of wheels on cobbles and later the drill of the roadmen lifting the cobblestones, the swell and roar and screech of voices. She would sit, mesmerized, on the top step, oblivious of the wind, until her hands grew red and cold and she would climb stiffly down to meet Khalil's jibe that she was becoming a worthy match for Mrs McNab.

Mrs MacNab honoured them with her presence one morning. She wanted to know if they sold birthday cards. Her brief visit gave her time to examine Janet, Mr Boland and Khalil in detail and take a poking glance through the open doorway into the back shop. She lingered awhile in front of a stand of philosophical and religious books, then propelled herself, inch by inch, out onto the pavement. 'I have a sneaking admiration for that woman,' Khalil said. 'She is as determined and unsubtle as a steam roller.'

And each afternoon at half-past four Tim came along the street, whistling and swinging his brief-case against his leg. 'What has he to be so pleased about?' Khalil said. 'I thought teachers were supposed to be a depressed race?'

At closing time Tim helped to carry in the trolleys; Khalil busied himself behind the counter, folding the brown paper and arranging the rolls of sellotape. 'These young ones are strong,' he said to Mr Boland. 'Look at their arms! Mine are too thin and weak to carry such large objects.'

Tim and Khalil accompanied Janet to the nursery to collect Sally, then they all returned to The Crescent to eat together. Most evenings Tim left them to go and meet Isobel. He had not yet managed to get rid of her. It was a

91

tricky business for she clung to him like a leech, and he imagined her flying into the arms of her sister Janet for comfort if she were prised loose. The wasted hours spent staring moodily across sticky tables frustrated him and he returned to the mews with an irritable tongue and his stomach awash with greyish-brown liquid.

'It's time you took a hold of yourself, man,' Murray told him. 'You're too soft-hearted. You need a touch of ruthlessness to get what you want in this life and get rid of what you don't want. You'll end up in a semi-detached planting bulbs in the garden and Little Miss Puppet darning your socks while she watches "This Is Your Life".'

'Very funny! And what do you do? You sit here night after night poring over the dead and done for, and you make damned sure no one will ever get near your socks. Not that they would want to!'

Mr Boland went one morning to a sale. He came back twice, once for his hat and the second time for his spectacles. It was only after he had finally gone that Janet saw he had forgotten his teeth. He kept them in a jam jar of water in the back shop. She hid them behind a stack of the *Waverley Novels* and settled down by the fire, leaving the communicating door into the shop open. It was a dark wet day. Water was streaming down the windows blurring the outside world. In the shop the lights were on, shining equally over the bright new jackets and old faded bindings. There were few customers. Rain made people hurry past, their collars pulled up against their necks, umbrellas angled against the driving wind. She was content to sit listening to the drumming of the rain and turn over the pages of the morning papers, enjoying the sanctuary of an inner room.

The tinkle of the bell brought her to her feet. A girl stood in the doorway, pushing the hood of her mackintosh from her face. She started and said Janet's name. Janet gave her a half-smile, trying to dig back into her memory for an identity for the pale face framed by soft light brown hair. Water dripped from the fawn coat; it made little plopping noises on the linoleum. The girl laughed nervously and pushed the hair from the nape of her neck. This gesture Janet remembered.

'Dolly!' she cried.

It *was* Dolly, almost unrecognizable, but nevertheless it was she. They went into the back room and Dolly sat beside the fire in a brown skirt and fawn twin set, fiddling with her single string of pearls. This new disguise intrigued Janet for in all her roles Dolly had never chosen to look dowdy. There was obviously a reason for it and as she laid her left hand on the arm of the chair Janet saw what it was: five diamonds hooped round her fourth finger.

'Well?' Janet demanded.

'Well,' Dolly repeated uncertainly, avoiding the green questioning eyes.

'So you're in love again?'

She shrugged. 'I'm engaged.'

'And?'

'And what?' Dolly sounded irritable. 'His name's Paul and he's a minister. Church of Scotland.'

Janet was unable to restrain a laugh, but Dolly was not amused.

'It's his birthday tomorrow. I came to buy him a book. My boss is away so I just slipped out for a moment. I work in an office further along the street.'

'So you're going to marry a minister, Dolly!'

Dolly frowned, then started to talk very rapidly, giving Janet no chance to comment. She spoke about the manse which was large and draughty, the carpet they had chosen for Paul's study, the curtains for the kitchen window, the three-piece suite for the lounge. She would have to take the Women's Guild; the Sunday School was a bit of a problem as they couldn't get enough teachers of the right type; they really ought to raise ministers' stipends; he was having a bit of trouble with one of his elders: the man thought they

93

were spending too much on church heating but Mrs Brownlee had been saying only last Sunday that she'd been simply frozen and that her teeth had chattered throughout the sermon; people didn't realize all the things a minister had to contend with; she was going to have her hands full what with sick visiting and then they were trying to raise funds for a new hall . . . Oh, and by the way, did Janet mind not calling her Dolly? It was rather a childish name, wasn't it? She preferred Dorothy. The pearls spun between her neatly manicured fingers. Janet was speechless.

She had forgotten that Dolly could become so immersed in a part that she did not know herself when she was acting. But was she acting? Perhaps this was the real Dolly at last. How could she know?

Dolly did not stay long. Before she left she bought Paul a book about crossing the Pacific in a canoe; he liked stories of adventure when he relaxed. Janet helped her on with her coat and murmured an invitation to visit her at the flat. Dolly said that she would come one evening when Paul had a meeting.

'Do,' Janet said, 'and bring your knitting.'

Dolly nodded. 'I never seem to get time for it these days. I'm making Paul a thick jersey to wear in his study. The draughts are something terrible, you've no idea.'

Janet stood at the door watching the fawn blur that was now Dolly fade into the slanting rain. If she wished to pursue her friendship with her she would have to go to Mrs Dodd's Drapery on the corner and buy a bag of wool and a pair of knitting needles. She hated the click of knitting needles and she always dropped stitches. Lack of concentration, Fiona said; you can save a lot of money by knitting jumpers. But Janet had no money to save.

She was astonished when Dolly did come to visit her. She liked the basement as much as Agnes Robertson had. Janet found it difficult not to call her Dolly and every time she forgot a spasm of annoyance crossed Dorothy's face. To Janet's inexperienced eye she seemed an expert knitter.

94

Muffin lay on her mistress's knee, hypnotized by the flash of the steel rods and the speed with which the wool flew off and on, off and on. Plain and purl, purl and plain, cable stitch, twisted rib, cast on, cast off. When anything from the past was mentioned, the face above the knitting went blank. Dorothy knew nothing of a Dolly with pink hair and false eyelashes and a string of lovers that sounded like the roll call for the Olympic Games. Janet was building up for one big yawn when Khalil arrived. Dolly remembered him, yes, distantly, with a stiff handshake and cold smile. She had to go now or she would be late meeting her fiancé. He was at a meeting about the church heating. The row was finished, the wool wound to a tight ball, pierced by the steel pins, and then all was wrapped in a white serviette and placed in a tartan bag.

'That was Dolly,' Janet said after Dorothy had thanked her for a pleasant evening, promised to come again, nodded to Khalil and taken away the tartan bag to meet the fiancé who was coming from a meeting about the church heating.

'Rubbish!' Khalil said. 'That was not Dolly. You were always gullible, Janet. You could be taken in by a policeman dressed up as your mother.' He surveyed the room. 'Have you any food? As I came across the Meadows my stomach rumbled three times. That is an ominous sign. If it rumbles a fourth time it means great disaster will befall me.'

He perched on the table in the long narrow kitchen whilst she whipped eggs into a creamy froth and scorched slabs of bread under the smelly gas grill. They were disturbed in the middle of their meal by three loud, evenly-spaced knocks on the front door.

'I will go,' Khalil said, hastily pushing a piece of egg into his mouth. 'It may be Tim.'

It was not Tim.

'How nice to see you, Janet,' Fiona said as her eyes quickly took in the litter of dishes in the sink and the grease clinging to the gas jets of the stove. 'We haven't

95

seen you for days. We've been wondering if you were still alive.'

'We've been out for a drink, just thought we'd drop in when we were passing,' Howard said, his eyes on a yellow stain on Khalil's tartan chest.

They stood in a line in the kitchen, there being no room for two abreast. Khalil picked up his plate and recommenced eating. Howard moved a little to the left and Janet saw that he and Fiona had not come alone. 'You remember my cousin George of course, don't you?' Howard said.

Janet smiled at George Bell, who was pinned against the end wall, and murmured a greeting. George raised his hand in salute and said: 'Nice to see you again, Janet.' His hair had thinned and receded since she had last seen him, heightening his already high forehead. He looked embarrassed as if he had been an unwilling party to the intrusion. Janet could hear him putting forward his objections and excuses, and being overruled, impatiently, by Fiona.

Khalil crunched a piece of toast, washed down the crumbs with a gulp of tea and suggested that they go into the living room. 'There is more room there and it is not necessary for us to stand here in Indian file,' he said. A murmur of assent ran along the line and George, being nearest the door, led the way. A glance at her watch reassured Janet: it would soon be time for Fiona and Howard to go home for cocoa and bed. But her hopes were ill-founded for it soon became apparent that they were determined either to outstay Khalil or to remain long enough to discover whether he lived in the flat or not.

'Just two rooms you have, isn't it?' Fiona said as she tried to make herself comfortable on the chair that had no springs.

Khalil squatted cross-legged on the floor, hugging his ankles. He accepted a cigarette from George's silver cigarette case; said in answer to Howard that, oh yes, he was a Muslim but he had fallen into wicked ways. Fiona frowned and tugged at a loose thread on the arm of the chair. She

96

was endeavouring to send her sister a message by eye-signal but Janet was refusing to co-operate. Fiona's eyes frequently said more than her mouth. Though she urged others to state their problems and thoughts she often chose not to put her own into words. She had a range of gestures and expressions as eloquent as any racetrack bookie; she could frown, beckon, shake her head with complete propriety for she imagined that what was unspoken went unnoticed except by the person to whom she wished to communicate.

They had a lengthy and uninteresting conversation about a film which no one appeared to have seen, agreed that September had been an unusually wet month – Howard quoted the figures – and hoped that it would not snow before Christmas. Then Khalil recited a new poem he had written entitled 'Laughter in Leith Street'. After that they had a few minutes' silence. The fire crackled noisily and a car swished past in the road.

'We were really hoping to have a few words alone with you,' Fiona said. 'George, as you know, is a lawyer.' She lowered her voice as she enunciated the last word so that it came out as something vaguely threatening.

Janet could see no connection between the two statements but then her brain often became stultified in the presence of Howard and Fiona. Khalil, who rarely took a hint, decided to take this one. He departed to the kitchen to wash the dishes.

'What's he doing here?' Fiona said at once. 'I thought he would have gone back to where he came from years ago.'

'Seems a decent enough chap,' said George who was a liberal.

'People like him are just spongers. Why should this country support a lot of wasters and down-and-outs?' Fiona leaned back and folded her hands in front of her stomach. 'We brought George along because we thought you might need some legal advice.'

'Legal advice?'

'To try and recover the money that photographer owes you. It's disgraceful employing you and not paying you. He shouldn't be allowed to get away with it.' She looked at Howard.

'It'll just encourage him to do it again,' Howard said.

'Don't be silly.' Janet spoke impatiently. 'It wouldn't be worth trying to recover seven pounds.'

'You said he owed you two weeks' money,' Fiona said. 'That's twelve pounds.'

'He paid me part of it.'

'You're lying,' Fiona snapped. She sat back and said more quietly: 'You ought to do something about it. It's the principle of the thing that matters. A warning letter from George might do the trick.'

'It's unlikely that any letter from George would persuade P. Smiles to part with seven pounds even if he had it. He'd put it in the drawer along with his unpaid bills and his pornographic photographs.'

'Pornographic!' Fiona said.

'Yes. Pornographic.'

George Bell, with the tact of his profession, intervened in what looked like developing into a family squabble and said that he would be pleased to call another evening and discuss the matter with Janet then. Tomorrow at eight?

'Very well,' Janet said.

Khalil, of course, outstayed them all. He accompanied Janet to the gate to wave them off.

Fiona wound down the car window. 'We'd like to see Sally some time. What about letting her come to us for a week-end?'

'I'll see,' Janet said, meaning no.

The car moved off. Janet and Khalil remained in the street for a few minutes leaning against the railings, enjoying the night. The moon was full and unshadowed, and the stars were white.

'So George Bell is coming back into your life,' Khalil said.

'Not necessarily. I wouldn't place such importance on his visit tomorrow.'

'No? His face is one that is easily read. I read it tonight.'

CHAPTER TEN

George Bell came at eight, as arranged. He sat in the springless chair, almost at ease, but not quite. Janet noticed that he had combed his black hair carefully so that each strand was put to good use. She pictured him in his bachelor flat checking details in front of the mirror: top pocket handkerchief protruding the right amount, tie straight, no dandruff on shoulders. He was not unduly vain, but a good appearance mattered to him.

The first moments were awkward. They stared into the fire. She wished she had some sherry to offer him: it would have made an appropriate beginning and eased their tension.

Gazing into the fire, she tried to recall how she had felt the last time they had been alone together, but could not. All she remembered was his baffled face when she blurted out her news. Before going to meet him she had rehearsed the scene, seeing herself as a woman of experience and sensibility, regretting what she must do, suffering because she was making him suffer, comforting him in his misery; but when the moment of truth had arrived she had merely blurted out the bald fact: 'I don't love you, George.' She had meant to tell him she admired him, respected him, and that the girl he married would be lucky. She had meant to leave a good impression of herself. She had been eighteen years old.

She decided to cut across the awkwardness, acknowledge it.

'What does one say to a man one – ' She paused.

'Jilted?' he suggested.

'Well – jilted – seven years ago. Does one apologize?'

99

'I think the operative phrase is "seven years ago". It's a span of time after which things and even people can be presumed dead. I don't think you need apologize.'

'Thank you. I'm not much good at it. The word "sorry" used to stick in my throat when I was a child.'

'You take after your father in that respect. Why do you look so surprised? He is your father, after all. You remind me of him in a lot of ways.'

'I do? In that case you must be glad I didn't marry you,' she said drily.

'I've never been glad of that.' He said it as a statement, and not as a means of trying to draw out of her how she felt towards him now. After so long he did not expect her to feel anything. He offered her a cigarette, took one himself, lit them both. 'One thing puzzles me, looking back – I understand why you broke off our engagement but not why you ever agreed to it in the first place. You were never in love with me.'

'No.' She wanted to return his honesty. She said: 'I was fond of you, I'd known you all my life. I was flattered, I suppose, that you who were so much older should want to marry me. And the night you asked me I was feeling warm towards the world in general. Afterwards I was alarmed by what I'd done.'

She had confided in Dolly. She had told her that she thought she did love George a bit but she didn't want to marry him or anyone else. Dolly, who had been involved with the Egyptian at that time, had been scornful. 'Love! That's not love. That's an old worn path you have between you, a right of way established by common usage. He's so dull, so Scottish, so reliable! I hate pipe-sucking men with both feet on the ground and the right amount of money in the bank. You'll have to be brutal and tell him.' And so Janet had told him.

'You were very young,' George said, excusing her finally. The subject was closed.

That first evening he stayed an hour. He said at once, on

100

the matter of Smiles, that it was not worth doing anything; he had merely humoured Fiona and agreed to come along as he wished to see Janet again. 'Fiona likes to dabble in good works,' he said with a smile.

After that he came regularly to the basement. As she came to know him again she found that he was likeable and pleasant company. He read widely and this alone gave them sufficient basis for friendship. He was unexciting perhaps – he was never carried away with enthusiasm and he seldom had an original idea – but he was relaxing to be with. He prided himself on being an honest man but did not parade his honesty as Howard and Fiona did. They had no time for social lies: the truth must be told whatever the cost, and you had to be big enough to stand up to it.

Janet wondered how George made out as a lawyer but thought it likely a quite different person would emerge when he sat behind his solid desk: a hard core of determination would lie at the back of his smiles and tactful words. He took her one evening to his office. The black lettering 'Robertson and Bell' on the frosted glass made her feel strangely nostalgic. The Robertson was Uncle John, father's eldest brother. As a child the words had filled her with awe and she had loved to come into the gloomy rooms and finger the rolls of parchment. The smell of dust and old documents remained, and the dark wood. Even in the after-hours atmosphere of his room with the quiet of the landing seeping round the half-open door, she sensed the change in his character. He spoke with definiteness, explaining various aspects of his profession, answering questions in a way that precluded argument.

She encouraged him to visit her: he was a link with a world outside basements and lack of money; he brought an aura of security with him and helped her keep her life in perspective.

George was pleased to visit her. He went mostly out of curiosity, he told himself: he was intrigued by the change in her circumstances, by the way in which her life had diverged from its inherited pattern. She had come from a similar background to his, but at a certain point along the line had taken a turn off. He disapproved of her intimacy with Khalil who used her belongings as if they were his own, and he disliked the run-down slumminess of The Crescent, the nosey slut of a woman who lived on the ground floor and never failed to see him arrive through the leaves of her potted plant, the gangs of kids who left their sticky imprints on his car; but his curiosity counteracted his animosity and he continued to come. He even took a pleasure in being able to bridge two ways of life: he was equally at home in Fiona's lounge and Janet's bed-sitting room. Coming into the hot stuffy basement, he had the air of a man on holiday; it was as though when he hung his coat behind the door he hung up his identity as George Bell, lawyer, cousin of Howard Bell.

Fiona was delighted at the renewed friendship. As she said to Howard: 'It could be the making of Janet. She's lucky to have another chance. And George would make an excellent father for Sally.' She phoned the bookshop regularly to extol George's virtues. She could talk on the phone for hours – it seemed a natural medium of expression to her – but Janet soon developed a way of dealing with this: she leant on the counter, mumbled at intervals into the mouthpiece and read steadily. On one occasion she read twenty pages of *Anna Karenina* and was so immersed that she forgot to make her usual noises.

'Are you there, Janet?' Click, click, click. 'Janet!'

'Yes, I'm here. That's fine, then.'

'Good. I'll collect Sally on Friday.'

Janet discovered that she had agreed to let Sally spend the week-end at Howard and Fiona's. She was not keen for Sally to go but the child liked Fiona and went off happily with her. It would be good for her to have a week-end alone, Janet thought: it would give her the chance to catch up on the ironing, clean the flat . . .

On Sunday morning she wakened early. She slipped out

of bed and walked over to the window, the grain of the coconut matting biting into the soles of her feet. As she drew back the curtains the church clock tolled seven times. Two small birds swayed on the railings but nothing else moved. She returned to the warmth of the bed.

Lying in bed she could only see a little of the pavement. As more light penetrated the room so the outside world began to move. The four paws of a ginger cat pattered along, one of its back ones trailing behind the other; a motor bike roared to life somewhere along the street; the clock struck the half-hour. The clink of milk bottles announced the arrival of the milkman. His black boots appeared at the gate, then his legs began to descend. He was whistling *Come Back To Sorrento*. From half-way down the steps he leant over and swung a pint of milk onto the window sill; his legs whisked upwards, and he left the gate open to swing in the wind. The marmalade cat ambled back and sat facing the road with its tail hanging down between the bars of the railing. Muffin sat up at the end of the bed, eyes wide and fixed, the pupils narrowed to a thin black line, head pushed forward, as she watched the dangling orange pennant.

Janet thought of Sally, and felt lonely. The morning stretched in front of her like a long grey tunnel. Sunday morning in The Crescent: no bustle to get to work, no children running late for school. Nothing, nothing, but the milkman on his rounds and a ginger cat swishing his tail. Not even the postman to push a dull circular through the stiff-flapped letter box.

A leaf blew down, then another. A piece of brown paper drifted along and a ginger paw snapped out and held it fast. The cat's pink nose moved down, twitching over it: then his pink tongue snaked out and licked last night's cold grease. Sunday mornings brought a wealth of fish and chip papers to The Crescent.

The clock struck eight. She dozed off.

The next thing she heard was the squeak of the gate.

Lifting her head she saw her typewriter and Tim's legs coming down the steps.

He rapped on the window. 'Hurry up and get dressed. We're going up Arthur's Seat.'

She hesitated, thinking of Isobel. Until now she had shelved the thought of Isobel and Tim. But there was nothing in her friendship with Tim to make her feel guilty and no reason why she should not go for a walk with him on a Sunday morning.

The sun came out as they reached the Queen's Park. Two small children were throwing a large yellow ball to one another in a slow, rather dignified manner; and a car swirled blithely past, exceeding the speed limit. Janet and Tim ran quickly up the lower slopes until, half-way up, they stopped, breathless, and looked down on the city. Smoke rose in thick plumes from the high line of tenements backing onto the park. They crouched down out of the wind.

'It's a good place this,' Tim said.

She nodded. 'I like to feel miles from civilization and yet see it all spread out before me.' She sat comfortably, feeling the dampness seeping slightly through her slacks, the freshness of the morning air on her face, the prick of the grass under her left hand. It was very quiet. The city seemed motionless, save for the drifting smoke. And then a church bell began to toll, its notes soft and clear. She tilted her head backwards to watch the flight of a gull, then looked at Tim to share the moment with him. But they were not sharing anything.

He was frowning at some thoughts which preoccupied him; he sat hunched forward with his eyes fixed unseeingly on a tuft of grass in front of his right foot. She sighed, lay back and closed her eyes.

He was aware that she had lain back, he was aware too of the tuft of grass which bent and swayed with the wind but they were only vague impressions that did not disturb his preoccupation. He wanted to say something to Janet, some-

104

thing that would establish a very special sort of relationship between them, but he couldn't do it. He was in love with her – he knew it now – and he was tired of sustaining the pretence that he was nothing but a good friend who loved her sister. But he wasn't free to speak. Isobel was like a flea crawling round his body nibbling at him, a flea that he couldn't catch and cast aside. She was dropping hints, unpleasant ones; unpleasant and alarming to him, but she seemed happy and untroubled, almost self-satisfied. She couldn't be sure, she said, not yet; they would have to wait and see but she was getting fatter and she had been sick a few times. He had been sick too when he thought of being tied to Isobel for life. Most times he did not believe it could ever happen, but sitting here beside Janet, he was afraid.

Suddenly Janet leapt to her feet, pulling him with her, and cried: 'Let's go up to the top.'

At the top the wind rushed in their faces, whipping up the colour in their cheeks. He put his arm lightly round her shoulder and they stood together, feeling the force of the gusts against their bodies. Janet laughed and the noise was whipped away by the wind. It was wonderful for her to stand on high in the middle of the city, to look over at the castle and down to the palace, to see the sun glinting on the Firth of Forth and the Fife coast beyond, to be elevated from 31B to this.

They descended slowly to the park. Tim asked Janet if she would have lunch with him at his flat and stood gazing down at the path whilst he awaited her answer. 'Aren't you seeing Isobel today?' she said uncertainly, but he was not to see Isobel until the evening and he was sure that she would not mind. Of course Isobel would not mind, Janet affirmed, for there was no reason for her to do so. She was annoyed at having made a slight issue out of something that was quite harmless and meaningless; it would make it worse if she refused. She said that she would be pleased to have lunch with him and meet the great historian who pounded nightly on her typewriter.

105

'Murray is away for the week-end,' he said.

He took her arm and led her out of the park. .

'It's so light,' Janet said, as they came into his flat. Golden sunshine was pouring through a large skylight onto the whitewashed walls. 'I can hardly believe I'm indoors.'

'That's because you're a basement dweller.' He lifted a pile of newspapers to uncover a chair. 'Bit of a mess, I'm afraid. But it's not as bad as it looks. Isobel clears up the place once in a while which infuriates Murray – he can't find anything for weeks afterwards.'

They had lunch at a card table in front of the open window. Sounds of children playing and the distant hum of traffic floated in on the afternoon breeze.

'Why didn't you get a job in Glasgow?' Janet asked. 'What brought you to Edinburgh?'

'I don't know. Just fancied a change. Nothing unusual in that, is there?'

'You weren't trying to get away from your family by any chance?' She laughed and he shrugged.

'I get on very well with my family. They're a bit over-powering at times and they're fond of noise, but they don't sit in judgment on one another.'

'I stand reproved!'

'I didn't mean it like that. Oh, I suppose I did want to get away from them in a sense. I wanted to live on my own but as long as I was in Glasgow my mother wouldn't have accepted that. She wouldn't have understood why I should pay good money for a flat when there was room in the family house.'

He was watching her face too closely. She said: 'Show me your pots.'

She liked most of them though confessed that she knew little of pottery. To her it seemed simple and the colours were translucent and warm. 'I only know if I like it or not.'

'That's all you need to know. Isobel dissects my work. She tells me what influences I'm under.'

106

'It's probably her mathematical mind.'

'Does Isobel have a mathematical mind? I've often wondered.'

'She's a mathematician!'

'You don't have to snap at me. She hates mathematics: she'd do anything to give up her course.'

'I don't believe you,' she said. He was no doubt right: he probably knew Isobel better than she did now.

'I'd like to give you something,' he said. 'Choose what you'd like.'

She knelt down to study the pots and he stood over her. She lifted a green bowl and he said: 'I knew you'd choose that.'

'Why?'

'It's the colour of your eyes.' He laid it on Murray's desk. 'I'll wrap it for you later.'

He asked if she would like to throw a pot herself and she enthusiastically accepted. They went down to the garage where he kept his wheel and kiln and he instructed her. She had not realized it would be so difficult: the end result looked like a shapeless amoeba. They laughed a great deal over the whole operation, and at the end of it Tim said he didn't think she would make a potter. They went back up to the flat to drink tea to assuage the dust in their throats.

Janet relaxed, feeling comfortable and pleasantly tired. With a sigh she saw that it was seven o'clock and time for her to be gone.

At that moment they heard footsteps under the window, then a knock on the downstairs door.

'Tim!' Isobel's voice came up to them, as clear as a bell.

Tim leaned out of the window and threw down the key. 'Don't look so worried,' he said to Janet.

'I'm not worried, but I shouldn't have stayed so long.'

Isobel stopped in the doorway, the smile on her face giving way to a look of perplexity. Her eyes swept the room, noting the evidence: two dirty plates, two cups, two sets of cutlery, ashtray full of cigarette ends marked with lipstick,

107

Janet's duffle coat thrown across a chair. She took a step backwards.

'I've been teaching Janet to throw a pot,' Tim said. 'She's not a very promising pupil.'

'She never was very good with her hands,' Isobel said.

She came into the room, took off her coat and threw it on top of Janet's. She had not known that Tim and Janet had met apart from that night in the café at Marchmont. Then she thought of Khalil. It would be Khalil's doing: she had always known he was a trouble-maker. But that did not excuse Janet. She avoided her sister's glance and wandered round the room looking abstractedly at the books and dishes. She was not going to let them see that she was disturbed at finding them together. She felt remarkably cool and knew that she was looking her best in her blue velvet frock. Janet was messy and untidy, and her make-up had disappeared. Isobel paused when she saw the green bowl on the desk. She wheeled round to face Tim.

'You've not given this to Murray?'

'No. I've given it to Janet.'

'But, Tim, you knew I liked it. I thought you knew I wanted it.' Her voice was high.

'You have it, Isobel,' Janet said quickly. 'I'd no idea you wanted it. I'll choose something else.'

'No, you have it. He gave it to you.'

'You have it.'

'I don't want it now.'

'It belongs to Janet,' Tim said. 'I gave it to her.' He took a sheet of newspaper, wrapped it round the bowl and handed it to Janet with a little bow. 'The matter is closed.'

'I must be going.' Janet reached for her coat.

'I'll walk to the bus stop with you,' Tim said.

'No, no, don't bother.'

'No bother.'

'Goodbye, Isobel,' Janet called. Isobel did not reply.

They walked down the steps in silence, Janet clutching the bowl in front of her. He closed the door behind them and took her arm. It was dusk and the mews was full of shadows.

'I've enjoyed today,' he said.

'I have too. But Isobel – '

'I'll reassure Isobel,' he said wearily, thinking of what lay ahead of him.

'Thank you. I don't want her to be upset. There's nothing for her to be upset about. I'm very fond of her,' she said primly. They turned into the main street and stopped at the bus stop. 'I don't think you should come again to The Crescent. At least, not without Isobel.'

A bus came round the corner. She took her arm from his and leapt onto the running board.

When she arrived home she found Fiona and Howard waiting in the car with Sally. They had been there for half an hour. Janet apologized and thanked them in one rush of breath, gathered up the child and took her down to the basement to be put to bed. Sally was tired and fell asleep at once. Janet unwrapped the bowl and placed it in the centre of the table where it would catch the light. It was a beautiful green and she was pleased that it belonged to her.

At eleven o'clock she was startled to find Isobel on the doorstep. Isobel said that she would only come in for a moment. She was smiling.

'I'm sorry I was a bit cool to you earlier, Janet. It was stupid of me to feel jealous, but coming in and seeing you together like that . . .' There was a far-off look in her eyes. 'But I know it didn't mean anything. I didn't want to go to bed feeling there was anything wrong between us.'

She wanted her happiness to be complete, without any flaw. To go to bed estranged from her sister would be like having a little stone in a comfortable pair of shoes. The world must be a good place and any disruption in it might threaten her happiness. Janet hugged her, and she gave a laugh of sheer happiness which could not be restrained in her body. She really loves him, Janet thought, and was afraid for her, for she knew that Tim did not love Isobel.

109

Isobel looked at the bowl, gleaming on the table. 'It's lovely, isn't it?' she said. 'I'm glad you've got it, Janet.' Her eyes said: I don't need it.

CHAPTER ELEVEN

The green bowl kept its place on the table; autumn dulled ready to give way to winter; Tim continued to come to the basement with Khalil as before.

One night, shortly after they had gone, Janet heard the gate open again. She sat up in bed and swore for she was tired and had been on the brink of sleep. Muffin, roused from her slumber in the sag of the armchair, yawned and began to wash her face.

The feet were heavy and clumsy on the steps. It was certainly not Khalil, who came and went noiselessly, nor did it sound like Tim, who had a light, springy walk. She decided that she would not open the door. There was a clatter outside the window as the feet came into contact with the dustbin. Now a voice muttering, a man's voice. A drunk more than likely. Not uncommon in The Crescent. A drunk mistaking his basement: they all looked alike. A quiet grovelling and more muttering whilst the lid of the dustbin was searched for and replaced, then a loud thump on the door. Muffin yawned again and stretched herself, unperturbed and uninterested. Janet pulled the bedclothes over her ears.

'Janet!' It was Howard. 'Let me in!'

He continued to bellow and beat on the door until she opened it.

'For God's sake!' she said. 'You'll waken the whole Crescent.'

'Fiona's had the baby,' he shouted. 'A boy, eight pounds two and a half ounces, twenty-two inches long, and it looks like me.'

'That's wonderful.' She kissed him on the cheek, as was

110

proper for the occasion, and drew back in astonishment at the stench of alcohol on his breath. She led him into the living room.

'Met some of the boys. Been out wetting the baby's head.' He stood in the middle of the floor, tipping forward on his toes, then rocking back onto his heels. He added in a hushed voice: 'Don't tell Fiona.'

'Fiona wouldn't mind.'

Her reassurance seemed to please him even though he knew she had lied. He grinned. 'She would want me to celebrate, wouldn't she?'

'Naturally.' She put her hand on his arm, afraid he would fall. 'Sit down, Howard, and tell me all about it.'

He sat in a chair with a foolish smile on his face and related the details of the confinement whilst she roared up the stove. He followed her along to the kitchen when she went to make coffee, talking incessantly. He leant against the sink with his elbow on the draining board. She carried the coffee back to the fire; he trotted behind. Like a dog, she thought. It was a totally different Howard to the one who carved the Sunday joint: he was dishevelled, sprawling, flushed with whisky and exhilarated by the birth of his child. His son would play rugby for Scotland at Murrayfield, climb all the 'Monroes', swim across the Forth and back . . . Fiona was marvellous, he declared, she could do anything. Janet agreed wholeheartedly.

Usually Howard sat upright in a chair, his legs crossed at a considered angle, his trousers hitched just a little above the knee to avoid undue creasing. Now he did not sit at all: he reclined, careless of the position of his body, a lock of hair falling over his face, the knot of his tie slack and squint, his open jacket revealing an unclean shirt, the lace of his right shoe loosed, the sole of the left one caked in mud. Janet sat opposite him, speechless and bemused by this brother-in-law.

He looked round at the jumble of books, toys, pieces of

111

clothing. 'You know,' he said, 'I rather like this little place of yours, Janet. It's snug.'

She smiled. It suited his mood for tonight but if he had to live in it he would have a nervous breakdown within days.

'You look like Fiona tonight.' He squinted at her. 'Sometimes I see no likeness at all but now I see it plainly.' He eased himself out of the chair onto the floor. 'But your eyes are green, aren't they?'

'Yes, they are,' she said hurriedly and moved her chair back an inch, keeping her eyes on his face. He shuffled nearer. She was hot and uncomfortable; she tried to push her chair back further but it came to rest against the side of the dresser and refused to move. He was breathing heavily and he was very close to her. She said that she would make more coffee. As she got up he put his hand round her ankle.

'You have nice ankles. Fiona's are too thick.'

She essayed a laugh that was intended to convey amusement and disbelief. The sound cracked at the back of her throat. 'Don't be foolish, Howard.'

'Very nice.'

It was ridiculous to have her right foot held prisoner by a vice of five fingers. Howard's fingers. She relaxed her foot; then tried to wrench it free, thinking to take him by surprise, but his hand kept its grip. His grin widened to something approaching a leer. She stared down at him and examined his face with curiosity. It's only Howard, she said to herself, he's had too much to drink and the whisky's lifted the lid off the suppressed side of his nature. To formulate this clearly in her mind calmed her.

'Now, Howard,' she said, 'be sensible and take your hand from my ankle. I want to go and make coffee.'

'Don't want coffee. Sit down.'

She sat down and he released her foot. He leaned against her knees, his head flopped back into her lap and his eyelashes settled on his cheeks. She laid her hands, palms downwards, on the arm of the chair and resisted the impulse to drum her fingers. He moved his head and rubbed his cheek against her knee.

'I love Fiona, you know,' he said.

'Yes, I know.'

His breathing became slower and steadier, his mouth sagged and he began to snore. Now the situation seemed funny to her. She laughed softly and smoothed his hair. The church clock struck three, bringing her back to the cold knowledge that in four hours' time she would have to begin another day. She pushed Howard away from her legs: he flopped forward onto the rug, groaning.

'Time to go home, Howard,' she said firmly.

She stood up and shook out the folds of her dressing-gown. He didn't want to go home, he wanted to stay with her. She protested, he wheedled, she coaxed, he groaned. He said he felt ill. She tried to reason with him but quickly abandoned that and spoke to him with controlled impatience as she did to Sally when she was being unreasonable. She stared down at Howard heaped on the floor like an untidy bundle. 'Very well,' she said. 'You can sleep in my bed. I'll sleep with Sally.'

She helped him undress and get into bed. He clutched her hand and opened his eyes wide. 'Stay with me. I won't touch you. I don't want to be alone.'

He looked pathetic and defenceless without the assurance of a clean shaven face and his mind beyond the grasp of his statistics and code of living. Suddenly she was ashamed of her lack of sympathy. She put out the light and crept into the narrow space beside him. She put her arm round him and within minutes he was asleep. For a little while she lay awake thinking of Fiona, and then her eyelids drooped.

She wakened a few hours later to see George standing by the door. His face was crimson. He lifted his hand as if to switch the light off again, then let it drop. Janet slid out of bed, pulled on her dressing-gown.

'How did you get in?'

'Sally.' He turned his head as the child bounded in behind him. 'She heard me knocking.'

Sally peered at the body in the bed and demanded to know why Uncle Howard was sleeping there and why he was not wearing blue and white pyjamas; on receiving no answer she turned her attention to a book about Andy Pandy. Howard's eyes flickered open with difficulty and focused on George.

'Andy Pandy always wears blue and white pyjamas,' Sally said.

'Does he, dear?'

'Of course,' Sally said scornfully.

'Well, Uncle Howard doesn't.'

Janet swept the curtains back with a rattle, pulled down the window and took a deep breath. Mrs McNab's slippered feet waddled into view, met up with a pair of bony ankles coming in the opposite direction, and all four extremities came to rest. Greetings were exchanged, followed by a soft splutter of whispers. A grubby handkerchief floated down to the pavement. A stir and commotion, a crackling of whale bones, and a fat beige hand was thrust downwards. Mrs McNab's two blank eyes stared straight into Janet's.

Janet repulled the curtains. The two men were still staring at one another as though hypnotized.

'I'm late for work,' she said irritably.

George cleared his throat. 'I've been looking for you half the night, Howard.' He paused. 'It's about Fiona — '

Janet swung round to face him. 'What about Fiona?'

'She's all right,' he said nervously, 'but the baby died. Its heart gave out.'

Fiona was sitting up in bed, wearing a pink lacey bed-jacket. She was holding her mother's hand and they were both crying.

Janet hesitated in the doorway with a bunch of flowers.

'Go away,' Fiona said. 'I don't want to see you.'

Agnes Robertson gave Janet a sorrowful look before

114

turning her head away to stare at a bottle of Lucozade on the locker top. Janet closed the door behind her and went over to the bed. She put her hand on the rail.

'Don't come near me!' Fiona said.

Janet said nothing. She moved to the long window that was open onto a balcony. It was a dark gloomy day; fog was rolling in across the Meadows, shrouding the trees, laying drops of water on the window sill. The dampness touched her face. Behind her the room was hot, overheated, and someone was crying.

'Go away!' Fiona cried.

Janet went then. The corridors of the hospital seemed endless, and overheated like that room the fog threatened. They smelled of polish and disinfectant. Her heels clicked along them like drumbeats amidst the murmur of cut-off voices, the squall of babies, the clink of instruments. She dropped the blazing chrysanthemums into a litter basket and went out into the chill moist air. She could still hear the shrill voice: 'Go away! Go away!' It pursued her up the slope of the hospital drive and along the street to the phone box at the top of Middle Meadow Walk.

She tugged open the heavy door and entered the musty cubicle. She thumbed through the directory and found the number she wanted. As she dialled her fingers slipped on the slots; she replaced the receiver and started again. Engaged! She collected her four pennies and waited till the second hand of her watch had made two complete circles. The next attempt was successful. A sharp staccato voice answered.

'Mr Bell, please,' Janet said.

'One moment, please.'

She rubbed the glaur from the tiny mirror above: her eyes were heavy and her skin sallow. She wondered if she could be getting jaundice. A duffle-coated student was circling the kiosk, eyeing her hostilely.

'Howard Bell speaking.' He sounded confident and businesslike.

'This is Janet. I've just been to see Fiona.'

'Oh yes?' His assurance had evaporated.

'Did you tell Fiona you had stayed with me?' She rattled the receiver rest. 'Howard, are you still there?'

'Yes, I'm still here. Listen, Janet, I had to tell her.'

'You knew it would upset her. You're a bloody fool!'

His voice was stiff. 'Fiona and I never lie to one another.' The student was clinking coins in his trouser pocket.

'No one was asking you to lie,' Janet said.

'But they knew I hadn't been home all night. They were trying to get in touch with me. Be reasonable!'

'You could have said you walked the streets.'

'I couldn't have walked the streets all night.'

'Why not? There's no law against it. People have done it before now.' She wanted to stick out her tongue at the student. He gave an exaggerated sigh and leaned his shoulder against the corner of the box. 'Did you tell her you had slept with me?'

' 'Sh, Janet, for heaven's sake! Watch what you're saying.'

'Is your phone tapped?'

'Don't be silly. But the operators—'

'Damn the operators!' I don't suppose they care whom you sleep with.' She put out her tongue at the student and he laughed.

'I can't talk about this over the phone. Can I meet you for a few minutes?'

'I don't think there's any point in that.' The mouthpiece was covered with drops of water. She wrinkled her nose at it and replaced the receiver. She pushed the door open. 'Sorry to be so long,' she said to the student. 'I was having a conversation with a Calvinist about sin.'

'That's all right.' He laughed. 'It's happened to me before now.'

She wandered aimlessly round the streets and eventually found herself outside a dully-lit café in a side street. Dirty net curtains draped the steamed-up window. It was cold and wet on the pavement so she went inside. The place was

116

empty downstairs except for the woman behind the counter. In a dead voice she asked what Janet wanted, her jaw scarcely moving. She slopped off into the back premises to find a cup of coffee, leaving Janet to lean on the glass counter and gaze at sick-looking cakes and curling triangular sandwiches.

When the woman reappeared she slapped a cup of grey liquid onto the counter and said: 'Sixpence.' That was all. She was quite uncurious: she did not even look up. Janet laid sixpence on the glass: the woman's hand came up, the fingers curled round the coin and slid it into the palm of her hand. Then she shuffled along to the till.

Janet walked up the stairs. A man without teeth was sitting in a corner. She sat down several tables away from him.

For a few minutes she sat with her elbows on the table, head in hands, letting her mind and body flop. When she looked up she saw that the toothless man in the corner was staring at her with small ferrety eyes. Every now and then a black-nailed hand came up and picked the bulbous nose but the eyes did not waver. She pushed her chair further back into the shadow of the room. It was not really a room but a gallery that looked down into the well of the café below. Downstairs the lights were on; she could see the grey head of the woman moving behind the counter and the row of sweet bottles against the greasy wall. The clink of money and the 'ding' of the till floated up into the dim silence above. On the stained oilcloth in front of her the cup of liquid lay cold and scummed. She lit a cigarette and watched the smoke drift away into nothingness. It was inevitable that Howard would tell Fiona he had spent the night in the basement: he would have been overcome with remorse at the idea that whilst Fiona was suffering he had been sleeping warm and comfortable against another woman's body instead of being ready and available to come to the hospital and share the suffering. He had let Fiona down at the time when she had needed him most. Janet's thoughts moved from Howard, about whom she did not care, to Fiona. It was inevitable too that Fiona would be resentful. Her principles were even higher than Howard's for they had seldom been challenged.

The man with the eyes and the nose but no teeth got up and staggered towards her. He put a hand on the back of her chair and peered into her face. His breath was heavy with methylated spirits. 'Gie us a fag, hen,' he whined. As she took one from the packet he snatched it greedily. She tossed another onto the table and left.

Fiona had been home from hospital for a week when Janet went to see her.

They sat facing one another across the hearthrug. Fiona was tight-lipped and puff-eyed: she looked like their mother. The tick of the golden hands was even louder than Janet remembered. She took out a cigarette but Fiona made no move to proffer the table lighter.

'Why are you staring at me like that?' Janet said.

The flood was released. Janet was pinned into the purple chair by the rush of words. Howard had been drunk that night but Janet had been sober, she should have called a taxi, put him into it and sent him home; he had been astounded when he awoke in the morning and found himself in Janet's bed. And then for George to come in and see him! Sally too: that was another thing. What would she think about it? Janet became riled for the first time. She said firmly that Sally thought nothing about it, that she had not mentioned the matter since. Such things lay hidden in a child's mind, Fiona said, they made an impression on the inner consciousness and came to the surface later. Everyone knew that the first seven years of a child's life were the important ones.

'So if Sally becomes a prostitute when she grows up it will be because she saw Howard in my bed?' Janet said.

'There's no point in us saying any more. But there's one

118

thing you should know: you needn't bother trying to get your hands on Howard. He doesn't even like you. He thinks you're selfish and irresponsible, that you have no sense of values, that your moral standards are questionable and that you're a trouble-maker.'

'I'm not interested in getting my hands on Howard,' Janet said calmly.

Fiona laughed, a high neurotic laugh that Janet would not have associated before with Fiona. 'But you've done it to me in the past,' Fiona said. 'When we lived at home and I brought someone in you always tried to take him away from me. I used to watch you flirting with him, talking to him with that little secret smile about your lips. I didn't have a chance when you were there. I was glad when you went away, right away.'

Janet stared at her. 'Do you mean you were jealous of me? And I was jealous of you! I was jealous because you were always being praised and held up to me as an example. "Look at Fiona," mother would say, "she's so neat and tidy, so good with her hands" – '

'Don't talk nonsense!' Fiona snapped.

'But don't you see how absurd it all was?'

'It wasn't that way at all. You twist everything.'

Fiona got up abruptly and moved to the window where she stood, back to the room, hugging her resentment, unwilling to part with any of it. She was allowing her misery to feed on it, to postpone coming face to face with her real misfortune. Janet saw this, pondered a moment, then said:

'The stupid thing is, Fiona, that we had no need to be jealous of one another: we've always wanted different things and different people. I know you're unhappy about the baby and I'm so very sorry – '

'I don't want your sympathy. You always got what you wanted without trying, you always landed on your feet in trouble. And now you've got a child you don't even deserve!' Fiona struck the window-sill with her fist. 'Leave me alone. Why did you come here today? To crow over me? Go away! Go away!'

Janet went.

CHAPTER TWELVE

She sensed the importance of Tim's visit even as she watched him hang his overcoat behind the door and take a bottle of wine from the inside pocket. There was a nervous quality about his movements, normally so relaxed, that set the alarm bells ringing in her head. And he was alone.

'You shouldn't have come,' she said. 'I've asked you not to. My relations with my family are complicated enough without Isobel coming in here and finding you.'

'Isobel doesn't own me,' he said. Not yet, he added to himself. 'I thought you were a great advocate of people not owning one another?'

'I'm an advocate of a lot of things and most of them only lead to confusion.'

He uncorked the wine, poured some into a cup and gave it to her.

'What's this in aid of?'

'Nothing in particular. Does everything have to have a reason? I thought you might need cheering up.'

'You must have second sight.'

'You are gloomy tonight. What's wrong?'

'I was thinking I ought to go away from Edinburgh.'

'You mustn't do that,' he said quickly.

'Why not?'

'I want you to stay.'

'What you want has nothing to do with it, Tim.'

'I suppose not.' He put his hand on hers briefly and then withdrew it. 'I wish that it did. I wish –'

'There's no point in wishing for things that cannot be.'

'Cannot?'

'Cannot. Give me some more wine and cheer me up. That's what you came to do, isn't it?'

'There's only one thing I want to do.'

'I don't know what you're talking about.'

'You don't want to know, you mean.'

'It's all the same in the end. Sit over there – let's have a few feet of coconut matting between us, a no man's land – and talk to me. Let us pursue this platonic friendship that's so valuable to us both.'

'It's cold over there,' he said. He sat on the floor by her feet, where Howard had sat the night he was drunk.

'I'm very fond of Isobel,' she said.

'That sounds like a statement, a rather self-conscious one. Am I meant to write it down or something?' He put his hand on her knee but she pushed it away.

'She was very gay when she was a child. She was the brightest thing in our dark household.'

'I should think your eyes were the brightest things. I bet they shine in the dark. Let's find out.' He jumped up and switched off the light.

'It's not properly dark so you can't tell.'

'Yes, I can,' he said, looking into her face. 'They shine in the firelight anyway.' He kissed her lips gently, then drew back for he was trembling. It seemed ridiculous to be trembling because he had kissed a woman. It hadn't happened to him since he was fifteen, playing Postman's Knock in a dim lobby with a round-faced girl with large eyes. When he had kissed her she had moaned and pulled him back to her. He remembered her now and smelt the smell of the lobby, musty, thick and exciting. And he remembered how he had trembled. Then she had said: 'What's the matter with you? You scared or something?', and he hadn't trembled any more.

Janet did not moan or pull him back to her. She said: 'Go away for God's sake!'

He returned to his seat on the matting.

'I meant go right away.'

121

'Have some more wine.'

She held out her glass and he poured out the wine too quickly, slopping some of it onto her forearm. He dried it with his handkerchief, letting his fingers linger over the warm skin of her wrist.

'You look rather Egyptian,' he said. 'Cleopatra!'

'And who are you?'

'I'm just Tim MacAuley. Couldn't ever be anything else. Why don't you come down to my level?' He put out his hand. 'You can't go on avoiding me.'

She slid down from the chair onto the floor. They faced one another, and his heart raced. He watched the light of the fire touching the smooth clear line of her jaw, and the heavy fall of dark brown hair against her slender neck. A delicious excitement filled him. He thought of burying his head in the hair, of covering her body with his, feeling her warmth.

'I've never wanted anyone so badly,' he said in a low voice.

'Not true,' she said.

'Yes, true.'

'You forget the other times. It's difficult to remember what one felt at a certain moment in the past. Memories are deceptive. We make of them what we want.'

For a moment he felt impatient and wanted to hit back but he kept quiet for it was no time to start an argument about memory. When she got her teeth into a theory she was as hard to pry loose as a dog from a bone. In a minute she would be quoting Sartre at him, or Freud. He held up the bottle of wine.

'There's a little left. It's for you.'

'Are you trying to lower my resistance or something?'

'Yes.'

They finished the wine and then they made love. She had known that it would happen, had known it from the moment he had come in and hung up his coat; she had known it since that first evening when he had come to the basement with Khalil and they had watched one another over the rims of their glasses.

'You won't leave Edinburgh, will you?' he said before he fell asleep. 'Anyway, where could you go?'

Where indeed?

She slept deeply all night and wakened in the morning with a sense of contentment and peace. Tim slept beside her with his hair tossed across the pillow. She touched his cheek lightly but he did not stir. She lay back against the pillow and surveyed the ceiling. Was this all she needed to make her feel relaxed and contented? And how long would it last? At once she cursed herself for letting the thoughts pass through her mind. She had a devil inside her that would not let her accept pleasure without question. The puritanical strain coming out in her, she thought wryly.

She sat up and swung her feet onto the matting. Their clothes lay in a heap on the floor; the stove had gone out and the room was cold; the hearth was littered with cigarette ends and spent matches. She dressed, cleaned out the stove, tidied the hearth. When she stood up she saw the green bowl on the table, and felt suddenly chilled. Tim grunted, moved a little and settled again. She looked at him dispassionately, wishing that she had never met him.

As she opened the front door to bring in the milk the church bells began to ring, reminding her it was Sunday. She carried the bottles along to the kitchen which smelt of grease and stale air. The sink was full of dirty dishes. Her stomach turned over, and she groaned. Muffin was honking on the outside window-sill, her green eyes glistening and indignant through the steamy glass. Janet pushed up the window and gulped thankfully at the rush of fresh air. The window came down with a bang, narrowly missing the cat's tail: the sash cord was broken. George had told her to get it mended. Damn him, damn everyone! And the water gushed ice cold from the tap, numbing her fingers and making no impression on the grease. Muffin padded up and down the draining board mewing piteously. Janet took

123

down a tin of cat food from the shelf and as she ground the tin opener round it Muffin rubbed against her arm, her cries at once transformed into a soft contented purr. Janet wished she were as easily pleased.

They had breakfast in the kitchen. Tim seemed very happy, so happy that he did not notice Janet's ill humour. He and Sally chattered and laughed as they filled their mouths with food. Janet drank a cup of tea and smoked a cigarette. Sally sat on Tim's knee and he told her a story about Muffin who eyed them all disdainfully from her perch on the draining board. She was quite unconcerned about the adventure that took her along the Bridges and down the High Street to Fishmonger's Close. She looks as cynical as I feel, Janet thought.

After Muffin had swallowed the largest fish ever to be landed in a Scottish port, Tim suggested that they go down to the Forth Bridge. 'It's a lovely frosty morning and the sun's shining. We'll go across on the ferry.'

Sally was delighted with the idea and ran at once to fetch her coat. Janet said that she was going to clean the flat. From end to end. She was sick of living in a pig sty.

'You can clean it when it rains,' Tim said.

'I'm going to do it now.'

'O.K. You clean the flat and I'll take Sally to Queens-ferry.'

Five minutes after Tim and Sally had gone, Isobel arrived, and for a moment Janet felt sick. Had Isobel seen them?

'Come into the kitchen,' Janet said, 'I haven't seen you for ages.'

Isobel sat at the table and fingered the spoon in the sugar bowl whilst Janet put on the kettle. She looked pale and tired.

'Where's Sally?'

'Khalil has taken her for a walk.' Janet turned to look out of the window. Why had she lied? There had been no need and she could easily be proved wrong. Washing hung straight and still in the back green: it belonged to her. She had put it out yesterday afternoon and forgotten it. Yesterday afternoon seemed a long way back.

'Seen Tim recently?' Isobel asked.

'Why should I see him?'

'I thought he came here with Khalil. He said he did.'

The kettle began to sing. Janet made tea, glad to have something to do with her hands. The gas went out with a loud plop. It was much too quiet in the kitchen; the only noise was the tinkle of the spoon against the bowl.

Janet could not stand the suspense any longer. 'What's wrong, Isobel?' she asked.

'It's Tim. I don't know what's wrong exactly but things aren't the same between us any longer.' Isobel spoke listlessly, her eyes fixed on the grains of sugar running off the spoon. 'I haven't seen him for days. He phoned yesterday and said he couldn't see me in the evening. It's the same old story: they get what they want from you and then they shove you onto the scrap heap like an old car and go off looking for someone new.'

'What are you talking about?'

'Men. They pester you to sleep with them and then they despise you for doing it.'

Janet sat down. 'Don't be ridiculous.' Her voice was too high. She knew it and brought it down a register. 'You've been reading the back pages of women's magazines.'

'But everything *has* changed. He cares less for me now, not more.' Isobel's eyes were wet. 'I made a botch-up of our first night together – I asked him how many women he had slept with. He was annoyed.'

'You shouldn't ask men things like that. It can only hurt you.'

'I know that now. But I didn't know it then. I kept pestering him. I couldn't bear to think of him touching any other woman in the way he'd touched me.'

'Was he – was he the first for you?'

125

Isobel nodded. She was crying now, the tears dropping slowly from her chin into the sugar. 'Janet, what am I to do? I love him.'

Janet took a gulp of hot tea. It stung her throat as it went down.

There was a knock on the front door. Janet jumped up, knocking her cup half-way across the table. She ran along the hall and pulled the door open, relieved to see that it was only Mrs MacNab who stood on the doorstep. Mrs MacNab didn't want to make trouble but Muffin was coming in through her kitchen window and eating her cat's food. People shouldn't keep cats unless they fed them properly. The matter could be reported to the R.S.P . . . . Here Mrs MacNab faltered and Janet took the opportunity to say that Mrs MacNab's cat often came through her kitchen window and ate her cat's food. Mrs MacNab stuck one slipper over the step and said that she didn't believe it. Janet said that she would have to believe it and slammed the door. Mrs MacNab growled as the door met her toe.

'Silly bitch!' Janet said as she came back into the kitchen.

Isobel was staring at the large tea stain creeping slowly across the table cloth. She tried to smile but began to cry again instead. Janet put her hands on her shoulders and wondered what words of comfort she could say that wouldn't stick in her throat. Isobel sat slouched over the table staring at the sugar bowl. It was one that Tim had made. Janet moved it, and Isobel sat up straight.

'I'm sorry,' she said and dried her eyes. 'I'm probably being a fool. Maybe everything will be all right. Thanks for putting up with me. I'm glad you've come back to Edinburgh.'

When Isobel had gone, Janet took the sugar bowl and buried it in the dustbin under the ashes. Then she set to work. She was so busy scrubbing the floor that she did not hear Khalil come in. She turned her head and saw his two feet placed neatly side by side. He took a step backwards.

'I'm in a foul mood,' she said, making another wide soap sworl on the floor.

'You didn't have to tell me.' He stepped carefully over the scrubbing brush and edged round the bucket. 'There was a glow of ill temper surrounding your hunched-up shoulders. Why do women always feel compelled to state the obvious?'

She flicked the brush upwards, sending a spray of grey water over him. He wiped his face with his arm and retreated to the far end of the kitchen.

'Has something happened? Are you removing the traces of a deadly crime? I thought perhaps you might give me a cup of coffee.'

She said that if he would help her clean the flat she would take him out and buy him some. He pulled up the collar of his overcoat. Since the frost had set in he had taken to wearing a long coat of navy-blue serge; it hung down to his ankles but this he liked for it kept the wind off his shins. 'I am very delicate but for you I will run the risk.' He removed the coat and pushed up the sleeves of his jacket. 'You have great energy this morning. It looks as though you have an extra supply of adrenaline pumped into your bloodstream. It seems a pity to waste it on this evil floor.'

When they had cleaned the flat to Janet's satisfaction, they went out. As they passed the church on the corner they saw Dolly going up the steps with a middle-aged woman in a high fur hat. She looked directly at them without a hint of recognition.

'We are the unrecognizables,' Khalil said, pushing his hands deeper into his pockets. 'We are not dressed for the Sabbath. Perhaps she did not care for my coat? Did I tell you I was swindled over it? I bought it in a nasty dark shop in the Cowgate for five shillings. The next day was a little warmer and I was in need of money so I went to another shop to sell it and the man said he would take it only for rags. He weighed it and do you know what he offered? One and sixpence! I was mortally offended. And whilst he weighed it he watched me with little yellow eyes in case

127

I should put out my foot to tip the scales. As if I would stoop to such dishonest practices!'

They walked to the High Street, Khalil grumbling all the way, asking petulantly when they might have the promised refreshment; but Janet wanted to go up to the Castle to look down on the city. 'You are always wanting to look down on the city,' he said. 'Why not look up to it for a change? If the wind asphyxiates me you will have it on your conscience for the rest of the week.' He toiled up the slope behind her, declaring that he felt like an American tourist in search of ancestors or ancient firearms; as they passed over the drawbridge he felt as Randolph must have done after scaling the Castle rock; when they came out into the wind that swept across the battlements and leaned over the balustrade he said he had no head for heights and that once he had been so misguided as to climb to the top of the Scott monument whereupon he had been seized with an attack of nineteenth-century vertigo and had had to be carried down and laid amongst the flowers until he recovered. 'Sal Volatile was administered to me by a man who said he was a poet. I had no reason to disbelieve him: he spoke in Lallans and as he stood over my body he addressed me with the words of his master:

> ' "Wee sleeket, cowerin', tim'rous beastie,
> O, what a panic's in thy breastie!" '

Janet laughed. 'Don't imagine that I will carry you down and lay you amongst the flowers.'

'Oh no! I would lie where I fell. I would probably land in the dog cemetery which would be a pity. For the dogs of course.' He rested his arms on the wall and put his chin on his hands. 'Let us contemplate the streets of the Princes, the home of the Shortbread Kings and the Baronets of Bombazine. It is a fine street, is it not, despite its vulgar moments? It has width and colour, gardens and a bandstand, a gallery of art with another tucked behind, and a big ugly hotel at either end. What more could a street

128

want? And now, have we paid sufficient homage? Can we go and get warm? For man cannot live on aesthetics alone: he must have coffee.'

As they recrossed the drawbridge he said: 'I think I shall write a poem entitled "There is Culture in the Capital and Capital in its Culture".'

They went to a café where they used to sit as students. It had been rejuvenated but the horse boxes had been left, which pleased Janet. As she warmed her hands round her cup and looked at Khalil over the tops of the sauce and vinegar bottles, she felt a faint stir of nostalgia that made her feel old and rather tired.

'I slept with Tim last night,' she said. She waited. For once Khalil was silent. He flicked out his tongue and then drained his cup. 'Well?' she said. 'Have you nothing to say?'

He spread out his hands. 'What am I supposed to say? I don't know yet what role you've cast me in. Your priest, your mother, your confidante? Or do we exchange whispered confidences as you and Dolly used to do in here? Do I tell you that last night I went up the Calton Hill and lay under the Acropolis with a girl who smelt of pancake make-up and Californian Poppy? The moon was white and the ground as cold as a mortuary slab. Of course I did not lie on the ground myself – '

'Khalil! Don't you ever take life seriously?'

'I take it seriously all the time. That is why I am so often amused.'

'I slept with Tim because I was lonely and depressed.'

'Reasons, reasons! Extraneous reasons. Must there be any? Art for art's sake. Love for love's sake. I shy from vivisection. Must you analyse yourself down to your component parts every time you do anything? After I have made love I do not wallow in a blood-bath of introspection.'

'It's different for you. A woman becomes involved. I don't want to be involved with Tim. I would be better off with George. I could keep myself apart from him more easily.'

'George! Bah! He is too antiseptic. His mother must have washed out his mouth with disinfectant every morning and given him a peppermint cream to take away the taste. Nothing would ever slip over his tongue that had not been carefully considered. I doubt if he ever has a tactless thought.' Khalil shook his head. 'You have such a passion for being honest with yourself that you only end up by bending backwards into self-deception. If you look hard enough you'll find motives and feelings that didn't exist at the time; but once thought, they do exist. What can I say about you and Tim? You have only told me half the truth and that is worse than none.'

'You are right,' Janet said.

'I thought perhaps you and Sally might like to go for a run this afternoon,' George said. He stood just inside the door. He shifted his gaze to take in Khalil and Tim, who were wiping their plates with hunks of bread, and extended the invitation to include them. He mouthed half-hearted regrets at their refusal.

'You go along, Janet,' Khalil said. 'Tim and I will wash the dishes. Since your newly found burst of housewifery we know that you don't like to have a dirty dish in the house.'

Janet avoided Tim's eye as she went out. He was leaning on the table smiling to himself. She heard him whistling as she followed George up the steps.

They drove southwards out of Edinburgh. Sally sat on the back seat lulled into quietness by the warmth of the car and the tiredness which had followed her exertions at South Queensferry in the morning. Janet felt lulled too, by the smooth purring of the engine and the afternoon colours of the winter sky: dust pink, turquoise, blue, white, yellow, grey, and black branches feathered against mauve clouds. On their right the sun was a great ball of orange light gleaming between a dip in the Pentland Hills. Looking into it she saw that it was pure yellow, but that the light it diffused was the colour of flame.

They went into the Moorfoot Hills and George stopped the car on the grassy verge at the side of the road. Sally was asleep so they got out and walked a little. Janet inhaled deeply. The cold air nipped at the flaccidity of her face, exhilarating her. She let her eyes sweep over the wide open country, delighting in the soft rounded tops of the hills, the muted greens and browns and russets of the moors, the dark chain of the Pentlands in the distance. The silence was startling, yet comforting. She was too much in the town amongst its pavements, grey stones, grind of traffic, smoky roofs. She wanted to turn and walk into the dark valleys of the hills, to walk and not stop until she was tired. But she could not go. Her sigh made George turn. His face was bronze in the setting sun.

'Would you like to live in the country?' he asked.

'I don't know. It makes me feel peaceful but basically I think I belong in the town.'

'I've often thought of buying a country cottage. I'd keep my flat in town too and have a foot in both worlds.'

'I think I hear Sally calling,' Janet said.

The thin call came to them across the empty space. George took her hand and they put their backs to the sunset. A partridge rose up in front of them with a screech and a flutter of wings. They watched it until it was swallowed up by the dusk.

'It can't be easy for you looking after a child by yourself,' George said.

'I manage. I could hardly say I led a hard life.'

'If you're ever short of money, you can come to me.'

'I'll remember.' She squeezed his hand, thinking that she was always short of money but that it was unlikely she would ever borrow from him. She might borrow from Khalil if he had any to lend, or from Tim who had little to spare, but from George who could give and not be left short she would not consider it.

Tim and Khalil had gone when they returned. Lying on top of the stack of clean dishes was a note from Tim. 'Last night was . . .' She read no more. Out on the moors she had forgotten last night. She crumpled the note and pushed it into the stove where it quickly burned and died.

George stayed for a meal. Afterwards Janet asked him if he would stay with Sally whilst she went out for an hour. He agreed without question and told her to take his car.

She drove down to the mews. Tim's flat was dark. She banged on the downstairs door but no one came. She returned to the car to wait.

Twenty minutes later she heard his whistle.

'For a moment I thought George had come to visit me. I'm glad it's you.' He tried to kiss her through the open window but she pulled back her head.

They went up to the flat. It was in the same state of disarray as before but it was cold without the sun slanting through the skylight window. Tim lit a paraffin stove and she hunched over it, warming her hands. She liked the smell of paraffin but now she found it impossible to enjoy anything. Her body was filled with the chill of the room and the intense white of the walls was making her eyes throb. A headache was building up at the back of her eyes.

'Why didn't you tell me you had slept with Isobel?'

He started. 'How did you know?'

'She came this morning when you were out with Sally.'

'I had no particular reason to tell you.'

'Let's at least be honest with each other. You know you should have told me.'

'Why the hell should I? For God's sake, did you want me to make a confession before I touched you? You're as bad as Isobel. "How many women have you slept with? How many?" '

Janet got up. 'I don't care about any of the women you've slept with, bar one. You can forget about last night. It was a mistake. My life's a chain of mistakes. But that particular one won't happen again. You can't expect to share me with Isobel.'

'I know that,' he said quietly.

132

She waited for him to speak again but he said no more. She moved to the door and then he said her name.

'Yes?' She looked back at him.

'Can I still come to see you?'

'Isobel's my sister.'

'I'm not asking to sleep with you again, just to come and visit you.'

'Don't come alone,' she said.

She ran out of the room, down the stairs to the car. She glanced up and saw him standing at the lighted window, looking down. She took the turning out of the mews too fast and scraped the back mudguard. When she got back George said not to worry and laughed because she was so upset.

CHAPTER THIRTEEN

Agnes Robertson dusted the chair with her glove before sitting down. She had put on an old skirt so she was not too worried. Once she had been foolish enough to wear black when she had visited Janet and had had to send the frock to the cleaners afterwards. It had been an expensive visit.

In the small cramped area outside the window Sally and three other children were playing at boats in an old zinc bath. The noise was deafening; they shrieked and screamed and beat the sides of the bath with stout sticks. Janet and her mother smiled warily at one another from opposite sides of the stove.

Presently, an argument developed amongst the mariners. A small boy with a hoarse thick voice claimed that his father had a real boat that could be sailed on the sea.

'That's nothing,' Sally retorted. 'My daddy's got two boats.'

'He hasne.'

'He has.'

'He has not.'

133

'He has sot.'

'Not!'

'Sot!'

'Not!'

'Sot!'

When the interchanges had lasted for five minutes without showing any sign of palling, Agnes Robertson put her fingers to her temple. Janet went to the window and told the children to take the bath into the back green. 'There's more room there,' she said.

'But there's no sea there,' Sally cried.

The other three were already half-way up the steps, dragging their boat behind them. They were used to being moved on. Sally scampered after them. As they manœuvred their craft round the gate she said:

'Anyway, I've got two daddies.'

'You canne hae twa faithers.'

'You can.'

'You can not.'

'Can sot.'

'Not!'

'Sot!'

'Ach,' said the hoarse-voiced boy, 'ye havne even got yin.'

'I have sot!' Sally shouted.

The children passed the railings, the bath going bumpety-bump on the pavement behind them.

'It's dreadful,' Agnes Robertson whispered. 'Poor child.'

'Don't be silly, mother! She's perfectly happy.'

'I wonder. Are you?'

'For goodness sake! Are you happy, mother?'

Agnes Robertson sighed. She said: 'You look tired, dear. Are you eating enough?'

'I never eat enough. You know that.'

'Maybe you need glasses. Why don't you go to the doctor's for a check-up? Your eyes are sunk in. It's this basement: there's not enough light.'

134

'I see perfectly well.'

'You read too much. I told you often enough when you were a child that you would regret it one of these days.'

'I don't regret anything, mother. Not anything.'

'Well, it's time you did. That's all I can say.' Agnes Robertson blew her nose, gently. 'I'm worried about Isobel. I think she's had a row with her boy friend – she's been moping around the house looking like death. I must say I'll be quite relieved if she has broken it off with him for your father and I didn't care for him much. Rather uncouth, I thought. Not at all like Howard and George. They have such nice manners and they're so considerate. No, no, I won't have a cup of tea, dear. Don't you think George is nice?'

'He's a big improvement on Howard anyway.'

'That's not a very nice thing to say about Howard. He makes Fiona an excellent husband. They're as happy as a couple of sandboys together. But this Tim person would never have suited Isobel. She'd have been throwing herself away on him. He hasn't much of a job either. She'll get over it. It was just a teenage infatuation. I've promised her a new coat for Christmas.'

'So you're not really worried about her at all?'

'Of course I am. Do you think I like to see her unhappy?'

CHAPTER FOURTEEN

Isobel and Tim parted in the middle of Princes Street.

'See you tomorrow,' he said and hopped on a bus as it swerved out from the stop. He had not even looked to see where it was going.

He had said that he had an urgent appointment but that she did not believe. People like Tim didn't have urgent appointments. Did he think she was a fool? She knew perfectly well that he was going off to get drunk. The meeting however had not been totally unsatisfactory: it had held a

grain of hope. He loved her, he *must* love her, she told herself fiercely. She stood on the edge of the kerb watching the
red lights of the bus dwindle. It was too early to go home.
She decided to go and visit Janet.

She crossed the street and stood at the back of a small
queue at a bus stop. It was a dreich night, fog and drizzle,
and her toes were slowly freezing. She stamped her feet up
and down whilst she waited.

She became aware of a flicker of movement to her right
and saw a little dark figure slide in behind her. She turned
right round, presenting her back to it, and pulled up the
collar of her coat.

'Cold evening,' Khalil said.

She grunted and edged closer to the man in front. Khalil
moved up after her.

'Allow me to keep the draught off you.'

She stared at the man's head: it was bald and shiny and
fringed with a few ginger hairs.

'Have you been waiting long?'

She continued to stare at the shiny head.

'I seldom travel by bus but tonight my feet need resting.'

She craned her neck out sideways: the long stretch of
street was empty.

'Nothing coming?' Khalil made sympathetic noises at the
back of his throat. 'The service must be poor at this time of
day. Did you ever hear my poem "Waiting at a Bus Stop"?'
He began to recite.

She was thankful that it was not broad daylight and that
there was no one in sight whom she knew. Khalil was no
concern of hers; nevertheless, she felt the colour welling up
in her face, flooding across her cheeks, bringing heat into
them. The man with the bald head turned round, looked
past her at Khalil, and then looked back at her. She made a
face, denying any responsibility for the brown-faced idiot
in the ridiculous long coat. The man tapped his bald pate
and she nodded. Khalil continued to spout about the lum-
bering of heavy tyres, buses the colour of dried blood . . .

136

She stepped into the roadway and peered east: a bus was coming.

It swooshed into the kerb, spraying their legs with dirty brown water. Isobel sprang onto the running board, Khalil followed. She clambered up the stairs, he came fast on her heels. At the top of the stairs she almost panicked: the deck was empty. She turned to go back down but he was standing on the top step blocking her way. He was gazing at her with a smile that seemed the embodiment of evil. He didn't look normal. Perhaps he was insane?

She slipped into a seat near the stairhead. He joined her. She decided that she had better humour him for he might be capable of anything. What did he keep in those big pockets in which his hands were bunched? A knife? She shuddered. But he wouldn't touch her, he had no reason . . . . Reason might not mean anything to him. She must pull herself together; her nerves were on edge. Of course he wouldn't touch her, not here on a public bus in the middle of Edinburgh. She would only have to scream and the conductor would run up to her rescue.

'Don't you like my poetry, Isobel?'

'I don't care much for poetry,' she mumbled. She cleaned a patch on the window and pressed her nose to the glass. The bus was moving so slowly, like an aged snail bound for its last resting place.

'Not any poetry?'

'No.'

He sighed.

They sat side by side, silent for the rest of the journey. When she reached her stop, she excused herself politely and he allowed her to pass. He followed her down the stairs. They left the bus together.

'Going to visit Janet?' he asked, falling into step beside her.

'Yes. Are you?'

'Later perhaps. First I have an appointment.'

'Urgent no doubt?'

137

'All my business is urgent.'

He lengthened his stride, marvelling at the swift tic-tac pace she could sustain in the spiky high heels. At the corner of The Crescent she stumbled on a cracked paving stone; he caught hold of her arm and steadied her. The arm was rigid with hostility. She snatched it free and ran ahead of him along the pavement. She vanished down into the gloom of the area of 31B.

Khalil walked slowly past, laughing softly to himself, bent on his urgent business.

Isobel found that Janet was out and was resentful: people were never there when you most wanted them. Dolly was baby-sitting. She sat by the stove, regarding a half-finished sock with a bovine air. At her feet Muffin rolled on her back playing with the ball of lovat wool that dangled from the end of the knitting. The complacency of the scene infuriated Isobel. She flung herself down on the settee.

'What's the matter?' Dolly asked. 'Been running?'

'I came up on the bus with Khalil. He frightens me.'

'He's odd but harmless,' Dolly said and started another row.

'Where's Janet?'

'Gone to the pictures with George.'

'George! That doughnut!'

Dolly held up the sock. 'Would you say that measured nine inches? I'm knitting socks for my fiancé, he suffers from cold feet. It's the draughts in his study: they're something dreadful.'

Dolly was launched. Isobel listened sullenly for half an hour, making no attempt to show interest. Eventually she could not restrain herself and burst out with the news that she was engaged to be married to Tim MacAuley. Dolly dropped a stitch.

'Janet didn't tell me.'

'She doesn't know yet.' Isobel felt a little sick but it was almost true: he had more or less said he would marry her.

'That is nice.' Dolly smiled. 'Marriage is an excellent institution. I can't think why Janet is so opposed to it.'

Dolly and Isobel talked of their respective fiancés, neither interested in what the other had to say but delighted to be able to talk copiously with someone who would not class her immediately afterwards as a bore. Isobel enjoyed herself thoroughly; she had not been so relaxed for weeks. The more she talked of Tim the dearer he became to her, and the more real her engagement. She talked herself out and lay back feeling like a deflated balloon. Now she did not want to see Janet who would quiz her and not accept the news so calmly. She took her leave of Dolly, who hoped they would meet another evening, and hurried home.

Murray looked at Tim over the top of his book. 'What are you doing in so early? I thought you had a date with Little Miss Puppet?'

'That's why I'm in early.' Tim frowned. 'I'm in rather a tricky spot. Isobel thinks she's going to have a baby.'

'That is tricky. But she'll make you a good wee wife.'

'I don't want a good wee wife.'

'Looks like you're going to get one whether you want it or not.'

'I don't have to marry her.'

'No. But you probably will. It's what any decent bloke would do, and you see yourself as a pretty decent bloke at heart. If it were me, I would have no such scruples. I have no expensive conceptions of myself.' Murray got up and went over to the table. He sawed off a wedge of bread, whistling cheerfully. He spread it with marmalade and sank his teeth into it.

'You've got a disgusting appetite.'

'It's not as disgusting as some of your appetites. I have to keep fit for my work.'

'There's more to it than just not wanting to marry Isobel.'

'I know: you love another!' Murray finished his bread and reached for the knife again. 'Those Robertson girls seem to have an aptitude for landing themselves in trouble. It shows a remarkable carelessness on their part, or on the men they associate with. I think you should go and talk it over with Janet before Isobel does. Aren't civilized people meant to discuss these things sensibly?'

'I'll run you through with that bread knife if you're not careful,' Tim said and departed.

He went up to *Greyfriars Bobby*, had a few drinks alone and then wandered round the streets until it was late. When he arrived at 31B he found George Bell and Dolly consuming toasted cheese and instant coffee. They were discussing bishops in the Church of Scotland. Janet was quiet, her coffee lay untasted by her chair. She knows, Tim thought.

It was close on midnight when Dolly and George left. After they had gone, Janet busied herself clearing away the dirty dishes. Tim followed her along to the kitchen.

'You're getting married, I hear,' she said. 'Isobel told Dolly.'

'There's nothing definite yet. She had no right to tell anyone.'

'I don't understand, Tim. Why – ' She stopped and said: 'She's pregnant, I suppose?'

He nodded.

On his way home he met Khalil who took him to a party in a tenement where the lavatories were communal and the smells obnoxious. As the night advanced the smells became less noticeable and a queue formed at the lavatory on the stair landing. Tim drank several glasses of cheap spirit, got involved in a fight with a drunk Pakistani, and wakened in the morning in a strange bed. There was also a strange woman in the bed. Her streaky red hair straggled across the grey pillow and a thin whine emitted from the gaping mouth. She looked ready to qualify for the old age pension. He retreated without rousing her.

He walked back to the mews where Murray held a piece of high stewing steak to his swollen eye and fed him a mug of thick gritty coffee that coated his tongue like a medicine.

'God man, do you go looking for trouble? I don't know how you manage it. You'll need to change your clothes. You stink. What happened?'

'Don't know. Don't want to know.'

Murray cleaned him up and put him into a taxi at the corner of the street. He reached the school as the bell was ringing. It went ding, ding, ding through his head like the clappers of hell. The green-painted, rust-revealing railings wavered and wiggled and pulled at his eyes; and behind them children shouted and screeched and surged across the grey asphalt. Suddenly the confusion melted, the shrieking mob dissolved into long straight meek lines, and silence fell.

Tim crossed the playground, ignored a few sniggers from the rear of the lines, and advanced towards the door marked BOYS, where the Infant Mistress stood with hands clasped.

'My dear Mr MacAuley, what have you been doing?'

'I fell down the stairs.' He attempted a smile but it proved impossible. He edged round her projecting left hip, barked his shins on a pile of milk crates just inside the door, and came face to face with the headmaster.

'This isn't your day for us, MacAuley. You were here a fortnight ago.'

The children had started to march in, keeping time to the clapping of the Infant Mistress's hands. Tramp, tramp, tramp went the feet and smack, smack, smack went the hands. Tim leaned back against the wall. As the boys passed they flicked their forefingers against their foreheads to show their respect.

'Nasty eye you've got there, MacAuley,' the headmaster shouted. 'You don't look so hot. Feeling all right?'

'Fine, just fine.'

The last child passed, the Infant Mistress smiled sympathetically, and Tim escaped through the door. He picked

141

up another taxi and reached the correct school at a quarter to ten. The headmaster there was off with 'flu, the Infant Mistress had measles, little Miss Grant had been sick in the staff room, and the visiting singing teacher had laryngitis.

'Thank God you've come!' the First Assistant said.

Tim's class had given up waiting for him. He paused outside the door, listening to the noise; then braced himself and entered. They were playing Cowboys and Indians: the Indians were shacked up on the high brown window-sills uttering warlike cries and the Cowboys were advancing towards them with deadly concentration. A little squaw with no front teeth shrieked as the door opened and toppled down amongst the Cowboys, laying three of them flat.

When order had been restored and the squaw sent to the lavatories to remove the blood from her face, Tim tore up black paper and distributed boxes of chalk. They settled down to draw clowns. Touring the room, he noticed that at least half of the clowns had black eyes. He went back to the desk and sat down. His right eye was almost closed and he could not see one side of the class. The noise coming from that section of the room told him that his pupils were well aware of the fact, but he could not think that it mattered. In the back row a boy with carrot-red hair was rapidly covering his own eye with crimson chalk; his neighbour gave it a touch of yellow for good measure and a snot-nosed girl in front leaned over his desk, showing a pair of grey-pink knickers under a yellow and black kilt, and encircled the lot with purple. Tim closed his good eye.

He was roused by a tap on his shoulder. There was an unnatural quiet in the room. He squinted up to see the First Assistant standing to attention by the desk.

The First Assistant cleared his throat and said: 'There's a telephone call for you, Mr MacAuley. A young lady. She wouldn't give her name.'

Tim hastened to the headmaster's room and picked up the detached receiver.

'Yes?'

'Tim, it's Isobel.'

'Isobel,' he muttered. Isobel! It was all her fault: the throb in his eye, the fug in his head, the sickness in the pit of his stomach.

'Darling, are you all right? You sound funny. What a job I've had getting hold of you! This is the fifth school I've tried. I couldn't remember which one you were at today.'

'Neither could I.'

'What? I can't hear you very well. Can you speak up a bit?'

'It doesn't matter,' he shouted.

'Good. Tim, do you love me?'

He took a deep breath and said very loudly: 'Isobel, I hate you.'

He replaced the receiver and went to tell the First Assistant that he was very sorry he would have to go home at once as he felt most unwell.

He slept all day and awoke when it was dark. He drank half a tumblerful of neat whisky which Murray kept in the cupboard for medicinal purposes, then examined his face in the mirror with revulsion but decided not to shave since he would certainly cut himself. He covered his swollen eye with a black patch and took the bus up to The Crescent.

Khalil was there, drinking beer and in good spirits.

'Behold the Pirate of Penzance!' he cried. 'The patch is rather theatrical but it makes an excellent disguise. I must remember it for some future occasion. I trust your friend looked after you well last night?'

'That bag!' Tim groaned. 'Some dark night I shall murder you, Khalil. You don't weigh much, I could easily dispose of your body, so be careful. And stop grinning at me. It makes my head hurt. You too,' he said, scowling at Janet.

'I'm not grinning,' she said.

143

'Our Tim does not take well to adversity,' Khalil said. 'It makes him peevish.'

'Peevish! I feel hellish. So would you be if you'd been through what I have in the last twenty-four hours.' He laid himself out on the settee and closed his eyes. He should have stayed in the mews. He didn't know why he had come here; he had no right to come now; he had come without thinking. He gravitated towards this basement as did Khalil and George Bell and even Dolly who, though she affected to despise it, found some comfort from the warm stove and the aura of seclusion the room held. Tonight there was no comfort in it for him. It reminded him of Isobel. Isobel! The name thumped through his pounding head. And seated tranquilly on either side of the stove were Janet and Khalil, regarding his body with amusement. They were in league with the devil, those two, mocking him, holding him up as an object of fun.

'I saw Isobel today,' Janet said.

There was going to be no peace. He swung his legs over the edge of the settee and sat up, supporting his head on his hands. He supposed he too should have seen Isobel today. What did it matter? He was going to see enough of her in the future.

'Do you want to be sick?' Khalil asked. 'Your face is a strange shade of khaki.'

'Isobel rushed into the bookshop this morning and burst into tears,' Janet said.

'Oh God!' Tim said wearily. 'She told you I hated her, no doubt.'

'And a lot more besides. She's very unhappy. She loves you, Tim.' Janet sighed. 'And she's not pregnant.'

'She's not?'

Tim lifted his head which, miraculously, had ceased to throb. Even his eye had become merely an area of discomfort and not a bore of pain. He lit a cigarette and enjoyed the taste. He looked round the room, rejoicing in the knowledge that he was free again, that he would continue to

144

come here in the evenings and watch the flames flickering inside the clumsy, ugly stove.

'Your colour has come back,' Khalil said.

Suddenly the full realization of what Janet had said came to Tim. To begin with it seemed as if a miracle had happened and then he understood: Isobel had lied to trap him into marriage! Indignation welled up in him, followed by red hot anger. He gave vent to it until brought to a halt by Janet.

'What right have you to judge when you don't understand? Isobel was miserable, she was desperate and she had to do something. She loves you. Doesn't that mean anything to you?'

'Does one have any responsibility towards the people who love one, if one doesn't love them?' Khalil murmured. 'I wouldn't know.'

'She's very unhappy,' Janet said.

'I'm not completely insensitive but what do you expect me to do about it?' Tim said. 'Marry her and become a martyr? I'm not cut out for that sort of thing. I can't be tied to her for life just because I've been to bed with her.'

'I blame myself in many ways,' Janet said. 'Things might have been different between you if I hadn't come back.'

'If you hadn't come along Isobel and I would never have lasted together.'

'I can't be sure of that. Neither can you.'

'I can. I knew it after the first time we made love. It was the last night of the Festival. I stood by the window watching the fireworks and I knew that it was no good. Maybe I should have told her then. It wasn't her fault and I don't think it was mine either.'

'She's young,' Janet said. 'She lacks experience, she says things that would be better left unsaid. You can't hold her innocence against her.'

Innocence, Tim thought! He doubted if Isobel knew the meaning of the word. From what he knew of her she was as shallow as a saucer and he was sure that she would soon find

145

someone else to take his place. He wished that Janet would let the subject drop. It had all been a rather unsatisfactory mess out of which he had emerged not particularly well. He knew that, but saw no virtue in poking the pus out of the boil, as Khalil had once said.

'Poor Isobel,' Khalil said. 'A little more humour, and life would be a lot different. If she could only laugh at herself!'

'None of us find it easy to laugh at ourselves,' Janet snapped. 'Even you. You mock yourself but underneath you think you're the most important creature that treads the earth.'

'Naturally. One has to believe that to survive.'

CHAPTER FIFTEEN

'I do like an old-fashioned Christmas,' Aunt Matilda said, as she wiped the gravy spots on the blue silk shelf of her bosom with a crumpled paper napkin.

'Say what you like,' Uncle John said with a belch into his port, 'but it's a time for the family.'

Agnes Robertson nodded and sat back in her chair, content. She looked round the table at them all. Fergus beginning to nod, the top button of his waistcoat undone, paper hat askew. Fiona giggling softly with the excess of food and drink, looking coyly at Howard who was awkwardly smoking a fat cigar. Isobel, peaked and drawn, gazing into her untasted glass of sherry as though in that amber pool she might find the solution to life. Grandmother Robertson watching everything, sharp-eyed. Three maiden aunts sitting in a row like Dutch dolls. George Bell, alert, smiling. Next to him, Janet, staring into the rising smoke of her cigarette, thinking . . . Of what? No one ever knew what Janet thought. And squatting in a corner by the window, half-hidden by the maroon velvet curtain, was her child. Sally clutched a bland-eyed doll against her chest. She

146

looked bored and confused by the density of so many large people who did not know what to say to her.

Fergus Robertson's paper hat slipped sideways onto his left ear; his mouth dropped open; his chin sank to his chest. A loud snore travelled across the table, causing one of the maiden aunts to wince. Agnes Robertson began to sort out the wreckage, sliding the cutlery onto one plate, the scraps of abandoned food onto another. Janet got up and helped her carry the dishes into the kitchen.

'It's so nice to have everyone together,' Agnes Robertson said. 'If only Robert had come! He doesn't seem to care whether he comes home or not.'

'It would be nice to see him again,' Janet said, to please her mother. She felt quite indifferent to Robert: she remembered him as a fat eleven-year-old with hot hands that left sweaty marks on everything they touched.

Agnes Robertson wrapped a large apron round her new frock and put on a pair of plastic sleeve cuffs. Janet stood by the draining board holding a drying up cloth in front of her, ready to pounce on the first gleaming dish as it would leave the workworn, sudded hands. Water filled the sink slowly.

Her mother turned off the tap, and the silence was overwhelming.

'Fiona seems to be bearing up well,' Janet said. 'About the baby, I mean.'

'Fiona's sensible.'

Janet made her pounce. The hot slippery plate slipped between her hand and the cloth. She tried to save it but succeeded in knocking it against the sink. It dropped to the floor in four clean pieces. She started to apologize but her mother cut her off.

'Better get rid of it before your father sees it.' Agnes Robertson ruffled the water with her hand. 'It's part of our wedding china, you know. We've had it thirty-five years.'

Janet carried the pieces out to the dustbin, glad to escape into the fresh air for a brief moment. The sun was dipping

147

behind the bare lilac trees at the bottom of the garden. As she poked the evidence well down into the rubbish she thought of the many times they had feverishly gathered up broken glass, rubbed salt on ink stains, stuck back pieces of wallpaper, all in an atmosphere of impending disaster — before father would come in.

As soon as they had finished the washing up it was time to start eating again. Janet's stomach rebelled.

'But you must have a piece of Christmas cake, dear.'

'You can't disappoint your mother after all the work she's had. She was up till two o'clock this morning finishing off the icing.'

Very well, just a tiny little bit. Rich fruit cake, thick almond paste and sweet white icing, washed down with a gulp of tea. No, no, she couldn't possibly eat a mince pie.

'But your mother's mincemeat is the best in the district. She won first prize for it at the Women's Guild.'

'Best mincemeat I've ever tasted,' George said.

'Well — just one.'

Sally was crumbling a piece of cake between her fingers, about to spit out the lump in her mouth. Janet leaned forward, ready to catch it as it came.

'We must have some carols after tea,' Grandmother Robertson said.

Aunt Mildred, who played the organ in church, allowed herself to be persuaded to go to the piano. She laid her rings on the sideboard in front of the photograph of Ian and his bride whom no one had ever seen and perhaps never would, flexed her fingers, and the Robertsons gathered round. Grandmother Robertson was given a glass of water and seated next to the pianist. In her youth she had had a fine contralto voice which had been heard soaring above the choir for many years; it wavered a little now but she still liked to sing. Her gnarled brown hands frightened Sally. She looked round for her mother who was not visible in the throng. Fiona took the child's hand in hers and told her they were going to sing about the baby Jesus. Sally stood obediently, her eyes level with a round fat bottom swathed in tight blue silk. It swayed very slightly from side to side. She prodded it with one finger: it was warm and solid and her finger bounced off it, leaving no impression. Over the tops of the heads she saw the glittering pink and silver fairy on the tip of the Christmas tree and wondered if it would be given to her to carry home in her pocket.

'Ready?' Fergus Robertson called.

'Still the night, holy the night . . .'

With a soft, secretive movement Agnes Robertson switched off the light. Now they were bathed in a candle-flickering glow of sentiment where all is forgiven and blood is thicker than water. The little smiles round the piano reassured them of this.

'. . . sleeping in heavenly rest.'

Agnes Robertson blew her nose. Sally pulled her hand out of Fiona's and sidled out of the room.

After the carols Uncle John suggested they play Twenty Questions. Janet looked at her watch.

'You can't go yet, dear,' her mother said.

Father was elected to be first out of the room. Janet jumped up when she heard his bark and ran into the hall. Sally was sitting with her bottom hard up against the banister post and her legs dangling astride the rail. She was staring defiantly into her grandfather's eyes.

'You're a bad girl,' he said. 'I told you not to slide down the banisters.'

The child slid from her perch and very slowly remounted the stairs. Fergus Robertson swayed a little on his feet. Sally clambered back onto the rail at the top.

'Don't you dare!' he thundered.

With a swoosh she sailed past him. His hand came out and caught her a hard slap on the back of the leg. She burst into tears and Janet caught her up into her arms.

Janet turned to face her father. A stream of words issued from her mouth; it was as though they had formed up

149

somewhere at the back of her throat and come gushing out of their own volition. Afterwards she could not remember what it was she had said. There was a gasp from the family knotted in the doorway.

For a moment she thought that her father would strike her and she almost wished that he would. His face changed colour and his mouth twitched. Then he pushed his way back into the room. His wife followed, her face puckered.

'I'll get your coat,' George said, 'and take you home.'

Janet stood in the hallway listening to the voices behind the closed door.

'She's storing up trouble for herself and no mistake. That child's quite undisciplined.'

'Needs a father's hand.'

'It's a shame, poor wee bairn.'

'It's Christmas day, Fergus . . .'

'She defied me deliberately. She's going to be just like her mother.'

'She's really quite a biddable child. We had no trouble at all with her that week-end she stayed with us, did we, Howard? She needs handling the right way. Janet doesn't seem to have the knack of dealing with children and she ought to have more sense than to let her mix with some of the people that walk in and out of her flat as though they owned it. There's an odd little Indian . . .'

'Ready?' George said.

'More than ready.'

In a house across the road the wireless was gushing forth 'Hark the Herald Angels sing'. Janet got into the car and slammed the door on it.

She was jerked out of sleep by the noise of the window being lowered. She sat up to see a figure coming feet first through the curtains into the room.

'It's all right. It's me, Khalil.'

She lay back on the pillow, her heart hammering against her ribs. He hoisted up the window, rearranged the curtains and switched on the light. She began to scold him for having given her a fright.

'I came to wish you a Merry Christmas even though it has just gone. Your chimney is too long so I had to use the window. I knocked several times but you must have been sleeping.'

'I was sleeping. I've had a terrible day.'

He sat down on the edge of the bed. 'So you didn't enjoy your family Christmas?'

'If it weren't for the fact that Fiona and I are twins I would be inclined to think that I was a cuckoo that had been dropped into the nest.'

'You're not the first to have such thoughts. Half the teenagers in the world think the same things.'

'I'm not a teenager.'

'That's true.' He brought a cigarette-end up from the depths of his navy-blue pocket and put it in his mouth. 'Nor me either. If I were to return home I, too, would be a cuckoo and I would quarrel with my father. He thinks that the peasants in his village are fortunate in being alive – though he would not be so indiscreet as to say so unless it were to his advantage – that too much education would give them ideas above their station, that too much food in their bellies might give them the strength to rise up, band together and demand something more of life than a hovel of mud and a pittance of rice. My father is not in favour of a New India or a new anything. He is a money-lender and he likes to hold men's souls in his hands. It is strange that men like my father should live.' Khalil blew out a stream of smoke from his mouth. 'Some day he will have his throat cut.'

He sat crouched into his coat, his eyes far away from the room, cigarette smoke blurring the outlines of his small head. Janet waited, hoping he would say more, but he straightened himself up and once more became the half-mocking, half-sarcastic Khalil.

'My penny tenement fell down tonight so I have nowhere

151

to sleep. I would have gone to Tim for asylum but he is in Glasgow for the festive season. So – '

'You can't stay here,' she protested.

Why not? There was a spare bed in Sally's room. She crawled into it, muttering. It was as cold as charity. She lay shivering, thinking of Khalil in her warm bed. One night, she told him, that was all. He stayed seven weeks.

George frowned. 'But, Janet, you can't have that fellow staying here.'

'Why not?'

'Well, I mean to say . . .'

'I'm not sleeping with him.'

'I didn't say that you were.' He spoke with careful patience. 'A woman living alone has to watch what she does. What will the neighbours think?'

'I don't give a damn what they think – other women take in lodgers.'

'But he's not really a lodger. He doesn't pay you anything, does he?'

'Would it make any difference if he did?'

'Of course not. But you've got Sally to consider.'

'Sally's very fond of Khalil: he makes her laugh.'

Seeing that Janet was not prepared to be reasonable, he abandoned the matter. He was stiffly polite to Khalil whenever they met though he despised any man who would take advantage of a woman in Janet's position. 'Don't keep referring to "my position",' Janet said good-naturedly. 'You make me feel like a leper outcast or someone who isn't responsible for her own actions.'

She made one or two half-hearted attempts to chivvy Khalil into taking some action but he had always just heard of a place that might suit him or he had an appointment with a friend who had just heard of a place, so she gave it up. The arrangement suited her well enough: he did all the shopping, getting everything at cut-throat level, he took the washing to the launderette, he proved to be a competent cook and he often took Sally to the nursery in the morning and collected her in the evening. The matron looked oddly at Janet when she went but this she ignored for she was used to people giving her odd looks. Later she discovered that Khalil had told the matron he was Mrs Crosbie's houseboy.

On New Year's Eve they were visited by George and Dolly. Dolly called in on her way to the Watch Night Service. She sipped a glass of sherry and ate a piece of Black Bun.

'Terrible stuff that,' Khalil shuddered, indicating the Black Bun. 'Once I made a great mistake: I ate a large slice and afterwards had a bath. I went down twice and was going down for the third time when I fortunately managed to grab hold of the soap dish.'

'I didn't know you ever had a bath,' Janet said.

'Hogmanay and Midsummer Eve. I shall have to do without tonight unless I use the kitchen sink.'

'I'm rather fond of Black Bun,' George said.

'It's traditional, isn't it?' Dolly said.

She told them that she was going to be married at the beginning of March, dusted the Black Bun crumbs from her fur coat, and wished them all 'A Happy New Year' when it came. Janet walked along to the corner with her.

'George is very nice,' Dolly said.

'Yes.'

'You could do worse than marry him.'

'I've no doubt I could.'

Janet walked slowly back along The Crescent. The windows were well lit; behind them the women would be doing their last minute cleaning and the men would be stacking up their bottles on the sideboards. The end of one year, the beginning of the next . . . She looked up to see Tim leaning against a lamp-post, watching her.

'Counting all your misdeeds? Or are you speculating on the nature and purpose of life? Are you wondering what

153

you're doing in this world, in this street, in that little basement?'

She laughed. 'As a matter of fact I was. Rather an obvious thing to do perhaps.'

'Did you reach any conclusions?'

'No. I was thinking that I didn't really belong in The Crescent any more than Khalil does in Edinburgh. I'm not a part of the community – I'm thought of as something odd and foreign. I live in a little sealed unit below ground, isolated.'

'Does it matter?'

'I don't know that either. It's temporary. That's the thing about it – it's not lasting. You, too, you don't know where you belong. Not with your family any more.' He began to protest but she continued: 'You left Glasgow because of it, didn't you? You found it overwhelming, all the aunts and relations asserting their right to know what you were doing. Lack of privacy, you said. You and Khalil and I, we're all in transit.'

'Isn't everyone?'

'Not unless you believe in a life after death. It makes me think of one of those games, a little enclosed box with holes in it and three silver balls you shake trying to get them into the holes.'

'So we're the little balls and we've not found our holes?' Tim sounded amused.

'Yes.'

'Well, I don't mind. I don't care much for holes. It's much more interesting to be rolling around. Don't you feel that too?'

'I do, but some day one stops and one's frightened of ending up in the wrong hole by mistake or apathy. 31B could be my hole. Heavens, I sound morbid tonight!'

'You know what it is? There's something lacking in your life, some extra dimension that would enrich it. Could it be me?'

'I thought you were in Glasgow.'

154

'You have a nasty habit of changing the subject when it's interesting,' he said. 'What are you afraid of?'

'Let's go and join George and Khalil,' she said.

She had already moved away from him and was opening the gate. She ran down the steps, paused at the door and called up: 'Are you coming? It's almost twelve.'

He leaned over the railing. 'You didn't answer my question,' he shouted, but she had disappeared inside.

CHAPTER SIXTEEN

On the twenty-fifth of January the Robertsons met together again. It was the occasion of the Women's Guild Burns Supper in the Church Hall. Janet had not wanted to go but had succumbed to George's pleading: he was most anxious that she should be reunited with her family; in addition, he was proposing 'The Immortal Memory'. It was indeed very much a family affair: Agnes Robertson had been in charge of boiling the turnips, Howard was addressing the haggis, Aunt Mildred was playing the piano and Fergus Robertson was proposing the Toast to the Lassies. Someone, Janet thought, had a sense of humour.

They sat on hard chairs quite unsuited to the human body at the sides of trestle tables which were disguised with sheets of white shelf paper and sprigs of greenery. The bleak hall with its dark wood and smell of dust brought back memories of Girl Guides, boring hours at Sunday School, youth club dances with pimpled youths ganged in one corner and shiny eager girls trying to look self-confident and nonchalant in the other. The girl who had been a part of all these things seemed no part of the person who now sat half-smiling at half-recognized faces. Facing her on the wall was a dignified portrait of the poet, suitable for the Women's Guild: he gazed down at them, his disciples, with an indifferent eye that held no trace of lust, debauchery or love of common man.

'So glad you could come, dear,' her mother said, squeezing her hand on the shelf paper. 'Your father's a bit hasty at times – you know what he's like.'

The skirl of the pipes drowned out the chatter. Eyes went to the doorway: coming majestically through was the solemn-faced piper, his lips pursed and swollen round the mouthpiece, tartan swirling round his strong hairy knees. In spite of her antipathy Janet felt a thrill run through her. She grinned. The noise was enormous. Two yards behind this resplendent figure came the minister's wife, wearing a tartan glengarry and carrying aloft a large white platter on which lay, steaming like a cannon, the mighty haggis. Janet was reminded of Salome carrying the head of John the Baptist, but no one else seemed to share her irreverent thought for they were all beaming happily upon the tableau and smacking their hands together to show their approval.

The haggis was set on the top table and Howard rose, kilted and sporraned, to address it.

'Fair fa' your honest sonsie face,
    Great Chieftain o' the Puddin' race . . .'

The haggis continued to steam, unaware of its impending doom. And then: 'Gie her a haggis!' Howard cried and stabbed it with a knife. He slit its belly wide open. Steam rose, the innards fell out, everybody clapped anew. They settled down to eat. Haggis and neaps, washed down with glasses of Vimto, followed by cups of tea and sweet cakes: it was enough to make Burns burst out of his frame. Janet struggled with the hot peppery mess and sticky lemonade, her mother urging her on. She tried to think of pleasant things: fields of golden corn, snow on the branches of trees, Muffin rolling on her back, Sally laughing at Khalil; but her mind clung tenaciously to the linings of sheep's stomachs. She had too much imagination, her mother had once told her.

'You can't leave that, dear,' her mother said now. 'It doesn't look nice. Try a little more. It's really delicious.'

156

When George began 'The Immortal Memory', Janet kept her head down. The speech was appallingly dull: a recital of the main facts of Burns' life, broken by snatches of his poetry. She had heard her father give the same speech, even the same quotations, ten years ago.

Lodged somewhere at the back of her throat was a haggis crumb; she concentrated on not choking. A trickle of perspiration ran down her back. The room was deadly quiet except for George's clear, well-modulated voice.

She allowed herself a tiny cough but it did not ease the situation. She longed for a good strong drink. She closed her lips tightly and swallowed hard, pushing back into her throat the great enormous cough that was building up, ready to erupt at the slightest slackening of her mouth. This had not happened to her since school Prize Days and long Sunday mornings in church.

God, would he never stop! He was quoting another poem. She swivelled her eyes to study the faces around her. They were listening as though spellbound! There must be something wrong with her. She caught Fiona's eye; Fiona glared and looked back at George. What would Burns have thought of all this? Janet glanced up at him but he did not seem to be thinking anything. Was there anything new to be said about him? These gatherings only served as an excuse for a string of clichés to be trotted out with all the hypocrisy and cant that attended them. And yet year after year the subject was stretched to its utmost like a piece of old elastic. It was tough but one day it must surely snap.

'Ae fond kiss, and then we sever;
Ae farewell, and then forever!'

She *had* to cough. It came from her like a clap of thunder. George paused. She coughed again and again. Soon she was immersed in a prolonged fit of coughing. Her face burned and her eyes streamed. A hot sticky peppermint was pressed into her hand. It was impossible for George to continue; he stood patiently, not quite managing to smile, fingering his sheets of paper. Janet pushed back her chair and fled. As soon as she was outside the hall, the coughing ceased.

She stood in the doorway, looking out into the street. It was snowing a little, light flakes of wet snow that would not lie. She put out her hand and felt them melt on the warmth of her skin. Opposite was a pub. She crossed the road, hesitated for a moment between the Cocktail Lounge and the Public Bar, and then went into the latter. It was no less dingy than the church hall but no one was reciting Burns. The barman looked a bit startled, said that maybe she wanted the Cocktail Lounge next door and smiled and poured her a drink when she said no, she didn't. She leant against the counter and a man who smelt of lime dust and mortar told her that he was a stone mason and his name was Sandy. He bought Janet a drink, then she bought him one. The barman said: 'You at the Burns do over the road?' and Sandy sang the first two lines of 'Scots Wha Hae'. A man further along the bar followed up with 'Caller Herrin' and the barman and Sandy had an argument about whether Burns had written it or not. Janet left them to it and returned to the hall, full of beer and without the suggestion of a cough.

'Where have you been?' George said, seizing her hand. 'I've been looking all over the place for you to come and dance the Gay Gordons.'

At the end of the dance they joined the rest of the family which was bunched up in a corner as though in quarantine.

'Where have you been?' Fergus Robertson said to Janet.

She remembered that she had missed him toasting the lassies and was sorry about it. It was unlikely she would ever have another opportunity to hear it.

Fiona leaned forward. 'You've been drinking! I can smell it on your breath.'

'I went into the pub across the road. Not a bad place really, rather much the sawdust-on-the-floor type but pleasant enough. I met a very interesting man called Sandy. A stone mason to trade.'

There was a short silence. Fergus Robertson was the first to find his voice.

'Do you mean to say you went into a public house alone?'

'Only tarts do that,' Fiona said.

'Then there is only one conclusion to be drawn from that statement,' Janet said.

'Janet is used to English ways,' George said, and was met with a cold, united stare.

'This is not England,' Fergus Robertson declared.

The piper was swelling up again. George turned to Janet. 'Come and dance. It's an Eightsome Reel.'

As he led her away, a buzz of voices rose behind them.

'Poor things,' Janet said. 'Their moral indignation is so easily aroused. Such a waste of energy.'

Janet had left Khalil baby-sitting but when she returned she found Tim reclining on the settee. He had relieved Khalil an hour ago as he had had to go out on business.

'Did you have a pleasant evening?' he asked.

She told him about it and he said: 'I don't know why you bother so much about your family. You did without them for five years so why can't you do without them now?'

'It's not as simple as that. I can't dismiss them so easily.'

'It annoys me to see them clipping away at you. What did they ever do for you? Chuck you out when you landed a baby! That's not what I call Christian conduct.'

'But they didn't chuck me out. I've never told you that they did.'

'But I always took it for granted –'

'You shouldn't take things for granted. They're not always what they seem.'

'So it would appear,' he muttered.

Janet moved about the room, tidying up Sally's clothes and toys.

'What did happen?' he asked.

'I left home of my own accord. I made my arrangements

and went. I left a note for my parents telling them why I'd gone.'

'Stuck to the pin cushion, no doubt?'

'No indeed. I propped it against a bottle of air-freshener on the hall table where mother would see it when she came downstairs in the morning. I did a real moonlight flit.'

She picked up a pair of Sally's shoes and began to clean them. He watched her carefully. It all sounded so cool, so calm. Surely it couldn't have been like that? How self-contained was she?

'Didn't you tell anyone you were going?'

'I told Dolly – and Isobel.'

'Isobel.' He shook his head, decided not to pursue that one any further. 'So you don't know whether your father would have turned you out or not.'

'I don't think he would: he's got too strong a sense of the family.'

'But it would have been hell living in the house afterwards?'

'Precisely,' Janet said.

CHAPTER SEVENTEEN

Mr Boland was nervous and preoccupied. He sat at the table in the back shop with a salami sandwich in his hand. Janet bent down and brought up the jam jar.

'Ah yes.' He grinned at her over the top of his spectacles and fished his teeth out of the jar. 'Thought there was something missing.' He clicked the teeth into position. 'Matter of fact, there was something I wanted to speak to you about.' The last words tumbled out of his mouth. Now that he had said them he became confused: he bit into the sandwich, put the jam jar under the table, refilled his cup and avoided Janet's eye. She waited, half-smiling to encourage him, whilst he chewed through the salami. When it was gone he said: 'I – er had a deputation last night from your neighbours in The Crescent.'

Her neighbours in The Crescent. Who were they? There was Mrs MacNab of course: she leaned against the railings for hours talking to women with bony ankles and splayed feet. Then there was Mrs Green who lived in 33B; her husband went to the dog track three nights a week, to the pub for another three and on Sundays he sat at home complaining because they had no television set. Mrs Green visited Janet sometimes; she scuttled down the steps, stayed for an hour or so and then scurried back up again and down into her own basement like a little fawn mouse running for cover. There was also a young girl with a pinched face, unhappy eyes and cheap red shoes. She nodded when they passed in the street and smiled at Sally. The rest of her neighbours Janet would not be able to recognize. Except by their feet. She looked at Mr Boland.

He removed his teeth and slipped them back into the jar. 'Never did care much for salami.'

'Have an egg roll?'

'Thanks. I'm fond of egg.'

'What did they want?'

'Oh yes. They came to complain.'

'About me?'

He nodded unhappily. Janet searched her memory. Had they been making a noise late at night? She didn't think so.

'They said you had a man living with you.'

'It's true,' she said.

He spluttered into the roll and pieces of egg showered the table. She felt sorry for him: he had probably told the deputation that he did not believe it.

'He's not really *living* with me – he's a sort of lodger. It's Khalil.'

'I thought it must be Khalil. They said he was an Indian.' Mr Boland was looking miserable. He dropped the remains of the egg roll into the waste-paper basket. Somehow or other his lunch was not a success today and usually

161

it was his favourite meal for his wife was not there to say: 'No reading at meals, Albert. You can go out to a restaurant if you want to read.' He looked at the piece of cherry cake in the bottom of the paper bag but decided he was no longer hungry.

'What's it got to do with them?' Janet demanded. 'It doesn't affect them in any way.'

'They said it was lowering the tone of The Crescent.'

Janet laughed and felt better.

Mr Boland did not laugh. He said: 'They said it wasn't good for the children to know that sort of thing was going on.'

'What sort of thing?'

'Well – er – you know what people say.' He looked even more miserable now. Janet said that she didn't know what people said. She felt as obstinate as a hedgehog refusing to uncurl. She wished the neighbours had come to her. 'I'm afraid, Janet,' Mr Boland said, 'I'll have to ask you – '

'Surely you're not going to let that bunch of hypocrites tell you what to do!'

'It's not so easy. You see, they can cause trouble if they've a mind to. They said that if they got no satisfaction from me they'd go to the police.'

'The police can't do anything. You needn't worry about that.'

'I don't know. The neighbours could make allegations against you.'

Allegation: 31B is a house of ill-repute. Men come and go at all hours of the day and night. Three men come: George Bell, a fairly well known Edinburgh lawyer; Tim Mac-Auley, an unknown teacher of art and maker of pots; Khalil Siddigi, an Indian who is well known and yet unknown. This is not good for The Crescent: it lowers the tone. People will say: 'The Crescent is a bad place, it is full of wicked people who do not walk in the light of the Lord.'

Janet saw the misery on Mr Boland's face and her anger evaporated. She said that she would tell Khalil to go.

162

As she walked home along The Crescent, she studied the tenements with renewed interest. Passing No. 11 she heard the sound of two voices, a man's and a woman's, quarrelling. Would they have found time to stop snarling and march up to Mr Boland's front door to complain? Probably not. High up somewhere a child was crying, a thin wail that was slowly weakening. The ginger tom that licked at fish papers slunk past, hugging the railings. One back paw still trailed behind the other. The girl with red shoes passed and said: 'Isn't it cold? Feels like snow.' Would she have complained? Or Mrs Green? No. It would be the busybodies: Mrs MacNab and her splayed-feet friends.

The lights were on in the basement and there was a rich smell of curry. Khalil, stirring the meat in the pot, took the news with equanimity. No phase in his life was ever permanent so there was no cause to be upset. He had heard that morning of a place that might suit him. After their meal he went off to negotiate, returned to say that he had been suited and then went away with the brown paper parcel which constituted his luggage. He did not say, of course, where he was going. He preserved his mystery in a way that was unshakeable. Where did he go all day? What did he do? Who were all these friends who were forever nameless? What were all these appointments he had that were so urgent? Janet wandered round the confines of the flat, unable to settle. There were no secret parts in her present life. They were all wide open: anyone could walk in. Khalil had his pubs and shadowy streets and unknown haunts, George his flat in the New Town and his office, Tim his mews and his schools. She saw little of these aspects of their lives but they could walk into any part of hers: they could come into the basement or the shop where she worked. These were the boundaries of her life: Mr Boland's bookshop and 31B The Crescent.

She sank down onto the window-sill and listened to the feet tapping the pavement. They all passed by. And then, she heard another pair of feet. They stopped at the gate. She rushed to the door.

'Tim,' she cried, 'I am glad to see you.'

He leapt over the rail and landed at her feet. 'I wish you'd say that every time I come to visit you.' He put his arm round her shoulder and together they went into the warm room. His face was flushed with the cold. She put her hand up and put back a lock of hair that hung over his forehead. He raised an eyebrow. 'You are in a tender mood tonight.'

'I've been feeling lonely. I was missing Khalil. He's gone. Why does he never get depressed?'

'He has no house, no furniture, not even a suitcase. He carries all he needs in a brown paper parcel.'

'That's not the real reason.'

'Perhaps not. He's fascinated by life, even as he once said to me, by man's aptitude for destroying himself. That keeps him from being bored.'

'You sound very happy tonight.'

'Is that an accusation?' He laughed. 'I sold some pots this afternoon and I finished a picture that pleased me. It's a long time since I've painted. I painted it for you, Janet. The Crescent at dusk. Would you put it on your wall? Over there, where it catches the little light there is in the room. Take down that monstrous poster of Sydney harbour. You don't want to go to Australia, do you?'

No, she didn't want to go to Australia. She wanted to stay here in Edinburgh, in 31B The Crescent. It wasn't much of a flat perhaps, the sun never shone into the rooms and dust swirled against the windows, but it was warm and comfortable and she could sit in it with the curtains drawn and talk to someone she liked. And Edinburgh, though it was a city where the east wind blew and where some of the people thrived on gossip and malice as in any other town, was a city whose streets were known to her feet and whose roofs and spires and green grass were known to her eyes. It was a city where she could live and bring up Sally.

164

Her nerves had slackened; the restlessness left her body. She put out her hands and Tim took them in his. 'Would you really give me your picture?' she said.

'I painted it for you,' he said again. His lips brushed her forehead and he pulled her towards him.

Later, before falling asleep with Tim's arms round her, she thought of the neighbours. She smiled and closed her eyes.

Tim, too, thought of the neighbours before falling asleep. God bless their malicious hearts, he thought: if they hadn't ousted Khalil, he and Janet might not have come together again so easily.

Janet drew back the curtain. The pavement was covered with snow, soft and white at the edges but already trampled and dirty in the middle. A pair of feet hurried past, zippered into high brown suede boots.

'It's been snowing,' she said.

'Good,' Tim said. 'I feel like snow. We'll build a snowman for Sally tonight.'

'It'll be dark.'

'It's never properly dark when there's snow. That's one of the good things about it.'

Janet let Sally stay up late and they built a snowman in the back green, watched by Mrs MacNab from the sink at her kitchen window. They named it MacNab and pelted it with snowballs until its head dropped off and it stood in the pale light, a fat white body without appendages. Then they skiffed through the Meadows making zig-zag trails in the fresh snow. On their way home they bought fish and chips and ate them greedily, defying the soft wet flakes that drifted down onto the warm food to disappear abruptly.

'I like the snowtime,' Sally said.

'I'm glad you have a child,' Tim said later, when they lay in bed watching the firelight fluttering across the ceiling.

'It gives us an excuse to do childlike things. We can build snowmen by the dozen, go to the zoo . . .'

'There are lots of things we can do,' Janet said sleepily, feeling as if she were embarking on a holiday.

'I love you,' he said, stroking the line of her jaw, 'and I want to know all about you. You don't talk much about yourself. Tell me . . .'

'Not much to tell,' she said and thought sadly: I'm lying to him already, keeping back from him what he wants to know.

They talked a little of their earlier lives but they soon agreed that someone else's reminiscences were more often boring than not, that they pushed you further apart rather than brought you together: they reminded you of all the times when you were not together, when you did not even know the other existed. Memories of school days, first loves, evenings spent and enjoyed with other people: these were everyone's prerogatives and poking back into them, lingering over names which no longer have faces becomes a self-indulgence, a 'those-were-the-days' sigh echoing at the back of the throat. You smile wistfully, knowing of course that not for ten thousand pounds would you return to any of it. Or would you?

'I don't know,' he said.

'I wouldn't,' she said.

'Neither would I. I'd rather be here with you.'

She was interested to hear him speak of Greece and Yugoslavia, but when he began to talk of himself and Nancy, the girl he had gone there with, she felt something akin to resentment that he should think it important to speak of these things when he was here with her in this room cut off from the white windy night and the rest of the world. It was not that she was jealous of Nancy who could speak fluent Greek and do Slav dances – though if she were to be honest she would admit that she would have preferred Nancy not to be able to do these things since she could not. Tim had been in love with Nancy, had even

166

thought of marrying her. What had happened? He shrugged his shoulders, and Janet admitted it to be a stupid question. Nancy was married now and had two children. He saw her occasionally in Glasgow and they stopped to talk. She had put on a lot of weight and in her fur coat looked a typical young bourgeois matron who would never fulfil the promise of her youth. Janet felt better. No, she wasn't jealous of Nancy: Nancy spoke to Tim in the street but she was here with him, her arm lying beside his, her leg touching his, her head on his shoulder. She moved restlessly as she realized the implication of such thoughts: she could too easily become dependent on him. She sat up and reached for the cigarettes.

'It's one of the tragic things about love affairs,' he said, 'that when they're over so little remains but a few memories, and if anything positive is left it's usually hate or resentment so that even the memories are clouded. It's not often a man and woman can love and cease to love and feel grateful for what they had, meet afterwards and talk together as two friends who know one another well. The ones we've ceased to love become the biggest strangers of all. You meet in the street, clear your throat, wonder what there is to say when once there was everything to say. You edge away from each other, inch by inch across the pavement, until one of you has the courage to say: "Well, I must be going. Nice to have met you." Then you hurry away, trying not to feel guilty or too relieved, and when you reach the corner you look back and find that she has looked back too. The face of a stranger looking over her shoulder. And you feel sad because you'll never be able to see her again as you once did. Another human being has dropped through the trap door of your life.'

'It's not like you to talk like this,' she said. 'You're making me feel cold.'

'It won't happen to us.' He laughed at the stupidity of the idea. 'This time my trap door is firmly bolted. You'd have to saw your way through to get out.'

167

She remembered his words later when the bolts flew off and the trap door dropped.

'We mustn't make a habit of this,' she said. 'You mustn't stay every night.'

Not every night, he agreed. If they didn't meet every day they would return to one another with renewed interest; to live in the other's pocket meant death to any relationship. Tim did not really believe it but was unwilling to disagree with Janet. Sometimes in the morning he would say: 'I won't come tonight', but she knew that before the day was over she would see him.

It was strange for her to be preparing herself for a man again, to stand before the mirror brushing a shine into her hair, to spend idle moments staring into her own eyes, smiling a little anticipating his smile. Fool! she would think and clatter the brush onto the table and rumple her hair, but when she heard his step she would rush back to the mirror and smooth it so that she went out to put her hands into his, confident and happy that he would look and admire.

'Why doesn't Tim move in here?' Khalil said. 'He pays for half a flat he seldom uses. Such waste distresses me.'

'We don't want to live together,' Janet said. 'If we did, petty little domesticities would begin to creep in. We'd snap about leaving the cap off the toothpaste and want to know the other's movements. We're free, and I know that when he comes he comes because he wants to and not because he feels obliged to or has nowhere else to go.'

'People in love are not free,' Khalil said.

'There are different ways of being in love,' she said with a smile.

One Sunday afternoon they came upon Isobel sitting on a bench in Princes Street gardens. Tim and Khalil escaped quickly along another path, taking Sally with them.

'We'll be at the Cuckoo Clock,' Khalil called over his shoulder.

Janet sat down beside her sister.

'Do you see much of Tim?' Isobel asked, staring after the swiftly retreating trio.

'He comes to the flat with Khalil.'

'Does he ever talk about me?'

Janet shook her head.

Two girls, arrayed in their Sunday finery and arms linked, passed chattering and giggling at some secret joke. A few yards behind came two youths whistling softly.

'I wish I really knew what went wrong between us,' Isobel sighed. 'He didn't tell me.'

'There was probably nothing to tell, Isobel. Some things can't be explained. It's a sort of disenchantment between two people. It's no easier to understand than the enchantment.'

Isobel nodded. She told Janet that she hoped to get a job in Manchester modelling teenage fashions. She knew she would not pass the end of the year exams so did not intend to try. 'I hate mathematics,' she said. 'It was father's idea. I want to get away from Edinburgh. I've had enough of it.'

It would be best for her to get away from Edinburgh, Janet agreed, and from home . . .

The following Sunday morning they all slept late in 31B. They sat over breakfast reading the papers and did not hear Isobel come in. The door opened and Janet looked up to see her standing there watching them.

Isobel took in the scene quickly: Janet in a dressing-gown and Tim in open-necked shirt with stubble darkening the line of his chin. She turned away.

Janet ran after her along the hall. The front door slammed in her face. She tugged it open and saw Isobel whirling up the steps. She ran along The Crescent as though she were running for her life. The door of the ground floor flat opened and Mrs MacNab shuffled out to pick up her pint bottle of milk. Tim's voice calling Janet came up from the basement. Mrs MacNab sniffed, closing one nostril.

Later in the morning Janet went to her parents' house. The garage doors stood wide open and the car was missing: they had gone to church. She let herself in by the back door and stood in the kitchen listening. A cheap enamelled alarm clock ticked loudly on top of the kitchen dresser and a tap was dripping into the spotless sink. She turned the tap off mechanically, wondering how it had been allowed to drip, and went up to Isobel's room. The door was locked but a sound behind it told her that Isobel was there. She knocked gently, then again a little louder, but still there was no answer. She began to talk but it was hopeless to say such things through a thick brown door.

She left the house and walked to the Meadows, where she sat on a bench under a tree and smoked a cigarette, clutching it tightly between her cold fingers. It began to rain; she watched the drops spotting the grey path and listened to them rattling amongst the bare branches overhead. They dashed against her face and slithered down her neck, making her shiver. The rain increased, and soon it stotted on the path with an angry hiss.

When it slackened, her body relaxed too. Her cigarette was sodden and useless; she threw it into the long wet grass behind her. The rain settled down to a gentle, soothing patter.

The night before she had left home, when she had told Isobel she was going, Isobel had wept and said: 'But you can't go away. What'll I do without you?'

As a child Isobel was loving and wanted to be loved. She was the only one in the family who had ever admitted it openly. It was to Janet that she had run when she was unhappy; and Janet, as she comforted her younger sister, had known a great surge of tenderness and affection. Isobel had given her something no one else in the stone villa had. And Isobel had always trusted her.

Janet returned to The Crescent.

'Does it matter about Isobel?' Tim said. 'She was bound to find out sometime.'

'She's my sister and I don't want her to misunderstand.'

'People always misunderstand one another.'

'But must they?'

She was moody and upset, and resentful that Tim was not more upset about Isobel. He didn't give a damn about her, he said, and he wasn't going to pretend that he did. They had a row and he left early. The halcyon days were over, she thought, and sooner than she had expected. She would continue to see him but it would not be quite as it was before.

She wrote a long letter to which Isobel replied by postcard. On it was written one sentence: Fiona was right.

'How could you?' Fiona's voice was inordinately loud and high. Janet held the receiver away from her ear. 'You don't seem to care what you do to people as long as you get what you want. I thought it was odd when Tim dropped Isobel suddenly. I told her all along that she couldn't trust you but she wouldn't believe me. She thought the sun rose and set – '

Janet put down the receiver and with one finger pushed the squat black instrument to the end of the counter as if it were an unexploded bomb.

'I think I'll clean the windows today, Mr Boland,' she said.

He blinked over the top of his spectacles. 'But it's Wednesday.'

'I know, but I feel I'm getting in a rut.'

'Very well, very well. Just as you please.' He returned to his reading but he was disturbed at having the pattern of his week broken. Whilst Janet was sluicing down the windows he wandered about the shop, flicking the air with his yellow duster.

As she was brushing the water off the pavement she saw

George coming across the road towards her. He lifted his bowler.

'This is a surprise,' she said. 'I haven't seen you for ages.'

He looked embarrassed and said that he had been busy, but she knew it was Tim that was keeping him away from the basement.

'I had some business nearby so I thought I'd call and let you know your father is ill.'

'Serious?' she asked quickly.

'I'm not sure. It's his heart. He has to rest.'

'He won't like that.' She clasped her hands over the top of the brush and leaned her chin on them. 'I was talking to Fiona half an hour ago and she didn't even mention it. She was too absorbed in another matter. You know what she is when she's morally outraged!'

'I thought you might go and see your father,' George said. 'You may not realize it, Janet, but he's very fond of you in his own way. He told me once, when he'd had a couple of drinks, that you were his favourite.'

'I'll go and see him tomorrow.'

She meant to go, and would have gone, if Dolly's life had not erupted and spilled over into hers.

CHAPTER EIGHTEEN

Dolly crouched on the floor like a wounded animal, with her back up against the dresser. Loud sobs burst through the taut hands which clenched her face. Janet, squatting in front of her holding her shoulders, was alarmed by the tremendous turmoil she could feel in the heaving body.

Tim fidgeted behind a newspaper, ruffled his hair, cleared his throat. Then he said he was going out, and went off up the steps whistling.

As Dolly grew calmer Janet tried to piece together what she was saying. Her engagement was broken off: this much she had already gathered. 'I can't go through with it, I

172

can't go through with it,' Dolly repeated over and over again until the refrain screamed through Janet's head. She was not surprised that the strain of keeping up such an act – and an act it must have been – had finally told and Dolly's self-control had snapped. It was the night before her wedding.

'I love him,' Dolly sobbed, 'but I can't go through with it.'

Did she love him? Janet wondered. How could she know? Dolly had claimed to love all the others too. Was this an act: this hysteria, this sobbing, this clutching at her arm when she tried to move away? To her the grief seemed genuine. She gave Dolly some brandy that had been left from the New Year and several cups of strong black coffee. There was nothing else she could do for her. She didn't know what to say; she couldn't mouth all the usual ululations, the trite clichés that spring to the lips unbidden on such occasions; she couldn't say that it was better for Dolly not to enter into a life that she wouldn't want for she didn't know what kind of life Dolly would want. She began to wonder if Paul existed, if the manse with the draughts and the new carpet existed, the church where people complained of the cold . . .

She persuaded Dolly to lie down on the settee and by the time Tim and Khalil came in, she had drifted into an open-mouthed doze. The two men had been drinking heavily to armour themselves against this new phenomenon. They eyed the sleeping body warily and Khalil shrugged his shoulders. Janet told them to keep an eye on Dolly and went out in search of the minister-fiancé.

The manse was dark and square, and set back from the road in a screening of high trees that sighed and trembled in the wind. The gravel of the path crunched under her feet and a drop of water splashed from an overhanging branch onto her face, startling her. A single light shone from an uncurtained upstairs window.

The bell jingled in the deep recesses of the house. A

173

creak overhead, then feet hurried on the stairs. His shadow loomed large behind the glass panel of the door. He looked disappointed and tired when he saw Janet on the doorstep but rallied a little when she explained who she was.

They went up to his study and Janet understood why Dolly had talked so much of draughts. She glanced upwards expecting to see a gaping hole in the ceiling, but there was none. Where did all the air come from? The new carpet was an old-fashioned design in navy-blue and red; it looked cheap and less than new. She studied Paul as he talked: he was a kindly, middle-aged man in a grey pullover and soiled dog collar. He could not understand what had happened; he had pleaded with Dorothy to marry him but without success. It was all most distressing. He spoke nervously, smoothing back the thin hair from his high forehead, his shoulders hunched forward to protect his chest from the cold air. Janet stayed for ten minutes.

'Tell her I still want to marry her,' he said as he shook her hand and said goodbye.

But when she mentioned his name Dolly began to scream.

'I think we should call a doctor,' Khalil said. He spread out his hands. 'What can we do?'

The doctor came, administered a sedative and promised to return in the morning. Dolly was calm when the doctor was in and seemed almost normal, although none of them knew any longer what the word meant. They sat up all night, holding back with endless cups of coffee the waves of sleep that threatened to engulf them. Dolly tossed restlessly, talking intermittently in her sleep. Through her haze of fatigue Janet felt as if she were listening to excerpts from their life in the horse-boxed café. Names of people scattered round the world, fragments of old conversations, and then: 'I can't go through with it, I can't!' And a burst of sobbing breaking her sleep.

'My teeth are on edge,' Khalil said. He threw a cigarette carton onto the fire. 'No more cigarettes and the coffee tin is empty. We've reached the stage of the morning when the body temperature is at its lowest and one could very easily believe one is going mad.'

When Janet was ready to take Sally to the nursery, Dolly had fallen into a deeper, quieter sleep. Khalil offered to stay with her as he had no demands on his time. He came to the bookshop at lunch-time to say that Dolly had wakened and seemed composed. She had gone off, saying that she would come back later to see them.

They did not see her for several days.

'Perhaps she won't come back again,' Tim said hopefully. Any form of mental disorder made him uneasy.

'She'll be back,' Khalil said. 'There aren't many other places she can go.'

She came on Sunday morning. Janet and Sally had risen early and gone into the back green to weed round some daffodil bulbs they had planted. They were thriving in the middle of the fawn-green waste, holding up their golden heads to the sunshine. The earth smelled fresh as Janet turned it over and extracted the weeds. Sally sat down to watch a worm wriggling between the plants. Janet straightened herself and stood with the sun on her back, facing the tenements. Mrs MacNab was rubbing the sleep from her eyes at her kitchen window, and in the flat above a man was shaving. She saw the froth on the underside of his chin and the glint of the razor as it moved upwards, leaving a clean track in the white. A window squeaked and she craned her head back: a string of washing came fluttering out of a top flat to flap against the blue sky. Sally was tugging at her skirt. She had cut a worm in two.

'It can still move,' she was saying. 'Why?'

Janet had to admit that she wasn't sure.

'Why aren't you sure?'

'I don't know everything, Sally. I don't know very much.'

'Why?'

'Janet,' Tim called from the back door. 'Dolly's here.'

The day was spoiled. Janet took a last look at the bulbs and the sky before she went in.

Dolly was unrecognizable at a quick glance: her hair had turned plum-red and her face was hidden under a thick layer of orange make-up. The sight of her, at first, took Janet back in time but only for a moment: this was not the old Dolly, this one was dead behind the eyes. She wore a tight black skirt and long pink sweater. She sat with the skirt wrinkled up past the knee revealing an expanse of thigh above the tops of her stockings. She smoked continuously, flicking ash into the grate with short, jerky movements. She talked very fast and flirted with Tim, who glanced longingly at the sunlight on the pavement.

And then, without warning, she collapsed onto the sofa. She lay prone, her hair streaming over the sagging drop-end. She stared at the ceiling. The effect was hypnotic: they all stared at the ceiling. Khalil thought he could detect a map of India etched in the dust; Tim said it was a parsnip. Janet thought she ought to do some spring cleaning but knew it was unlikely she would get round to it.

When Dolly had had enough of the ceiling she got up and sat by the stove and for a little while came alive again as though someone had breathed life into her body. She talked at them, rather than to them, for the flood of words paralysed their brains and numbed their tongues. It was the same gabble of reminiscences every time.

'The details of someone else's love life are extremely boring,' Khalil said. 'I can't feel envy or excitement. There's a great pit of blackness inside me when she starts to speak.'

After Dolly had disposed of Paul, the manse and the church heating, she moved to the window where she crouched on the sill and gazed up at the street. Tim and Khalil started to play chess and Janet tried to read but her eyes kept edging back to the face at the window. It was the face she would remember Dolly by afterwards: side profile, the chin rather sharp, cheeks hollow and flushed, slits of

176

eyes under half-closed lids, forehead hidden under the tumble of ludicrous red hair. All the other faces of Dolly escaped Janet in later years; they floated vaguely in the outer edges of memory but refused to come into focus.

'When I look at her I feel like Lautrec,' Tim said.

'We could have done with a day at the sea today,' said Khalil, who rarely opted for anything in the open air. 'My nerves are going phut, phut, phut, like the engine of an old car.' He moved a pawn. 'I have been making a study of the nervous system and have convinced myself that it is ridiculous to ask too much of it.'

'I agree.' Tim lowered his voice and said: 'Janet is watching her, fascinated.'

Khalil nodded, decided to move the pawn back again. Tim had not noticed anyway. 'She's watching part of her past life crumbling up. It is always fascinating to do that. And that past includes Sally's father.'

Tim's head jerked up. 'You know who he was?'

'I am pretty certain that I do but I would never say. Why should I? I was not told. But I'm sure Dolly was. That is largely the bond between them.'

Dolly stayed with them all day and went away as night was closing in on the street.

CHAPTER NINETEEN

Fergus Robertson died in the early hours of Monday morning. No doubt, if he could have selected the time of his passing, he would have chosen to go on the Sabbath, but the matter did not rest with him alone. He died peacefully with his wife and doctor by his bedside.

'He was a fine man,' the doctor said on the doorstep before he hastened away to snatch an hour's sleep. Light was streaking the sky in the east. 'He will be sorely missed.'

Agnes Robertson nodded. When she had closed the door behind him, she stood in the hall listening to the quietness of the house. She wondered whether to wake Isobel but decided to let her sleep on. She pulled up the long green wet tongue of the air-freshener, sniffed its odour automatically, checked that *The Monarch of the Glen* was straight – it had not moved recently for some reason – and went into her blue and white kitchen. It was the room she liked best in the house; the bright floor, clean white walls, gleaming pots and pans, the stainless steel sink, the row of beaters and whisks and spatulas, the old-fashioned mahogany dresser, all gave her immense pleasure and satisfaction. This morning, more than ever, they comforted her. They had not changed overnight. She made herself a pot of tea.

Whilst she waited for it to infuse – she always gave it four minutes from the time of pouring on the boiling water – she wept quietly, more from a sense of duty than anything else, for Fergus's death was not quite real to her yet. Later it would strike her with full force but after a long night of sitting hunched by the bed she was too tired to be anything other than vaguely aware of it.

The tea refreshed her, brought back heat into her body. As the chill left her stomach, her back, her limbs, her brain thawed too. Fergus was dead: she was alone. She had leaned on him for thirty-five years, sheltered behind him; she had not taken one major decision in her married life. There were so many decisions to take now, so many things to do, to arrange. The enormity of the task bewildered her, so capable in her housewifely duties but so ignorant of anything beyond her garden walls. And then she thought of Fiona and Howard, and her anxieties subsided. They would take care of everything.

She went at once to the phone.

Gradually the news spread. Blinds were drawn in the street, voices hushed as the Robertsons' gate was passed by, the telephone rang incessantly in the study. In diverse parts of the country, in Dunkeld, Glasgow, Wick, the Isle of Skye, relatives ripped open yellow telegrams, looked out

178

their mourning, consulted train time-tables. In the Central Highlands Robert Robertson packed his bags, knowing his days at the school were numbered. He was glad enough of an excuse to leave: he disliked being organized, no matter how pleasantly.

Fiona and Howard, too, put on their mourning.

'You realize something will have to be done about mother, don't you?' Fiona said as they drove over to the stone villa. 'The house is too big for her to stay on in with Isobel going away.'

'And too expensive.'

'It's going to be a problem.'

'It is indeed. She wouldn't take in a lodger, I suppose? No, no, of course not. I wasn't being serious.' Howard paused and said heavily: 'There is our spare room.'

'That would never do. It's sweet of you to suggest it, Howard, but I know mother wouldn't want that. She's much too independent. No, I'll think of something.'

'I'm sure you will, dear.' Howard braked behind George Bell's car. 'I see George has beaten us to it.'

Fiona and her mother collapsed into one another's arms.

'Best leave them to it,' Howard said to George as he closed the drawing room door on their grief. 'We'll get down to business.'

They went into the study.

Isobel was left to wander round the house like a disconsolate wraith. Her grey eyes were enormous in her small white face, she noticed, as she passed the various mirrors. She did not want to look into the mirrors but she could not help it: it was a habit. She felt hopelessly inadequate: she was not suffering as she thought she should, she was unhappy but not desperately so, and she had no role to play. Her mother had even waited for Fiona to come to break down completely. Isobel could not think of one single thing to do that would not be inappropriate in a house of death. She supposed that soon Janet and other relations would appear, but the prospect was not consoling.

The study door opened and George put his head round it. He asked if she would take the death notice to *The Scotsman* offices. She agreed eagerly; then remembering, nodded more solemnly.

It was a great relief to leave the house behind, to have something to do at last. When she had delivered the notice, she decided to take a walk along Princes Street. There was no need for her to return to the house so soon; she would not be missed.

As she walked along from the East End towards the West End, she thought how fine the street looked in the morning sun. She would be sorry to leave but knew she would not hanker after it. She did not mind that Manchester would be bigger, dirtier, noisier; she liked busy cities for they meant people, things to do, places to go. Edinburgh was too staid for her, too restricting, and there were too many Robertsons around.

Suddenly she halted, drew in her breath. She moved closer to the shop window. In the middle of a display of underwear was an underskirt which took her breath away: it was frilled and flounced, of different shades of pink, very pale at the top gradually deepening to bright shocking pink at the foot. It was beautiful. It would be very daring to wear such colours with her chestnut hair. She noted the price, sighed, walked on.

A few steps, and she halted again. She pulled out her purse, quickly counted the money, holding her breath as she got down to the coppers. There was just enough!

She ran back to the shop.

'Lovely, isn't it?' the assistant said as she crushed the frills into a bag. 'Don't worry, madam, it won't crease. It'll drop out as good as new when you hang it up.'

Isobel emerged from the shop, slightly dazed, clutching the bag. In the middle of the underwear display was a blank space.

As she moved out into the main stream of pedestrians again, her pleasure turned sour in her mouth. She had forgotten her father was dead. It was terrible but it was true: she had forgotten. She was horrified to think that she had bought a frilly underskirt only a few hours after he had died. She was ashamed. Her cheeks burned. She wanted to throw the bag into the nearest litter bin. She saw one ahead; it looked like a giant flower pot. She hesitated, but passed it by. It would be an awful waste of money, and she had spent her last penny. She would have to take it home with her even though she knew she would never wear it.

She walked home: she had no option.

When she opened the front door she found the hall jammed with people. She put the bag behind her back.

'What have you got there?' Fiona demanded, pouncing on it at once. She had eyes like a jackal's. She looked at the name of the Princes Street store splashed across the bag. 'What have you been buying?'

'Give it to me,' Isobel cried, trying to snatch it back.

In the tussle the underskirt fell out of the bag and lay on the floor in all the glory of its pink flounces. A cry of horror rose from the assembled company, then silence descended.

'Do you mean to say that you went out and bought *that*,' Fiona said, pointing, 'and your father lying dead up there? Just as well mother's asleep.'

'Terrible, terrible,' Uncle John muttered. 'No sense of propriety.'

'I didn't mean to buy it,' Isobel wailed.

'Don't be daft!' Fiona said. 'Were you sleep-walking or something? Don't you care at all?'

'I do care, I do!'

'It doesn't seem like it,' Aunt Matilda said, drawing up her bosom another inch.

'Leave her alone,' Janet said as she came out of the drawing room. She bent down and picked up the underskirt. She shook it out. 'Why shouldn't she buy something pretty on the day her father dies?'

'I don't need you to stand up for me,' Isobel shouted. She

pushed through the relations and ran up the stairs to have her first real cry of the day.

'If it had even been black!' Aunt Matilda said.

The funeral was followed by the inevitable family lunch where they all glanced uneasily at one another over plates of cold meat and Aunt Matilda's sweet brown pickle and tried to smile when they encountered Agnes Robertson's lost, sad gaze. 'Hasn't Robert grown?' Uncle John said in an effort to open up a conversation and Robert looked sullen and stuffed an overlarge piece of boiled ham into his mouth. It was a short meal: no one but Robert was hungry. The relatives started to disperse to Dunkeld, Glasgow, Wick, the Isle of Skye. Agnes Robertson went to lie down.

When the washing-up had been done, Janet went for a walk over the Pentlands. For once there were no demands on her time: she had the day off from the bookshop and Sally was at the nursery.

It was a crisp March day; pale sun shone on the grass and heather. Only a few wispy clouds smeared the clear sky. As she walked the odour of the new wood of the coffin and the banks of flowers that had surrounded it in the drawing room left her nostrils; they were filled instead with the freshness of the air and the raw, unperfumed smell of the grass. It was a long time before she could go again into a florist's shop for the heavy cloying smell of massed flowers nauseated her more than rotting garbage or choked drains, and on Friday mornings she moved her eyes quickly past the greengrocer's.

A man was dead but life was continuing. She was tramping over these quiet hills, hands in pockets, body warm and slightly damp with the exertion of the climb up from the road; birds were hovering over the ground searching for food; a hare was louping from hillock to hillock, its ears bent back in the breeze. She stopped a moment to watch its crazy antics.

The man who had died was her father. She had known

him only as a father and not as a man. What kind of a man had he been? She would never know now. Underneath his hard exterior he must have suffered and loved, had moments of despair, doubts, longing, uncertainty. The sadness she felt was not because she would miss him – she could not deceive herself into thinking that for she knew she would not – but because she had never really known him or perhaps had never tried to. Their real contacts with one another had been brief and isolated and had not led to anything permanent. Once when she was a child he had come into her bedroom; he had thought her to be sleeping but she had been awake and felt him tuck the covers round her shoulders and kiss her gently on the forehead. The next morning she had waited eagerly for some further sign, thinking that his action the night before had marked some magic turning point, but he had snapped at her for not eating her porridge and she had decided sadly that she must have dreamed his visit. Another time when he was worried because her mother was ill he had put his hand over hers and smiled into her face. In time she knew that she would remember only the better aspects of her relationship with him and the bitter memories would be pushed further and further back until they were almost forgotten and could be thought of dispassionately.

The other part of her sadness was that she had not gone to see him before he died. Dolly had put it out of her head: that was her excuse. She plucked a blade of coarse grass and twisted it round her finger. It was always possible to find an excuse.

'You must go and live with mother,' Fiona said on the phone the following morning. 'It's the most obvious thing for you to do. Robert is getting a job on an estate up north somewhere and Isobel is going to this job in Manchester and you can't expect her to give that up. After all she's had a hard time lately and she's got her whole life ahead of her. Mother can't afford to keep that big house on alone. You

183

could live in a decent house instead of that damp basement.'

'I couldn't help finance mother's house. The rates are colossal.'

'How much does Mr Boland pay you?'

Janet told her and held the phone away from her ear whilst Fiona expostulated.

'You must be mad!' Fiona said.

'I get the flat too.'

'The flat! How much do you think that's worth? A pound a week at the most. He ought to pay you for living in it. Apart from anything else, it's unhealthy for Sally. You don't seem to bother about that. You'll have to get a decent job. There must be something else you could do. Take a secretarial training. Secretaries are well paid. You ought to be able to earn more than twice as much as you're doing now and then you'd be able to help mother and Sally wouldn't have to go to that ghastly nursery. It isn't fair on the child: she's shoved out all day and she's developing a dreadful accent. It would be much better for her to be at home with mother and think of the advantages to yourself: your meals ready when you come in, your washing done, a nice house to live in and a garden. It's only fair to mother for you to go and live with her, and yourself and Sally.'

Janet said that she would think about it, and rang off.

Return to the house where she had grown up to a life outgrown? Mother calling her in the morning, setting her breakfast in front of her, telling her to hurry. Going out to work in an office, returning to a meal hot from the oven, putting Sally to bed. Then sitting with mother on opposite sides of the fire, doing their knitting, watching television. 'Did you have a good day, dear?' And anecdotes of Sally's doings. 'Why don't you have your friends in, dear? Remember, it's your home too.' Dolly, Khalil, Tim: how could they visit her in mother's drawing room? And sitting in the cold bedroom to escape mother's fond glance for an hour, fingers numb, shins mottled and red from the electric fire, back icy. Mother opening the door: 'What are you doing in there, dear? Why don't you come down to the fire? I won't disturb you.' Useless to explain that one must have a little privacy, that one must sometimes sit alone. It was all impossible.

But what of Sally? A good home for her, a more settled existence. But did she want Sally brought up as she had been with her mother's values stamped on her? She knew that she did not.

Agnes Robertson came to The Crescent that evening to offer her daughter a home. She was confident that Janet would not refuse for why should one refuse something which would straighten out many difficulties and bring added material comforts? She had thought it all out so carefully that she had come to believe her plan was already accepted and all that was required to set it in motion was for Janet to tell Mr Boland she was moving and pack her bags. She was pleased that she was going to be able to do something for Janet and Sally and that she would have them to fill the empty space left by Fergus's death.

For a moment Janet's resolution wavered and then she said: 'I'm sorry, mother . . .'

Her mother stared at her, unable to believe she had heard correctly. Tears gathered in the red-rimmed eyes. She was completely bewildered.

'You surely don't intend to spend the rest of your life in this basement?'

'Of course not. I don't intend to spend the rest of my life in any one spot.'

A sigh escaped Agnes Robertson's lips and they fell silent, watching the restless violet flame hovering over the orange coals in the stove. Muffin yawned and stretched her back legs. She looked at the two bowed figures and then leapt noiselessly onto Agnes Robertson's soft lap. She began to purr.

'You always wanted to be different from anyone else,' Agnes Robertson said sadly as she absentmindedly fondled the cat's ear. She didn't care for cats for they left their hairs behind them, but this evening she felt too weak even to push away a cat. 'Fiona says you scorn a nice comfortable house just because it's in the suburbs and the same as the one next door, and that you prefer this place because it's uncomfortable and shabby and you think it's more Bohemian or something like that.'

Janet waited until she could speak patiently. 'Fiona talks a lot of nonsense. It's not a case of wanting to be different. I just want to be me, that's all, and not what other people would like to make me into. There are hundreds of people living in places like this and my flat is just the same as the one next door, I'm not living here because I think it's Bohemian but because I get it for nothing and it happens to suit me for the time being.'

'I'll have to give up the house. Where can I go?'

Janet suggested she buy a small flat: it would be warmer and easier to keep clean than the house. It was easy for Janet to talk of new beginnings, her mother said, for she was thirty years younger.

'But you'll have to begin again, mother,' Janet said desperately. 'Other women have had to face it.'

Her mother thought her hard and selfish, and the tears welled up again. Janet felt as soft as butter pounded by a wooden mallet. She wondered if her mother was going to spend the whole evening weeping over Muffin's body. Muffin was unperturbed and drifted into sleep. Janet watched helplessly, unable to say the words which would stem the tears. She was glad when Dolly arrived.

Dolly looked terrible. The black skirt needed pressing and the pink jumper was turning grey. Her eyes were haggard and pouched, and her nails had been bitten to the quick. Out of her tartan bag she produced, not a fat white sausage containing knitting, but a quarter bottle of whisky. She offered it around and, on having it refused, poured the contents into a cup and drank. Agnes Robertson soon left.

At the door she begged Janet to reconsider, to remember

Sally, to think of the house where she had been brought up. 'It would mean such a lot to me, Janet, to have you live with me.'

Janet kissed her mother and said that she would think it over but knew that she would not change her mind now. After that her mother always looked at her with reproach: Janet had let her down at the worst moment of her life. In a way it was true, Janet conceded.

She returned to Dolly.

'Family crisis?' Dolly asked, lighting a cigarette from the stub of the last one.

Janet told her about her father. 'What about you, Dolly, have you any family?'

Dolly shook her head. 'My parents were killed in a car crash when I was small. I was brought up by a grand-mother. She's dead too now.' She tossed her hair back from her neck and, with the gesture, tossed aside all thoughts of death. She was in love again. She spoke breathlessly, her eyes shining. He was in the American Air Force, he had a Cadillac, he had a wonderful flat with central heating and the most wonderful bathroom she had ever seen. All the rooms were so warm that you could walk naked from one to the other. He was calling for her here at nine. Janet listened with forced concentration. Dolly was trying hard to recapture her former gaiety but failing miserably.

The Cadillac called on time; it stopped outside and blasted its horn. Janet pulled the curtains back and looked at its wheels in the gutter. 'Bring him in for a few minutes,' she said but Dolly hurriedly began to powder the end of her nose and fluff excuses into the clouds of powder. They were in a hurry, they were due at a party . . . Janet smiled wryly and surveyed the room, knowing it would not be up to the standard of the flat where you could walk about naked. Dolly thought the basement just a little far down-hill.

'See you soon,' Dolly said.

She tripped up the steps with her tartan bag over her
187

arm, the door of the car opened and closed, and the wheels rolled off out of sight.

CHAPTER TWENTY

It was a day of blustering wind, sudden downpours of rain and intermittent blinks of weak sunshine, more like March than May. In the middle of the morning the sun finally retired, dispirited, leaving the gale to sweep the streets. Doors and windows rattled and shook under the onslaught. Janet was alone in the shop. She felt restless and confined by the walls of books and the grey weather outside. There was nothing to be done, no books to wrap or sort, no customers to talk to. She found it difficult to immerse herself in a book; she read a few pages and then her thoughts turned to Khalil, who had been very quiet and withdrawn of late, or to Isobel or Fiona or her mother. The villa had been sold, complete with fitted carpets, and strangers had moved in obliterating the traces of the Robertsons who had lived there for thirty-five years. Isobel had gone to Manchester, and Agnes Robertson had moved temporarily into Fiona's spare room. She was getting ready for a trip to Canada to visit Ian; she was buying clothes and making lists, trying to rouse enthusiasm in herself for the project.

Janet sighed and went to fill the kettle. She was making tea when Khalil came into the shop with his arms full of books.

'I've brought back all the books I've borrowed,' he said, dropping them onto the counter. He shook a scattering of raindrops from his hair. 'You see, I always return what I borrow. Eventually.'

They sat in the back shop and drank the tea. Rain lashed the window. Khalil said that Janet looked tired, that her eyes were heavy. 'You ought to take life more lightly. Don't worry so much!'

She thought that he did not look well himself but did not

say so. He was subdued and preoccupied. He got up and moved about the small cluttered room, touching books, turning over pages.

'We're both restless today,' Janet said.

'It would seem so.' He sat down on a pile of books. 'This job is beginning to bore you. It's a dead end – there's nothing in it for you. It was all right at the start but now –' He got up and resumed his patrol. 'But I am not the one to talk of these things.'

Tim had said the same the night before: 'Do you want to be a shop assistant all your life?'

'What are you going to do, Janet?' Khalil asked.

'I could take a degree, I suppose, externally from London or I might be able to get a grant to go back to the university here. I've been thinking about it for some time.'

'And then?'

'Teach maybe. I would like to teach.'

He looked at the clock on the mantelpiece. 'The pubs will be opening up. It's a tantalizing thought. Come out for a drink.'

'The shop –'

'Shut it! Please. Just for half an hour. There are no customers anyway. No one is going to collapse of literary starvation for the sake of thirty minutes.'

She locked the shop and they went to the pub further along the street, next to Mrs Dodd's Drapery.

'Let's be gay,' Khalil said as he set the glasses on the table. 'It's necessary.'

'All right,' she said. 'Why not?'

He lifted his glass. 'To you, Janet.'

'And to you, Khalil.'

'To us both!'

They drank, and she smiled at him, troubled.

'I think I must have been drinking something very strange last night – I was in a curious bar down by the docks with some friends – for today I am feeling sentimental. I would never have thought it possible! As I came along

189

The Crescent I met the MacNab and I felt tender even towards her. I smiled at her. Yes, I have been known to smile so there is no need to look incredulous. I smiled and said: "A wild day, Mrs MacNab." I know that the politest Western greeting is a comment on the weather, and I wished to be polite to Mrs MacNab.'

'And Mrs MacNab? Did she say: "Aye, but it'll be worse before the day's out"?'

'No, she scowled and sniffed, one nostril closing in true MacNabian manner. Then she turned her head away at an angle of forty-five degrees so that she could still see me without giving the appearance of doing so. And I felt very happy. If she had smiled at me it would have turned my whole conception of the world upside down, and that I could not cope with today. Muffin was sitting by the railings viewing the universe with a detached air; she pretended not to know me so I respected her mood and did not know her either.'

Janet finished her drink and brought out money to pay for another round. Khalil scooped it from the table and paused before going to the bar counter. 'There is one little thing I have to ask you, Janet, and it's better that I ask before we become too gay.' He ran his tongue over his lips. 'Could you lend me five pounds? I know it's difficult for you and I would not ask you if I were not desperate.'

'Five pounds,' she echoed. She *had* five pounds for Mr Boland had paid her that morning. Khalil was waiting anxiously, jingling the coins in his left hand. She took the money from her purse and gave it to him.

'Thank you. Thank you very much.' He pushed the notes into the top pocket of his blue tweed jacket. 'I may not be able to pay you back for some time.'

'It doesn't matter. Consider it a present.'

'No, no. I will repay it some day.'

Some day, she thought. What did that mean?

Gaiety eluded them. Khalil tried hard to generate it; he

described an incident that had happened in the curious pub at the docks but his voice was flat and empty, and his laughter forced. Several times he closed his eyes, pressing his fingers against the lids.

'What's wrong, Khalil?'

'Nothing's wrong. Why should there be?'

'You seem strange today.'

'It's my liver. Haven't I ever told you about my liver?'

'You haven't ever told me much about yourself. I don't really know *you*, Khalil, do I?'

'Some of me. That's all we ever know of anyone. We manage to keep our real selves well concealed. There's a lot about you that I don't know, that you've never told me. I couldn't sleep last night – my liver again! – so I lay and thought about you.'

'And what did you think?'

'That you need someone, that you and Sally need to belong to some larger unit: you're too small and too vulnerable on your own. I think you should stay with Tim. Not many things have happened to him, he hasn't been hurt much, he had a happy childhood; but he knows about people and living. Some people can go through one thing after another and at the end of it they still don't know very much. Hurtful experiences do not necessarily make a man aware even though they should. Sometimes we begin to worship experience as an end in itself and not look to see what lies beyond it.' He laughed, flicking out his tongue. 'Hark at Khalil, the wise old sage! Pronouncing on life, giving advice. I will be a preacher yet. Vanity of vanities! And I have more need of advice than any other man I know.'

'Your talk's making me feel apprehensive, and cold inside. I've never known you so sad.' She looked at her watch and said: 'I'll have to go – it's almost one.'

He walked back to the bookshop with her and they stood in the porch out of the wind. He took her hand and held it between his two thin ones.

'There's Mr Boland,' Janet said, thrusting the key into the lock. 'He'll have a fit – the shop locked and me stinking of gin!'

'Goodbye, Janet,' Khalil said. 'Take care of yourself, and the little one.'

When she looked round he had gone. It was the last time she saw him.

In the evening, Tim said: 'Saw Khalil after school today. He was waiting for me at the gate when I came out. He wanted to go up Arthur's Seat. He'd never been to the top. We went up and at one point I thought he'd never make it: he was panting like a steam roller and sweat was rolling off his face. When we got down we went and had a beer together.'

'Did he borrow any money?'

'Five pounds. I had to draw it from the Post Office.'

As the days passed and there was no sign of Khalil, Janet became more and more worried. Tim said that she was being foolish as Khalil was liable to reappear at any time; nevertheless, he went out one evening and toured all the places where he might be found. He combed the pubs round the university, down the High Street, Leith Walk, along Rose Street and he called at two houses where Khalil had taken him to parties. He did not find him. And everywhere it was the same: 'Haven't seen Khalil for days.'

The next morning Janet received a postcard of Blackpool beach. On the back was written:

'The east wind of Edinburgh, even in the month of May, became too keen for the trickle of blood that courses through this bag I call my body. I have, therefore, come south and west to this great port of pleasure where I have gained remunerative employment: I am to work the big dipper. At last I am to be a man of importance! Every day I shall hold the lives of thousands of people in these hands! Some day when the sun is shining on the grey walls of your city I shall return. Khalil.'

Janet read it twice, then put it behind the clock on the mantelpiece.

As she came back along The Crescent that evening with Sally she saw a large black car standing outside 31B. Two men were sitting in the front seat smoking. She tightened her grip of Sally's hand. Even at that distance she knew it to be a police car.

When they reached the gate, the men got out. They were in plain clothes. One showed identification papers and asked if they might have a word with Janet. She took Sally down to Mrs Green who said that she would give her tea. Janet's throat was dry as she came back up the steps. The men were looking away from her, hands in pockets, as if she were no concern of theirs. The leaves of Mrs MacNab's potted plant moved.

They descended to the basement in silence. Janet apologized that the room was rather cold but she had let the fire go out as she was trying to save coal . . . Her voice trailed away. It seemed to belong to someone else, not to her sitting there on the edge of a chair taking a cigarette from a proffered packet, trying to hold it steady in the flame of a match and not succeeding. Don't be a fool, she told herself sharply. You've done nothing. Why should the word 'police' set your nerves jangling, your hands trembling, your head buzzing. Relax! Sit back! They can't do anything to you.

The men placed themselves strategically: one sat opposite her to ask the questions, the other faced obliquely so that he could watch her being questioned. She knew that this was deliberate but could not keep her eyes from swivelling from one to the other.

'We're making enquiries about a Mr Khalil Siddigi.'

She had known it would be this. Say something. 'Oh yes?' Smile. Lean forward a little. Look interested but detached. Look as though you're not concerned about any enquiries the police might have to make, but that you're always ready to help.

193

'He is a friend of yours?'

Careful now. Think before you speak. You've got Sally to consider. 'Well, I knew him quite well about six years ago when we were both students at the university. We often sat together in cafés and so forth. There was usually a crowd of us – you know how it is with students: you sit around with a lot of people you don't really know –' Stop! You're saying too much, talking too fast. The man was looking at her expectantly: he wanted more. 'I've been away from Edinburgh for some years. I returned last September.'

'Have you seen Mr Siddigi since you returned?'

'A few times, I suppose. Couldn't say exactly how often.' Smile again. Cross your legs. Take a long draw on your cigarette. You're doing all right.

'I see.' The man was leafing through some papers that she had not noticed before. He pulled one out. 'The address we have on our files for Mr Siddigi is: c/o Crosbie, 31B The Crescent.'

Count up to ten. One, two, three –

'Mrs MacNab, your upstairs neighbour, tells me that an Indian answering to the description of Mr Siddigi lived here, if not continuously, at regular intervals.'

Did Mrs MacNab use those words? At regular intervals? No doubt Mrs MacNab had had plenty to tell the men: that would account for all the sheaves of paper. What was the answer to that one? Think. Think hard. No thoughts to think.

'Is Mrs MacNab's information correct?'

'Well, in a way.' She moistened her lips and went on in a rush: 'When my mother was leaving her house I went to stay with her for a few days to give her a hand packing up, so I let him stay here: he kept the place aired and at that time he had nowhere to live and then there was the cat –' She looked round, hoping that Muffin would appear to confirm her statement. There was no sign of Muffin.

'I see. When did you last see Mr Siddigi?'

'Oh, let me think now.' Frown. Scratch your head. 'A

194

week ago perhaps. He came into the bookshop where I work. Mr Boland's Bookshop. Just round the corner.'

'We have reason to believe that he has left Edinburgh. Have you any idea where he might have gone?'

Don't look at the mantelpiece. Don't! No matter how much your eyes might want to go there. Don't let them do it. Keep them on the man with the papers on his knees. Is the postcard sticking out from behind the clock? Don't look to see. Are the people dotting the sand visible, the words 'Esplanade, Blackpool'? Blackpool. Why did Khalil go to Blackpool? Was he really there? The card had been posted there yesterday: the postmark said so. Blackpool . . . Liverpool . . . ships. Khalil in a ship. Yes, that was where Khalil must be. Perhaps at this moment leaning against the rail watching the sun setting on the horizon. No, he would be looking eastwards towards the land and the stretch of water gradually widening between him and the shore.

'Mrs Crosbie, have you any idea where we might contact Mr Siddigi?'

'I'm afraid not. He never did say where he was going or what he was doing.'

'I see.' The papers rustled. 'Could you give me the names of any of his friends or acquaintances?'

'I'm afraid not. He never mentioned anyone by name.'

'I see.' He coughed. 'Did you know anything about his activities?'

'I'm afraid not.'

The man pursed his lips and frowned. Could he hear her heart beating?

'In that case, Mrs Crosbie . . .' He got to his feet heavily.

Janet was surprised that her legs supported her when she stood up. She escorted the men to the door.

'Thank you for your help, Mrs Crosbie.'

'Not at all.'

'If you have any information that might be of use you can get in touch with us in the High Street. Good evening.'

'Good evening.'

She closed the door and leaned back on it. The palms of her hands were wet and clammy. She rubbed them dry on the sides of her skirt.

'Why don't you say something?' she demanded. 'You've been sitting there as calmly as though I've been telling you about a Sunday School outing.'

'Why don't you cool off?' Tim said. 'And sit down instead of pacing up and down like a panther.' He caught her hand and pulled her down onto the settee beside him. 'There's no need to be quite so worked up about it. Khalil can look after himself. But it annoys me to think that he used your address and got you mixed up in whatever it is he's involved in.'

'That doesn't matter. At first I was furious and even a bit frightened, but after the police went that didn't bother me. Trust Khalil: he borrows your money, uses your address and then walks out and leaves you to face the music. I could see the expression on his face if he were to walk in now: innocence betrayed! "What, me? I would not do such things." ' Janet laughed.

'I'm glad you can still laugh. The question is: what are these things he was doing?'

'Or supposed to be doing. Whatever it was, it wasn't lucrative – money didn't exactly bulge in his pockets.'

'Why didn't you ask the policemen what it was all about?'

'Would they have told me?'

'They might.'

'I didn't want to know.'

'You must be curious about it,' Tim insisted.

'There are certain things that I would rather not know of a person. I only want to know the things of Khalil that I knew personally; I don't want to learn things that are hearsay and unproved. How would I know what was true? And I don't want to have to pass judgment on him.'

'So Khalil keeps his secrets,' Tim mused, and Janet smiled.

196

She had no more visits from the police. Several times she thought a man was watching the basement from the opposite side of the street; he leant against a lamp-post reading a newspaper. She pottered about in the area with a sweeping brush, watching him. He was hatless and coatless, and he kept his face hidden behind the paper. Men did not usually stand about in The Crescent reading but he might have been waiting for the girl in the red shoes or someone else who lived in one of the tenement flats. He was too obvious to be a watcher, Tim said; if he were one he would not stand so openly announcing his intentions for all The Crescent to see. Twice she had the sensation of being followed, once quite strongly when coming up Middle Meadow Walk after dark. Footsteps on the path echoed behind hers, keeping step. She quickened her pace and the echo quickened too. At the top, in the safety of the busy lighted street, she stopped to look back: the path was empty. But as she turned, a shadow moved beneath a tree.

Gradually she forgot to think about it, and the man with the newspaper was not seen again.

CHAPTER TWENTY-ONE

Tim was in a restless mood. He had something on his mind: he wanted to ask Janet to marry him but was uncertain how to lead up to it. The temper of the evening was wrong, somehow, for a proposal of marriage, but he had decided to ask her before he came out and knew that he would not sleep that night unless he did. He paced the floor whilst she watched him, sitting curled up in a corner of the settee. He wished she would ask him what was wrong but knew she would not. They had exchanged a few sharp words earlier on—he had said he was tired of Dolly mooching around the place and she had said that she had no intention of turning away an old friend just because he was annoyed —and since then there had been an unspoken irritation

197

between them. She sat there like the sphinx, imperturbable. He wanted to shake her out of her composure. He said:

'I don't know how you can be bothered to have George Bell hanging around you, breathing down your neck.'

'George? What made you think of him? Anyway, he doesn't breathe down my neck and I happen to like him.'

Much better stop, he told himself, he was being childish and she would only despise him for it. But he carried on: 'Your family are pretty keen on him. They want you to marry him, don't they?'

'Yes.'

'Well?'

'Well what? I rarely do what my family want.'

Nor anyone else for that matter, he thought.

She picked up a book.

'George would make you a good husband,' he said. 'He's reliable and he's got quite a lot of money. He could afford to send his children to good schools.'

She yawned.

'George would make *you* a good husband.'

At that she laid the book aside. She asked if he had turned himself into a marriage bureau because, if so, he had better desist for she was not interested. He was pleased to see he had ruffled her a little.

'Why not marry George? He'd solve a lot of your problems.'

'I don't ever intend to remarry –' She broke off.

'Remarry?' he said slowly.

She recovered her composure at once. 'Yes. I've been married before.'

He had stopped beside the alcove. He flopped down onto the bed like a rag doll. A mirror was propped up on the ledge over the bed. He looked and saw the reflection of a young man with untidy hair and a slack, oafish expression on his face. That is me, he said to himself. He tightened his mouth.

'I don't understand,' he said. 'Perhaps I'm being stupid but I don't understand. We're talking about you, aren't we?'

'It's a long story, as they say.'

'I'm sure it must be.'

'And yet – it's very short.'

Her head was turned away from him: he could not see her face. He waited.

'Sally's father was called Derek Crosbie,' she began. 'I was in love with him. When I knew I was expecting his child I told him and he at once offered to marry me, but I realized that he didn't really want to. I loved him too much to force him into marriage with me: I didn't want him to be resentful because I'd taken away his freedom and I didn't want him to come to hate me. This is what I thought, at least. I didn't know, but I felt that this was how it would be. And of course there was my pride! I didn't want a man against his will. So I decided to go away. I went to London and he followed me. By the time he found me I was not so sure of myself, I was alone and felt lonely, and I still loved him. So I said yes.'

'You mean you were married to Sally's father?'

'What is so strange about that?'

'Nothing,' Tim muttered. 'I can't quite take it in yet. So Sally is not illegitimate?'

'No. And my poor family are all sweating away because they think she is! What difference does it make? Her circumstances are the same: she lives with her mother and has no father.'

Janet lit a cigarette and he saw that her hand trembled. He wished again that he could see her face but to get up and move his seat would create a disturbance in the room.

'What happened with you and Derek Crosbie?'

'We had a month together and in that month we had the beginnings of something good. I saw that he would come to love me: he was very young and had been loath to tie himself down in marriage so soon. We could have been happy.' She took a long draw on her cigarette. 'And then, one morning, he went out to post a letter and was knocked down by a motorbike. He died in the ambulance on the way to hospital.'

His mouth was dry. He wanted to say he was sorry but knew that the words would sound futile and less than he meant.

'So you see' – her voice had hardened – 'it's really quite a short story, after all.'

'But why didn't you tell your family?'

'I wouldn't give them the satisfaction of knowing I'd done the "decent" thing. They wouldn't give tuppence for the life or death of Derek Crosbie. All they'd care about is that I was made into a "respectable" woman and Sally was born on the right side of the blankets. They would so much prefer me to be a widow – such an eminently respectable status that is! – than an unmarried mother. Why should I pander to their self-righteousness?'

He understood how she felt. He said so. She was miles away from the room and from him: he saw it in the set of her head and shoulders. She scarcely registered what he said. He lay right back on the bed: Khalil's map of India was still etched in the dust of the ceiling. Why had she not told him before of her marriage? He realized for the first time how alike she and Khalil were: they made unassailable fortresses of themselves; they said you could come thus far and no further and if you didn't comply with their rules you could go away. She had loved a man called Crosbie, she had married him and borne his child but she had not even mentioned him when they had talked of their earlier lives. She had told him only of the trivialities and the things that didn't mattter and had kept back all that did. She withheld a part of herself from him all the time. A grain of resentment crept in, edged out some of his sympathy.

'Does anyone else know all this?' he asked.

'George knows.'

'George!' He shot off the bed, went over to the settee. 'You told George,' he shouted.

'It came out somehow. He wondered why I used the name Crosbie. His lawyer's mind started to work.'

'You told George but you didn't tell me!'

'I didn't have to tell you,' she said, on the defensive now in the face of his anger.

'I had a right to know.'

'What right?'

'I love you. Isn't that sufficient reason? Surely that gives me the right to know the important things in your life?'

'This is what I was afraid of: rights, demands, possession!'

'All right,' he said, 'you've been hurt once. Badly! But you can't go on nursing your hurt for ever. Now go ahead and tell me I'm a callous bastard.'

'I'm not nursing my hurt. And don't you stand there telling me how to cope with the tragedies of life! I doubt if you've ever been really hurt. You have an affair with Isobel and shake yourself free of it like a dog coming out of the sea and shaking the water off its coat. Half an hour afterwards all was forgotten.'

'Forgotten! You'll never let me forget. You want everything on your terms. You'll give me your body and your love up to a certain limit. It's a fixed point and you've got a board up: No Trespassing. On the back there's a set of rules and at the bottom it says: Trespassers Will Be Persecuted!'

'Don't shout. You'll waken Sally.'

'If I could waken you it would be more to the point.'

At that moment she hated him and felt quite dispassionate about it. 'I'm more wide awake at this moment than I've been for the past few months,' she said. 'So I've got a board up. All right: you can read. You've read it. If you don't want to accept my terms you can go.'

'If I go I won't come back.'

'That sounds like a threat, and I don't like being threatened. I'm not sure that I would want you to come back.'

Tim moved to the door. He opened it and said: 'You seem to think you can do without anyone.'

'I have Sally.'

'Poor Sally,' he said quietly. 'You're going to make an awful lot of demands on her. And in fifteen years' time she won't need you any longer. You'll still have a lot of years left to live.'

He went out into the hall and closed the door behind him. The front door squeaked as he tugged it open. The hinges needed oiling; she must do it. His broad back blocked the window as he passed in front of it, darkening the room. He put his hand on the rail and, looking straight ahead of him, climbed the steps. His head moved out of sight, then his arms and the hand that gripped the rail; gradually his legs began to disappear. His feet went slowly past the green railings. And he was gone.

He has gone, she said to herself. It doesn't matter. Let him go. It was bound to happen some day. The breaking-up of friendship or love is much quicker and surer than its formation. In a few minutes, with a few words, everything could be destroyed. Had been destroyed.

She was shivering. She opened the doors of the stove and knelt down in front of its warmth.

During the long summer evenings she came to know the people of The Crescent better. She sat by the window until it was quite dark and the feet that passed were only dim shapes hurrying and quickly gone. Then she would pull the curtains and flood the silent room with light and wonder what there was she could do in the small, overcrowded space. For now that there were no people in it, it seemed cramped.

But whilst there was daylight she had a preoccupation: feet. She became an expert on feet and shoes and ways of walking. Toes turned outward, toes turned in, fallen arches, sagging ankles, wobbling heels. Then there were the children and their games. Roller skates, their little wheels revolving frantically with monotonous clatter, up and down, up and down, never tiring. Tops, crimson, violet, turquoise, lemon, whirrs of colour spurred on by little snaking whips. After the tops came hopscotch: one leg dangling, the other hopping, legs scissoring and closing over the grey pavement. Marbles glistening and rolling, spun from grubby fingers. Footballs, laceless, with burst bladders, thumping the pavement, striking the railings, dropping down into the area pursued by a string of small boys. Skipping ropes swinging under bounding feet. One, two, three a-leerie . . . There was much to see and hear.

Not enough.

Mrs Green was always pleased to come in and sit by Janet's window. 'It makes a nice change. You go on out, dear. You're looking peaked. A drop of air'll do you good.'

If Janet could have conquered her pride she would have looked openly for Tim and gone down to the mews but since that was too much for her she wandered round the streets hoping to meet him – accidentally. She saw him a dozen times walking along Princes Street with his long even stride or coming round the sweep of the Mound towards her or standing, hands in pockets, looking into the window of a junk shop in the High Street. Her face would grow warm, her heart begin to thud and lurch, a pain would creep behind her ribs, her feet would go faster and faster and then – she would see that the man was too young or too old, that his hair was black or he had no hair at all, that he was too short or he wore the wrong cut of jacket. As the evenings passed and he did not come to her, her pride hardened and set and soon it was unthinkable that she should seek him out.

Each night she thought that she would surely sleep. She *had* to sleep. She went to bed exhausted; her head ached, her body refused to sink into the sheets, her eyes felt as if there was sand behind the lids. She lay on her right side, on her left side, on her back, on her stomach. She tried to relax systematically starting from the feet up but as soon as she reached the knees she realized that she was not concentrating, not thinking about each part of the body as she tried to make it flop. She had never believed in counting sheep: it worried more than it soothed. She recited poetry but this she could do with one part of her mind leaving the other free to wander. She tried to think of nothing at all. To empty her mind. Her brain reeled at the idea.

After a while the sheets were unstuck, the pillow hot and lumpy as though filled with pebbles, the blankets scratched and clawed at her skin. Then she would get up and smoke a cigarette, perhaps drink a glass of milk, eat half a biscuit, wash her face, brush her hair, read. If everything else failed she went out.

It was strange to emerge into The Crescent in the middle of the night: the street seemed unreal and the hush on the air unnatural. No matter what the hour a light shone from at least one window. Someone else was awake. A few sounds when she listened: a baby crying, distant hum of a car, the bang of a door.

In the main street the shops looked dead and unrelated to the places where the women bustled in the daytime. The bookshop was a tomb for old words. A few things moving: a policeman flashing a torch in a dark doorway, a taxi rattling homeward, a cat padding . . . always a cat. A curtain flapping at an open window. And herself walking. But she could not see herself.

Back to the tousled bed to doze off into a heavy sleep just as the alarm clock began to shrill on the shelf above her head. Head thick, mouth dry, eyes shot with red and sore: that was how she started each day. To begin a day and continue in such a condition seemed impossible but she was amazed how her body rallied. By the time she and Mr Boland sat down in the back shop to drink their morning cup of tea she could feel life coming back and hope returning.

Hope was always there, but Tim did not come.

She missed him but in a way she missed Khalil more. Her relationship with Khalil had been without emotion; it had

204

been stable and secure and could not be replaced by George or Tim or anyone else that she knew. Khalil had been her safety valve; he would listen and not judge, he would accept her in whatever mood she had upon her, they could disagree but not quarrel and part on angry words. She missed him in the corner of the bookshop and by the stove in the late evening. She missed him too because she could not talk of him to Tim.

She knew that she was slipping into a pit of apathy and that if she went much deeper, it would take something drastic to lift her out of it. Knowing this, she continued to sit by the window.

One evening as she sat, a large yellow marble rolled along the pavement and stopped an inch from the railings. It flashed in the sunshine like a piece of gold. A small boy appeared; he squatted on his haunches and lifted the marble carefully. Looking down, he saw Janet watching him. For a moment they gazed into one another's eyes and in those few seconds she saw what the boy saw: a pale-faced woman behind the window of a basement with no marbles to play with.

She drew the curtains and turned into the room. She found paper and a pen and wrote to London University asking for a prospectus for external degrees. She was going to make something of her life: she was not going to sit in a basement like a rotting cabbage and go each day to dust books and wash windows. She was going to control her own destiny, she was tired of being blown hither and thither by the wind like the chip papers of The Crescent.

Purpose and direction came back into her days; she had ceased to be disorientated. She worked every evening and enjoyed the discipline of study. Her brain reawakened and became sharp after the years it had been allowed to grow soft. And she could do without anyone but Sally: the knowledge was a relief.

When Tim had gone, she had phoned George and told him not to come for a while. Now she phoned and said that

she would like to see him again. He resumed his weekly visits
and on Sundays took them out in the car. They played on
the sands with Sally and ate ice-cream cones along the front
at North Berwick and Gullane with a few thousand other
people fleeing the town on fine Sundays. Coming out of the
car with their rugs, picnic baskets, buckets and spades, they
looked like a family. Janet was conscious that the same
thought was in George's mind. Agnes Robertson came to
the basement and told her daughter that a woman needed
a husband, and a child a father.

In the middle of June her three daughters accompanied
her to Prestwick Airport to wave her off to Canada. Isobel
had come up from Manchester for the occasion. She looked
older and more composed than before; she spoke quietly,
saying that she liked her job quite well and she had made
several friends. Fiona bounced along between her and
Janet, addressing them in turn, doing her bit to 'keep the
peace', as she told Howard afterwards.

The farewells were mumbling and unsatisfactory, and
infuriated Janet who wished that the expedition could be
looked upon as an adventure and a new experience, and
not as a further excuse for the shedding of joint tears.
When the tears had been spilled and promises to write
exchanged, Agnes Robertson went through the barrier in
the wake of the other passengers towards the aircraft. She
climbed up the steps and paused to wave at the top before
she was swallowed up by the gleaming silver machine. It
was the final disintegration of their branch of the family.
No more Christmas dinners with Aunt Mildred pounding
on the piano, Uncle John belching, mother smiling fondly
on them all . . .

The three sisters stood a little apart from each other and
watched the plane take off. How was it, Janet wondered,
that so many people could drop through the trap door of
her life in such a short time? Isobel, father, Khalil, Tim;
even Dolly seemed to have disappeared. And now her
mother was soaring through the sky to another continent.

It was doubtful if she would return. She had three daughters but not one willing to offer her a home. Janet thought of Tim's words: 'In another fifteen years Sally won't need you.' It was up to her to see that she wouldn't. The speck of silver had gone from their sight. Fiona was chattering on about it being the best thing for mother to have a complete change, and it would be so nice for her to see Ian's children.

'I wonder if she'll ever come back?' Isobel said. 'What is there for her to come back for?'

'What a funny thing to say,' Fiona said. 'She's got lots to come back for. She knows she can live with Howard and me whenever she wants to.'

They returned to the park where Fiona had left the car. As Isobel was getting into the front seat her skirt lifted to reveal a bright shocking pink frill. Janet grinned and caught her eye. Isobel looked down, then up at Janet again. Her face broke into a smile.

For a short time Janet's days rolled forward as easily as the little wheels of the roller skates passing her window, and a lot more quietly. Hearing their approach, she would look up briefly and smile. A more ordered life suited her, she decided. A certain part of her rejoiced in this living almost to a time-table, knowing that she could plan an evening and not have it disrupted by the squeak of the gate and a thump on the door. Another part of her recoiled at the idea of returning along The Crescent every evening after work with the sure knowledge of what the hours ahead held, but this part she could hold in check. Self-discipline, she thought, and felt a glow of self-righteousness.

And then, one evening, Dolly reappeared. Her face was gaunt and grey, and the red hair had taken on a purplish hue. She staggered as she came into the room. She sat on the window-sill, clutching her tartan bag, and stared at Fiona who had called to deliver a frock she had made for Sally. Fiona rose immediately.

'I must go, Janet.'

'Hello, Fiona.' Dolly let out a cackle of laughter.

Fiona nodded to indicate that she had heard and preceded Janet into the hall.

'You shouldn't let that creature come in here,' she said. 'She's disgusting.'

When Janet went back into the room she found that Dolly had emptied the contents of the tartan bag onto the floor and had turned the bag inside out. She was shaking her head and mumbling:

'Can't find it. I've lost it. I've lost it.'

Janet knelt down and repacked the bag. 'Where have you been, Dolly?' she asked.

'Been?' Dolly looked blank. 'I've lost it. I must go and find it.'

'Stay a few minutes.'

Dolly licked her lips and looked round. 'Have you a drink?'

'I'm sorry . . .'

'I must go. I've lost it. I'll come back when I find it.'

She came back on Sunday morning.

Janet and Sally had been for a walk in the park and when they turned into The Crescent on their way home they saw Dolly standing beside the open gate of 31B. Janet waved and called a greeting. As they came up to her, the church bells began to chime, slowly, softly, the notes lingering on in the air. Something seemed to burst in Dolly's head: Janet saw it in her eyes.

'Come down to the basement, Dolly,' she said, taking her arm.

'Don't touch me,' Dolly screamed. 'Don't touch me!'

She pushed Janet away with the flat of her hand. Janet landed on her back in the area. When she looked up she saw a blur of faces: Sally's white and terrified, Dolly's grey and distorted, and higher up, beyond them, was Mrs MacNab's moon-shaped one with spikes forming a ruff across her throat making her look like a corpulent Mary Queen of Scots. Beyond that face again was the sky, the same sky that she had seen earlier from the park with Sally but looking now curiously dark and strange. As she slipped into unconsciousness she heard two distinct sounds, quite separate, yet merging together to form a duet: Dolly laughing and Sally screaming.

CHAPTER TWENTY-TWO

Janet lay in her hospital bed with her head swathed in bandages and her left arm in a sling. She lay and fretted, depressed about the insecurity òf her life. An accident proved how insecure it was, and how non-independent she was. Fiona had given up a temporary teaching post to look after Sally.

'Now don't you worry about that,' Fiona said as she smoothed the sheet on Janet's bed. 'We've got to help each other out, haven't we? That's what families are for. And as for the financial side of it – well, I only went back to teaching to get some money for a holiday abroad, but when it comes to the bit, I'd much rather know that Sally was being properly cared for than go to Majorca. So you're not to think about that aspect of it at all, and when you come out you must come to us to convalesce. You've got to take care of yourself in future. This just proves you can't go on leading the kind of life you've been leading, associating with all sorts of odd people like that horrible girl.' She shuddered. 'She's locked up now anyway, where she can't do any more damage. I'm sorry for her and all that but nevertheless . . .'

After a visit from Howard and Fiona, Janet's temperature soared.

George came with sheaves of gladioli and boxes of beribboned chocolates, and Mr Boland visited her one Sunday afternoon with an armful of books and a bag of oranges that collapsed half-way up the ward. The fruit rolled along the polished floor and disappeared under beds and lockers. When the last of the oranges had been recovered by him and two nurses, he arrived at Janet's bed, hot and flustered.

He sat on the edge of the upright chair and said that he was managing quite well in the shop and she mustn't worry. That was everyone's theme song.

When the day came for her to leave the hospital, she was as excited as a child; but after an hour at Fiona's her excitement had petered away and she sat in the purple chair almost wishing she were back in the narrow bed watching the stiff white aprons of the nurses crackling up and down the ward. Sally, who had given her a brief hug on arrival, seemed indifferent to her presence. That was the way of children: Janet knew it but found it difficult to accept. Sally had become acclimatized to the bungalow, its L-shaped sitting room, the pink light in the hall, the open garden leading to the wrought-iron gate; and Janet resented it. Her resentment was directed not towards Sally, but towards the objects themselves. And of course towards Fiona. Fiona smiled complacently, soliciting Janet's gratitude with every cup of tea and every cushion she tucked behind her back. She talked to Sally about the children next door, and they dissolved into laughter over a private joke. 'Sally has made a lot of nice little friends,' Fiona said. 'This is a good place for children. Plenty of companionship of their own age and type, which is what children need.' She talked to Sally of plans they had made for the next day and of what they had done the day before. Janet was excluded. She grew more and more miserable. She had nothing to offer Sally but a dark basement and a scruffy back green.

Sally tripped on the edge of the rug and banged her head on the fender. Janet moved out of the chair, then sank back: Sally had gone to Fiona. Fiona had her arms round her and was murmuring into her hair. A jealousy such as Janet had never known before surged up in her. She went quickly into the bathroom and locked the door. She sat on the clothes basket and wept with sheer self-pity. When she had exhausted her ready supply she called up more, digging back into the worst spots of her past to prolong the tears.

Having convinced herself that life was a series of misfortunes joined by slight lulls and she but an object tossed mercilessly from one squall to the other, she felt remarkably better. It was a long time since she had wept so fully. She dried her face on the end of a blue towel marked HIS, and leaned back against the cool tiled wall. A spider was crawling round the top of the bath, its legs moving slowly and rhythmically over the white porcelain. She watched it until her eyes were hypnotized and she had to jerk them away to break the spell. An orange duck with one eye stared at her from the top of the lavatory cistern. She had to get out of this house as soon as she could.

The evenings were worse than the days. The golden hands recorded the passing of the hours with agonizing slowness.

Whenever she spoke to Sally about The Crescent and the basement the child began to cry and even to scream. Fiona said that it was impossible for Janet to take Sally back there: she remembered it as a place where a horrible woman with red hair had pushed her mother down the steps. Janet turned on Fiona with rage, accusing her of harbouring the image in Sally's mind. Fiona accused Janet of ingratitude. To Janet it was all very tedious and wearing – and frightening. During sleepless hours of the night she became obsessed with the idea that she had lost Sally, that even if she found a beautiful house with a garden and children next door, Sally would not want to come with her, that she would scream if she tried to remove her from Fiona. This obsession led her to another one: that she was a person who lost everyone and could keep no one. A house with a garden was impossible: she had ten shillings and sixpence. She was living off Howard and Fiona, and in return they were getting Sally's affection. When she slept she had nightmares and when she awoke, she was bathed in perspiration.

As soon as she felt strong enough she went to the bookshop. A young girl in a bunchy blue skirt and white blouse was sitting at the counter reading a magazine. Mr Boland was out, she said, he would be back shortly. Janet lifted a book at random from the shelves and over the top of it studied the glossy mane of hair that tumbled on the girl's shoulders. She had been replaced. In such a short time every space she had filled had been occupied. She was completely dispensable.

Mr Boland bustled in and greeted her cheerfully which reassured her a little. They went into the back shop and he removed his teeth and put them into the jam jar. Janet relaxed. She said that she could start work again the following week. Mr Boland looked startled. He stammered and fiddled in his pockets. Then he spoke. Fiona had told him Janet would not be coming back, that six pounds a week was a ridiculous sum for anyone to live on let alone support a child, and that the basement was unhealthy. He had engaged a student for the summer. 'But you can have your job back in October if you still want it,' he said anxiously. It was now the beginning of July. She could not live on ten and sixpence for three months.

'The flat?' she said quickly. 'Does the girl have it?'

No, the basement was empty and she could still live there. But what use was it when Sally would not go there?

From the bookshop Janet went to the mental hospital where Dolly was a patient. She dreaded the visit, yet felt it was something she must do. The psychiatrist attending Dolly had written asking her to come, as he thought she might be able to help. He was a small man with piercing blue eyes, and easy to talk to. She told him all she knew of Dolly.

Then he said: 'She's a virgin.'

'I don't understand.' Janet frowned. 'You say that Dolly is a –'

'Virgin,' he repeated. 'You're surprised?'

She was certainly surprised. She also felt a fool since she had just told him all the tales of Dolly's love life. Told him a lot of lies, in fact. But the men – they had existed. She had seen them. She remembered the Norwegian in his thick oiled sweater and the two hundred and twenty-three dirty milk bottles, the Egyptian coming towards her and Dolly up South College Street with his long sloping walk, the smell of garlic and peppermint on his breath . . . She put her hand to her head: it was throbbing. What had she really known about Dolly that had enabled her to sit in front of this table and toss bits of information about her life across it?

'I'm confused,' she said. 'Tell me about Dolly.'

'She's not an orphan,' the psychiatrist said and paused to allow her to absorb this further bit of knowledge. 'Her parents live in Caithness and they have never been involved in an accident.'

She could no longer be surprised. Anything she knew might be fact or fiction. They were not two separate categories to be put at the top of a list. Truth or falsehood? As the psychiatrist talked Janet realized that Dolly had ceased to be a person: she had become a case. It was not that he spoke clinically or without compassion but nevertheless Dolly was a psychiatric case in a mental hospital and it was unlikely that she would ever be anything else. Janet need never again ask: who is Dolly?

Dolly was the only child of a farmer and his wife who had married late in life. They were staunch members of the Free Church of Scotland; they kept the Sabbath to the letter and they brought their daughter up strictly. When she was seventeen she used to meet a boy from the village in secret. One evening her father found them lying in the barn together and had set about them in a terrible rage. The boy had slipped off and her father had struck Dolly across the face and told her never to come into his house again. It hinged so closely on Victorian melodrama that Janet found it less credible than the story of the car accident and being brought up by a grandmother. Dolly had left home and come to the university on a county grant.

The rest fell into place. Dolly going desperately from man to man, weaving her fantasies, making herself out to be the whore her father believed her to be. And then in the end: Paul. She had wanted to marry him but on the eve of the wedding had not been able to go through with it.

'She had built up the sexual act into such a monstrosity in her mind that when it came to the point of facing it, she broke down,' the psychiatrist said.

Janet nodded wearily.

'Would you like to see her?'

She did not want to, but she went. Dolly was heavily drugged and stank of sickness. She lay back on the pillows, her eyes glassy and lifeless. After Janet had spoken, she seemed to recognize her. She struggled to sit up and Janet put a pillow behind her back.

'Dolly, do you remember Derek Crosbie?'

'Derek Crosbie. Yes, yes.' Dolly sounded excited. 'You were in love with him.'

'I married him.'

'You went away. I sent him after you. I told him where to find you.'

'I know. I want to thank you. You would never let me speak about the past before.'

'Derek Crosbie,' Dolly mused. 'Where is he now?'

'Dead.'

'Dead? That's funny. Everyone I know is dead.' Dolly glanced furtively round the room and whispered: 'Have you seen the doctor? He's handsome, isn't he? Tell you a secret. Promise you won't tell anyone.'

Janet promised.

'Cross your heart.'

Janet crossed her heart.

'Last night when the lights were turned down' – Dolly giggled and arched her eyebrows – 'he came in and made love to me. I've fallen in love with him.'

Janet swallowed deeply. 'That's nice,' she said.

'Promise you won't tell.'

Janet promised.

'Cross your heart.'

Janet crossed her heart.

A nurse beckoned from the doorway. Janet patted the hand on the coverlet and backed thankfully away from the bed. She returned to the bungalow, exhausted and depressed.

That afternoon, Fiona offered to adopt Sally. The scene reminded Janet of her mother offering her a home after her father's death. Fiona listed the advantages: they were very fond of Sally and she thought she could say without being unduly immodest that Sally was fond of them, they could give her a good home and it would leave Janet free to do as she wished. After all, it was difficult for a woman to bring up a child alone. Janet could go anywhere in the world she liked, live in any kind of house – and with any kind of man, Fiona thought, but restrained herself from saying – and she would know that Sally was safe and well cared for. She could come and visit Sally too, whenever she liked.

Janet had gone off into one of her trances. Her eyes were glazed: she was thinking. Fiona, accustomed to her sister's odd ways, waited patiently. She had talked the problem over with *The Seekers* and they had had a lively discussion. They had decided that the child was the most important factor so the question must be looked at purely from her viewpoint. It was unanimously agreed that Sally would have a better home, better clothes, food, holidays, education with Fiona and Howard than she would with Janet. In addition, she would have the advantage of living in a normal family group and she would be settled and secure. One member had put forward the question of a mother's love but had been squashed by Fiona who said that she already loved Sally as though she were her own child.

Janet sighed and emerged from the trance.

'I suppose Sally would forget me in time,' she said slowly. 'I would be a sort of special aunt who appeared at irregular intervals with expensive presents and sad smiles, an embarrassment to all concerned.'

215

Fiona laughed, nervously. She repeated the good points and stressed that she was thinking only of Sally. She urged that Janet should do the same. 'It might hurt you a great deal to give her up,' she said softly, 'but one day you may be glad you were strong enough to do it.' She laid her hand on Janet's arm.

The touch of Fiona's hand brought Janet to her senses: she was appalled by the thought of the very thing they were discussing. Give Sally to Fiona! She threw off Fiona's hand.

'I couldn't do it,' she cried. 'I'll never give Sally up no matter what I have to do to keep her. No matter what,' she said again and meant exactly that. As she left the room she heard Fiona say something about selfishness or possessiveness or one of these things.

Howard, who was having a week's holiday at home, was in the garden clipping the front hedge which reached to his knees. Janet walked past without looking at him though she was aware that he was watching her over the top of his clippers. As soon as she was out of sight he would rush in to hear the verdict. On the corner she met a silly woman with protruding teeth and eyes who stopped to tell her that she had heard so much about her and admired her very much. 'It takes courage to stand alone,' she said. Janet stared at her. Before the woman had finished paying her tribute, they were joined by two others pushing little wheeled baskets in front of them. They inquired after Janet's health, they were so glad she was almost back to normal and how was dear wee Sally? They smiled at Janet and then at one another. Janet regarded them impassively and silently – some of Fiona's cultured friends no doubt – and then excused herself abruptly.

She *had* to do something. But what? First of all she needed money. How to get it? She thought at once of George who alone seemed to want her. She remembered him offering to lend her money one Sunday afternoon out on the moors, remembered too that she had thought she would never accept, not foreseeing this moment of extremity. She circled the block, ignored the waves of the three women on the corner, and went back into the house. She had made her decision. She told Fiona that she was going to spend a couple of days in the basement clearing up and packing, then she would come and take Sally away. Fiona said: 'It's up to you,' and went into her room. She had been crying.

Howard said to Janet: 'Don't you think you should reconsider our proposition?' He had finished the hedge and was now washing the lunch dishes.

'Sally belongs to me,' Janet said, 'and I don't intend to reconsider anything.'

She put on her coat and went out. The three women were still there. They waved again and stuck out their necks to watch her go along the street. On the way to The Crescent she phoned George and asked him to come to 31B that evening. Then she spent the rest of her money on a bottle of wine.

CHAPTER TWENTY-THREE

She had been afraid of returning to the basement, afraid of the damp ghosts and the chill silence and the sight of Mrs MacNab's legs at the railings. Now she was not afraid: she was too full of determination. She deliberately looked at no special part of the room until she had made a fire and roared it into a hot orange blaze. The cold left the room quickly, and the crackling flames made a pleasant cheering noise. She looked round. Dust covered the table, the books, the toys in the corner. She ran her finger over the green bowl; it was filled with pencils, beer tops, pins, a shrivelled apple, a piece of purple chalk, a ball of mustard wool. Beside the door hung Tim's painting: The Crescent at dusk. She turned it round to face the wall.

Then she went out into the back green. She whistled, and soon Muffin came padding towards her and landed in a

217

heap at her feet, rolling on her back, presenting her soft grey underside for tickling. She looked sleek and well-fed: she would have been looked after by Mrs Green and doubtless, too, she had made several smash-and-grab runs through Mrs MacNab's kitchen window.

Janet returned to the living room with Muffin. They both lay down on the settee. The cat began to purr, Janet closed her eyes.

She slept deeply and without dreaming, and woke to see George standing in front of the fire, a questioning look on his face.

'The door was open so I just came in,' he said. 'Are you all right?'

'I'm fine.' She smiled at him and he smiled back a little uncertainly. He had come straight from his office for he still wore his city suit.

She gave him some wine in a thick knobbly tumbler.

'Celebration?' he said, raising his glass, ready to drink to whatever she suggested.

'Not exactly.' She took a long drink: it was sharp and clean. 'I want to borrow some money. I've got none.'

He was incredulous. Yes, she said, it was possible for people to have no money at all. He at once took a cheque book from his wallet and scribbled across a cheque. He held it out to her. Would that do to be getting on with? A hundred pounds. Ten pounds would have relieved the immediate pressure on her life but a hundred made her mistress of it again. She could rent a large sunny room and feed Sally whilst she looked for another job.

Overwhelmed by his generosity, she leaned over and kissed him. His face relaxed into a smile.

'You're very good to me, George. You always have been.' She folded the cheque and tucked it under a corner of the green bowl. 'I'll pay you back, I promise.'

'No hurry.'

When they had drained the bottle of its last golden drop, George asked her to marry him.

'I know you're not in love with me,' he said, 'but I've always hoped you were fond of me.'

'I am fond of you, George.' She put her hand over his. 'You're very good and kind.'

'You make me sound dull.'

'No, no.'

'You find me dull,' he said sadly.

'I certainly don't,' she protested vigorously.

'I'm glad of that. I'm fond of Sally too, you know. I would give her a good home and send her to a good school.'

Janet smiled. 'I know you would.'

'And I'd hire a housekeeper or maybe one of those continental girls so that you could go back to the university. You'd like that, wouldn't you?'

'Yes.'

'I'm all for women having their own interests and developing their lives outside the home. I don't believe they should be shut up in the house all day. I'm not very good at this. I feel I must sound like a salesman, and I don't want to sound like that.'

'You sound very sweet.'

He coughed. 'I expect you'd like to think it over?'

'I've thought it over many times. You must have realized that.'

'Of course.' He fingered his chin. 'And what have you thought?' he asked, not looking at her.

'I've thought yes.'

He started. 'You mean – '

She laughed. 'Is it a shock to you? Perhaps you didn't expect me to take you seriously?'

He pulled her towards him and kissed her quickly. She had never seen him so animated. He laughed boisterously and talked without ceasing. Would she like a week-end cottage in the country? Or at the seaside? Sally might prefer the seaside. Would she like to live in his flat or should he buy a larger house in the suburbs? Should they tell Howard and Fiona soon?'

219

After a while he grew quiet, and they sat close together on the settee, basking drowsily in the heat of the stove, listening to the few sounds in the street. Sometimes she thought he was asleep but when she looked she saw that his eyes were half open and he was smiling.

'We'll have some children, won't we, George?' she said. 'It will be good for Sally, and we'll be a real family.'

'Sounds fine to me.'

When midnight struck, he said that he must go.

'Please stay with me,' she said.

'I'd like to,' he said gently, 'but you know what your neighbours are like. I wouldn't want them to talk about you.'

'All right,' she said, knowing that it would be a mistake to ask too much of him.

He kissed her goodnight at the door, under the shadow of the stairway. 'Go back and keep warm. You've got to look after yourself. I'll see you tomorrow.'

She pulled the curtains aside to watch him drive off. She had made an important decision, and as with any decisive action had come a certain satisfaction. She felt quite calm and even the panic of a moment ago at the thought of being left alone had passed. The car had gone. She put up her hand to close the curtains, then let her arm drop. Another pair of feet stood on the pavement where George's had been a moment ago. Something turned over inside her.

The gate swung open and slowly the feet came down the steps. When he was at the bottom he stopped and they stared blankly at one another through the glass. Then he opened the door and came into the room.

'Tim.'

'Hullo, Janet.'

She remained at the window, her back half turned to him. He moved round the room, touching various objects as though he were checking up on his memory.

'I've been standing on the opposite side of the street all evening, waiting for George to go.'

'You must be cold,' she said.

She kept her face well away from him. The window was dusty and spattered with dried raindrops. Did the girl in the blue skirt and white blouse clean the windows of the bookshop every morning? Did she sit on top of the step ladder in the sunshine and see the fruit in the boxes and the flowers in their cans?

'I thought George usually left at eleven?' Tim said. 'A respectable hour.'

'Tonight was a special occasion.'

'I see.'

What did he see? she wondered. What did she see for that matter? Only a blur of railings and a strip of pavement and the cracked cement of the area standing out in the shaft of light from the window.

'You've been away. I've been round several times in the last week. I spoke to Mrs MacNab yesterday – she said you went away in an ambulance. And she sniffed. I've been worried.'

'I had an accident. I fell down the steps. I'm fine now.'

'I went to the bookshop twice. There was a strange girl at the counter and both times Mr Boland was out.'

'I'm not going back to the bookshop. I'm going to marry George.'

Silence now in the room. Even the fire seemed to have died.

Tim cleared his throat. 'I hope you'll be very happy.'

'Thank you.'

'That is the correct thing to say, isn't it?'

'I think so.'

Two feet passed the window. Mr Green going home. The creak of his gate as he tried to open it quietly.

'I'm going to Italy next week,' Tim said. 'For a month.'

'That'll be nice.'

'I came to ask if you and Sally would like to come with me. But I didn't come in time.'

He started to move about again, coming into her line of vision and then moving out of it, casting shadows when he blocked the light. Suddenly he came up behind her and put his hands on her shoulders.

'You're not in love with George, are you?'

'No.'

'Then you can't marry him.'

'Don't be silly.'

'You're selling yourself!'

'We all sell ourselves at some point or other.'

'Now you're going to start taking refuge in evasive answers. How do you think George will feel when he finds out you've married him for his money?'

'George knows now. He's no fool. You and Khalil always tended to underestimate him. And I'm not just marrying him for his money. That's what you'd like to think, but it's not as simple as that.'

'I'm sure it's not at all simple. You can't let anything be simple, can you?'

'George is familiar to me, just as Edinburgh is. We understand one another; it will be easy for us to belong together. We'll have a peaceful life, and why not? I feel in need of some peace.'

'Peace! You'll be bored living with him,' Tim said, desperation building up in him. He had lost her and didn't know what to do to get her back. He felt helpless. 'Before long you'll find the boredom intolerable.'

'I won't be bored. I'm going back to the university.'

He dropped his hands from her shoulders and moved away. He stopped in front of the blank back of his picture.

'You're a coward,' he said.

'Probably.'

'You're afraid to love me in case you get hurt. You want to play safe, don't you?'

'You and I wouldn't last together, Tim.'

'We're not going to get the chance to find out, are we?'

She stood motionless, unable to explain to him what she was only realizing herself fully now. If she married him, it would be a second-rate imitation of her marriage with

222

Derek Crosbie and might easily fail, and Isobel would always be there, between them; whereas with George she would have something quite different, where there would be no illusions to prop up, no pretence, no effort to keep alive feelings that barely existed. It would be a freer association where they would not expect to possess one another completely, where they would each be dependent and yet independent. And it would be a solid relationship that would last. She had a need of something permanent: it was a need built into her since birth, and if it went unsatisfied, she would drift meaninglessly through life. She realized it all with relief for it would lessen the hurt when Tim finally went.

'I'm sorry,' she said.

'For God's sake, don't start apologizing! That's the end. I'll be getting along.' He tossed a postcard onto the table. 'That's from Khalil.'

This time she did not watch him go: she drew the curtains, locked the door and stood behind it until she heard the gate click shut at the top of the steps. At that moment the temptation to run after him was so strong that her resolution almost toppled; but she resisted. 'It is best this way,' she said aloud. Then she went to the table and lifted the card. It was a glossy one with serrated edges: the Eiffel Tower floodlit. She turned it over.

'After the big dipper I found I had a taste for heights. There was only one thing to do. Pinprick marks my position. Tell Janet not to be alarmed: there is no radical change in my nature, except in this one respect.

'I am journeying slowly eastwards. K.'

She found the pinprick with her finger: it was at the topmost part of the tower. She crumpled the card quickly and thrust it into the middle of the fire. She would never see Khalil again. She might meet Tim in the street; they would speak for a moment, then move on, and if she looked back she might find that he had looked back too, and she would see the face of a stranger.

223